KISS
of the
SPIDER
WOMAN

KISS
of the
SPIDER
WOMAN

by MANUEL PUIG

Translated from the Spanish by
THOMAS COLCHIE

 Vintage Books · A Division of Random House · New York

First Vintage Books Edition, August 1980
Copyright © 1978, 1979 by Manuel Puig
All rights reserved under International
and Pan-American Copyright Conventions.
Published in the United States by Random House, Inc., New York
and simultaneously in Canada by Random House
of Canada Limited, Toronto.
Originally published in Spain as El Beso de la Mujer Arana.
Copyright © 1976 by Manuel Puig.
Published in the United States by Alfred A. Knopf, Inc.,
New York, in April 1979.

The author wishes to thank
The Center for Inter-American Relations
for assistance in the translation of this book.

Some chapters appeared in slightly different form
in *Fiction* and *Triquarterly*.

Library of Congress Cataloging in Publication Data
Puig, Manuel.
Kiss of the spider woman.
Translation of El beso de la mujer arana.
Reprint of the 1979 ed. published by Knopf, New York.
I. Title.
[PZ4.P9786Ki   1980]   [PQ7798.26.U4]   863   80-12179
ISBN 0-394-74475-6

Manufactured in the United States of America

KISS
of the
SPIDER
WOMAN

—Something a little strange, that's what you notice, that she's not a woman like all the others. She looks fairly young, twenty-five, maybe a little more, petite face, a little catlike, small turned-up nose. The shape of her face, it's . . . more roundish than oval, broad forehead, pronounced cheeks too but then they come down to a point, like with cats.

—What about her eyes?

—Clear, pretty sure they're green, half-closed to focus better on the drawing. She looks at her subject: the black panther at the zoo, which was quiet at first, stretched out in its cage. But when the girl made a noise with her easel and chair, the panther spotted her and began pacing back and forth in its cage and to growl at the girl, who up to then was still having trouble with shading in the drawing.

—Couldn't the animal smell her before that?

—No, there's a big slab of meat in the cage, that's all it can smell. The keeper drops the meat near the bars, and it blocks out any smell from outside, that's the point, so the panther won't get excited. And noticing the anger of the wild animal the girl begins to work more feverishly, with faster and faster strokes, and she draws the face of an animal that's also a devil. And the panther watches her, a male panther, and it's hard to tell if he's watching to tear her to pieces and make a meal of her, or if he's driven by some other, still uglier instinct.

—Nobody else at the zoo that day?

—No, almost nobody. It's winter, it's freezing. The trees are bare in the park. There's a cold wind blowing. So the girl's practically by herself, sitting there on the folding chair she brought out herself, along with the easel to clip her drawing paper to. A little further off, near the giraffe cage, there's some boys with their schoolteacher, but they go away quickly, the cold's too much for them.

—And she's not cold?

—No, she's not thinking about the cold, it's as if she's in some other world, all wrapped up in herself drawing the panther.

—If she's wrapped up inside herself, she's not in some other world. That's a contradiction.

—Yes, that's right, she's all wrapped up in herself, lost in that world she carries inside her, that she's just beginning to discover. She has her legs crossed, her shoes are black, thick high heels, open toed, with dark-polished toenails sticking out. Her stockings glitter, that kind they turned inside out when the sheen went out of style, her legs look flushed and silky, you can't tell if it's the stockings or her skin.

—Look, remember what I told you, no erotic descriptions. This isn't the place for it.

—Whatever you want. Okay then, she's wearing gloves, but to get on with her drawing she slips off the right one. Her fingernails are longish, they're painted almost black, and the fingers are white, until the cold begins to turn them slightly blue. She stops working for a minute, puts one hand inside her coat to warm it. It's a heavy coat, black plush, very padded in the shoulders, but thick plush, more like the coat of a Persian cat, no, a lot thicker. And who's there behind her? Someone tries to light a cigarette, the wind blowing out the flame of the match.

—Who is it?

—Wait. She hears the striking of the match and it startles her, she spins around. It's a guy, kind of good-looking, not a pretty boy, just a likable face, hat brim turned down and a baggy overcoat, full-cut trousers. He touches the brim of his hat by way of introduction and apologizes, tells her it's sensational that drawing. She sees the guy's okay, face gives him away, he's the quiet, understanding type. With her fingers she touches up the hairdo a little, partly messed by the wind. It's cut in bangs with curls, and down to the shoulders, that's how they used to wear it, with little curls at the ends too, almost like a permanent wave.

—I picture her dark-looking, not too tall, really nice figure, and she moves like a cat. A real piece.

—Who didn't want to get aroused?

—Go on.

—She answers that he didn't frighten her. But with all this, and the business of fixing her hair, the page works loose and the wind blows it away. The fellow runs and catches it, he brings it back to the girl and offers an apology. She says it's nothing, and by the accent he can tell she's a foreigner. The girl explains to him she's a refugee, she studied fine arts in Budapest, when the war broke out she left for New York. He asks her if she's homesick for her city, and it's as if a dark cloud passes over her eyes, the whole expression of her face darkens and she says she doesn't come from a city, she's from the mountains, way off in the Carpathians.

—Where Dracula comes from.

—Mmm-hmm, those mountains with dark forests, where wild beasts live who go mad with hunger in the wintertime and have to come down into the villages to kill. And people are scared to death, and hang sheep and other dead animals in their doorways and make vows, for protection. After all that, the fellow wants to see her again, and she tells him she'll be back to draw again tomorrow afternoon, like almost every day recently, whenever there's been sun. Then you see him in his studio, he's an architect, the next afternoon with his architect colleagues and his assistant, a young woman, who's an archi-

tect too. But when three o'clock comes and not much daylight's
left, he gets the urge to put away his compass and ruler and
go over to the zoo, almost directly across the way in Central
Park. The assistant asks him where he's going, and why he's
so happy. He treats her like a friend but it's obvious that deep
down she's in love with him, even though she hides it.

—She's a dog?

—No, friendly face, chestnut hair, nothing out of this world,
but nice enough. He leaves without giving her the pleasure of
knowing where he's going. It upsets her but she doesn't let
anybody see and buries herself in work so that she doesn't get
more depressed. At the zoo it still hasn't begun to get dark yet,
it's been a day with very strange light for wintertime, everything seems to stand out more sharply than ever, the black
bars, the white tile walls of the cages, the gravel looks white
too, and the leafless trees gray with no leaves. And the blood-
red eyes of the beasts. But the girl, whose name is Irena, isn't
there. Days go by and the architect can't forget her, until one
day walking down some fashionable avenue something in the
window of an art gallery catches his attention. They're showing
works by an artist who draws nothing but panthers. The architect walks in, Irena's there, getting congratulated from all
sides. And I don't know exactly what happens then.

—Try to remember.

—Wait a minute . . . I don't know if this is when someone
gives her a greeting that scares her . . . Anyway, then the
architect congratulates her too and notices something different
in Irena, something like happiness, she's got no dark look in
her eyes like the first time. And he invites her to a restaurant
and she walks out on all those critics, and they go off together.
She looks as though she can walk down the street for the first
time, like she'd been a prisoner, and now she's free to go
wherever she wants.

—But you said he takes her to a restaurant, not wherever
she wants.

—Hey, don't take me so literally. Anyhow, when he stops in front of some restaurant, Hungarian or Rumanian, something like that, she starts feeling funny again. He thought she'd enjoy being taken someplace like that, with her own kind of people, but it backfires on him. And he figures something's going on and asks her. She lies and says something about memories of the war, which is still going strong at the time. Then he tells her they can go someplace else for lunch. But she realizes that he, the poor guy, doesn't have much time, he's on his lunch break and has to go back to the studio later. So she gets a grip on herself and walks into the restaurant, and everything's fine, because the atmosphere's relaxed and the food's good, and she's back to feeling how pleasant life is.

—And him?

—He's happy, because he sees how to please him she got her complex under control, just the way he planned, to go there in the first place, to please her. The kind of thing when two people get to know each other and things start working. And he's so swept off his feet by her he decides not to go back to work that afternoon. He tells her how he happened by the gallery by chance, that he was actually out on another errand to buy a present.

—For the other girl, the assistant.

—How did you know?

—Didn't, just guessed it.

—You saw the film.

—No, I swear. Go on.

—And the girl, Irena I mean, says that then they can go do that errand. Well, right away, he wonders if he has enough cash to buy two identical presents, one for the assistant's birthday and another for Irena, so he can win her over completely. On the way Irena says how this afternoon, oddly enough, it doesn't make her sad to see it getting so dark already, when it's only three in the afternoon. He asks her why the nightfall upsets her, is it because she's afraid of the dark.

She thinks about it and answers yes. And he stops in front of the store where they're going and she stares at the window uncomfortably, it turns out to be a petshop that only sells birds, marvelous, in cages you can see from the window there are all kinds of birds happily flying from one perch to another, or swinging back and forth on swings, or pecking at little shreds of lettuce, or birdseed, or taking sips of cool water, freshly changed for them.

—Wait a minute . . . Is there any water in the bottle?

—Mmm-hmm, I refilled it when they let me out of the john.

—Oh, that's all right then.

—You want a little? It's nice and fresh.

—No, just so there's no problem with tea in the morning. Go on.

—Don't worry so much, we have enough for the whole day.

—But I'm getting into bad habits. I forgot to bring it along when they opened the door for showers, if it wasn't for you remembering, we'd be stuck without water later on.

—There's plenty, I'm telling you . . . But when the two of them walk into the petshop it's as if who knows what walked in, the Devil himself. The birds go crazy, flying at the bars of their cages, blind with fear, beating their wings. The owner doesn't know what to do. The little birds squawk with terror, but it's like the squawking of vultures, not some little birdsong. She grabs the architect by the arm and pulls him outside. The birds calm down right away. She asks if he'd mind her leaving. They make a date and separate until the next night. He goes back into the petshop, the birds go on singing peacefully, he buys a little canary for the other one's birthday. And afterwards . . . well, I don't remember so clearly what comes next, guess I'm tired.

—Go on a little more.

—Just that I get sleepy and forget the film. What do you say we go on with it tomorrow?

—If you really don't remember, better go on tomorrow.

—I'll pick it up in the morning then.

—No, it's better at night, during the day I don't want to be thinking about such trivia. I've got more important things to think about.

— . . .

—If I'm not busy reading and I'm still keeping quiet, it's just because I'm thinking. So don't take it personally.

—No, it's okay. I'm not going to disturb you, don't worry.

—I knew you'd understand, I really appreciate it. Good night.

—Night. Sweet dreams of Irena.

—I prefer the assistant.

—I figured that already. Ciao.

—Good night.

—We left off where he went back into the petshop and the birds weren't scared of him. It was her they were scared of.

—I didn't say that, you thought that up yourself.

—All right, what happens?

—Well, they go on seeing one another and they fall in love. She fascinates him incredibly, because she's so strange, on the one hand so openly affectionate, and always looking at him, caressing him, putting her arms around him, but as soon as he wants to hold her close and kiss her she slips away and barely lets his lips brush against her. She asks him not to kiss her, just to let her kiss him, very tender kisses, but like a baby's, with her lips so soft and fleshy, but shut.

—Back then, there was no sex in movies.

—Wait and you'll see. The thing is that one night he takes her out to that same restaurant again, which isn't first-class but very quaint, with checkered tablecloths and everything in dark wood, or no, it must be stone, no, wait, now I know, inside it's like being in a log cabin, with gaslight and just candles on the tables. And he lifts up his glass of wine, his goblet, and proposes a toast, because tonight a man who is very much in love is going to commit himself to marry if his chosen one will accept him. And her eyes fill up with tears, but from being so happy. They touch goblets and drink without saying another word, just holding hands. All of a sudden she lets go of his hand: she's seen someone coming over to their table. It's a woman, beautiful-looking at first sight, but a second later you notice something really strange about her face, something frightening and yet it's hard to know what it is. Because it's a woman's face but it's also the face of a cat. The eyes slant up, and so peculiar, I don't know how to tell you, she has no whites to her eyes, her eyes are completely green in color, with black pupils at the center, and nothing else. And her skin very pale, as if she had a lot of powder on.

—But you told me she was pretty.

—Yes, she's beautiful. And from the strange outfit it's obvi-ous she's European, her hair fixed in a sausage roll.

—What's a sausage roll?

—Like a . . . how can I explain it to you? a chignon . . . a coil of hair something like a tube that goes around the head, over the forehead and all the way around in back.

—Doesn't matter, go on.

—But come to think of it maybe I'm wrong, I think she had more of a braid around her head, that's more like that part of the world. And a long dress down to the floor, and a fox stole over her shoulders. And she comes to the table and looks at Irena as if with hatred, or not quite, more the way a hypnotist looks, but an evil look in every way. And she speaks to Irena in an incredibly strange language, pausing there by the table. And he, being a gentleman, gets up from his chair at the approach of a lady, but this minx doesn't even look at him and says something else to Irena. Irena answers her in that same dialect, but very frightened. He can't understand one word of what they're saying. Then, so he'll understand too, the woman says to Irena: "I recognized you instantly, but you know why.

Be seeing you . . ." And she walks away, without having so much as looked at the guy. Irena is petrified, her eyes are filled with tears, but dark tears, looking like filthy water from a puddle. She gets up without a word and wraps a long scarf, a white one, over her head, he drops some money on the table and walks out with her, taking her by the arm. They don't say anything to each other, he sees that she's frightened. Looking over at Central Park, it's snowing lightly, the snow deadens every sound and noise, the cars almost slide down the street, very quietly, the streetlamp lights up the pure white snowflakes that are falling, and it's as though way off somewhere the cries of wild animals can be heard. And that's not so unlikely, because just a little distance from there is the city zoo, in that same park. She can't seem to go on, she begs him to hold her close. He holds her in his arms. She's shivering, from cold or from fear, although the distant cries seemed to have died down. She tells him, almost in a whisper, that she's afraid to go home and spend the night alone. A taxi comes by, he signals it to pull over and the two of them get in without saying a word. They go to his apartment, not talking the whole way there. His building, it's one of those old apartment houses, very well kept up, carpets, very high-beamed ceiling, dark wooden staircases all hand-carved, and there in the entranceway by the foot of the stairs a giant palm set into a magnificent urn. It must have had Chinese motifs. The palm is reflected in a tall mirror with a very elaborate frame, also carved like the staircase. She looks at herself in the mirror, examines her face, as if searching for something in her own features. There's no elevator, he lives on the first floor. Their footsteps can barely be heard on the carpet, like out in the snow. Apartment's huge, with everything turn-of-the-century, very proper, the fellow's mother had it first.

—And him, what's he do?

—Nothing, he knows there's something going on inside the girl that's torturing her. He offers her a drink, a cup of coffee, whatever she'd like. She doesn't want anything, she asks him to sit down please, she has something to say to him. He lights up his pipe and gives her the warm look he has all the time. She can't get herself to look him in the eyes, she sits resting her head on his knees. Then she begins to tell how there was some terrible legend back in her mountain village, that always terrified her, even as a kid. And this part I don't remember too well how it goes, something to do with the Middle Ages, something about villages that once were cut off for months and months by the snow, and they were starving to death, and all the men had gone off to the wars, something like that, and the starving wild beasts of the forest came right up to the people's houses, I don't remember exactly, and the Devil appeared and said a woman had to come outside if they wanted any food from him, and one woman, the bravest, went out to him, and at his side the Devil had a ravenously hungry black panther, and the woman made a pact with the Devil, so as not to die, and I don't know what happened but the woman had a daughter with the face of a cat. And when the Crusaders returned from the Holy Wars, the soldier who was married to this same woman came home, and when he tried to kiss his wife she tore him to pieces, as if a panther had done it.

—I don't really get it, it's very confusing the way you tell it.

—I can't remember right now, that's all. But it doesn't matter. What Irena tells that I do remember is that they were still giving birth to panther women in those mountains. Anyway, by that time the soldier was dead but a fellow Crusader figured out it was the wife who murdered him and set out to follow her, and meantime she escaped through the snow and at first the tracks she left behind were a woman's footsteps until close to the forest they turned into a panther's, and the Crusader followed them and struck deep into the forest where it was already night, and in that darkness he saw two bright green eyes of someone lying in wait for him, and with his sword and dagger he made the sign of the cross and the panther lay still and turned back into a woman, lying there half asleep, as if hypnotized, and the Crusader backed away because he heard other roaring coming near, the wild beasts aroused by the woman's smell and coming to eat her. The Crusader made it back to the village more dead than alive and told them everything. And the legend is that the race of panther women never died out and remains hidden in some corner of the world, and they all seem like normal women, but if a man happens to kiss any of them, the woman can turn into a savage beast.

—And she's one of those panther women?

—All she knows is that the stories frightened her terribly when she was a girl, and she's always lived with that fear of being a descendant of such women.

—And the one back in the restaurant, what'd she have to say?

—That's just what the architect asks her. And Irena throws herself into his arms, crying, and says the woman was only saying hello to her. But then no, she gets up her courage and tells him how in the dialect of her own village she told her to remember who she was, that the sight of her face alone was enough to make it obvious they're sisters. And that she'd better watch out for men. The architect bursts out laughing. "Don't you realize," he says to her, "she saw you were from the same part of the world because people from the same country always recognize each other. If I see an American in China I go out of my way to say hello. And because she's a woman and maybe a little old-fashioned, she tells you to watch out, don't you see?" That's what he says, and it's enough to calm her down. And she feels so peaceful now, she begins to fall asleep in his arms, and he lifts her onto the sofa that's right there, fixes a pillow under her head, and brings a blanket from his bed for her. She's fast asleep. Then he goes to his room and the scene ends with him in his pajamas and robe, good but not too expensive-looking, a solid color, and he's watching her from the doorway, the way she's sleeping, and he lights up his pipe, standing there pensive. The fireplace is lit, no, I can't remember, light must be coming from the lamp on the night table, in his room. When she finally wakes up, the fire's gone out, hardly any embers left. Dawn already breaking.

—The cold wakes her up, just like us.

—No, that's not what wakes her up, I knew you'd say something like that. The canary singing in the cage wakes her. Irena's afraid to go near it at first, but she hears how happy the little bird seems to be and that gives her the courage to go up close. She looks at it carefully, breathes a deep sigh of relief, satisfied because the little creature isn't afraid of her. She goes to the kitchen and makes toast with butter, and that crunchy cereal they have up there and . . .

—Don't talk about food.

—And pancakes . . .

—Really, I'm serious about it. No food and no naked girls.

—Okay, so she wakes him up and he's happy to see her so comfortable in his home and he asks her if she wants to stay and live there forever.

—He's still in bed?

—Mmm-hmm, she brought him his breakfast in bed.

—Me, I never liked to have breakfast right away, the first thing I have to do is brush my teeth. Sorry, go ahead.

—Okay, so then he wants to kiss her. And she won't let him get close.

—He must have bad breath, he didn't brush his teeth yet.

—If you're going to make fun, there's no reason to tell you anything more.

—No, please, I'm listening.

—He asks her again if she wants to marry him. She answers yes she wants to with all her heart, and she doesn't want to ever have to leave that house again, she feels so at home there, and she looks all around and the drapes are dark velvet to block the light out, and so to let the light in she draws them open and behind them there's another set of lacy curtains. Then you get to see the whole turn-of-the-century decor. She asks who picked out all the lovely things and I think he tells her how much his mother had to do with all that, every piece of furniture, how she was such a good mother and how much she would have loved Irena, like her own daughter. Irena goes over to him and kisses him almost with adoration, the way one kisses a holy saint, you know? On the forehead. And she begs him please never to leave her, she wants to be together with him always, all she could ever ask for is to wake up each morning to see him again, always by her side . . . But, to become a real wife to him, she asks him to give her a little time, until all those fears have a chance to subside . . .

—You get what's going on, don't you?

—That she's afraid she'll turn into a panther.

—Well, I think she's frigid, she's afraid of men, either that or she has some idea about sex that's really violent, and so she invents things.

—Wait, will you? He says okay, and they marry. And when the wedding night comes, she sleeps in the bed, and he's on the sofa.

—Keeping an eye on his mother's furniture.

—If you're going to laugh I won't go on, I'm telling you this in all seriousness, because I really like it. And besides there's something else I can't tell you, that makes me really like this film a lot.

—Tell me what, what is it?

—No, I was about to bring it up but now I see you're laughing, and, to tell you the truth, it makes me angry.

—No, I like the picture, but you have the fun of telling it and I just want to chime in once in a while too, see what I mean? I'm not the type who knows how to sit around and just listen all the time, you get what I mean? And all of a sudden I have to sit quiet listening to you for hours on end.

—I thought it helped you pass the time, and fall asleep.

—Yeah, that's true, absolutely, it does both things, it passes time and puts me to sleep.

—Well?

—Only, if it doesn't rub you the wrong way, I'd like us to discuss the thing a little, as you go on with it, so I get a chance now and then to rap about something. Doesn't that seem fair to you?

—If it's so you can crack jokes about a picture I happen to be fond of, then the answer is no.

—No, look, it could be just a simple discussion. Like for example: I personally would like to ask you how you picture the guy's mother.

—If you're not going to laugh anymore.

—I promise.

—Let's see . . . I don't know, a really good person. A lovely lady, who gave her husband every happiness and her children too, always managing everything perfectly.

—Do you picture her doing housework?

—No, I see her as impeccably attired, a dress with a high collar, edged in lace to cover the wrinkles on her neck. She has that marvelous thing of certain respectable ladies, which is that little touch of coquettishness, beneath all the properness, on account of her age, but what you notice about them is the way they go on being women and wanting to please.

—Yes, always impeccable. Perfect. She has her servants, she exploits people who can't do anything else but serve her, for a few pennies. And clearly, she felt very happy with her husband, who in turn exploited her, forced her to do whatever he wanted, keeping her cooped up in a house like a slave, waiting for him—

—Listen . . .

—waiting for him every night, until he got back from his law firm, or from his doctor's office. And she was in perfect agreement with the whole system, and she didn't rebel, and she fed her own son the same crap and now the son runs smack into the panther woman. Good luck with that one.

—But tell the truth, wouldn't you like to have a mother like that? Full of affection, always carefully dressed . . . Come on now, no kidding . . .

—No, and I'll tell you why, if you didn't follow me.

—Look, I'm tired, and it makes me angry the way you brought all this up, because until you brought it up I was feeling fabulous, I'd forgotten all about this filthy cell, and all the rest, just telling you about the film.

—I forgot all the rest, too.

—Well? Why break the illusion for me, and for yourself too? What kind of trick is that to pull?

—I guess I have to draw you a map, because you sure don't get the idea.

—Here in the dark he starts drawing things for me, well that's just wonderful.

—Let me explain.

—Sure, but tomorrow, because right now I'm up to here with it, so skip it till tomorrow . . . Why couldn't I have the luck to get the panther woman's boyfriend to keep me company, instead of you?

—Oh, now that's another story, and I'm not interested.

—Afraid to talk about such things?

—No, not afraid. Just not my bag. I already know all about yours, even if you didn't tell me a thing.

—Well I told you what I'm in for, corruption of minors, and that tells it all, so don't start playing the psychologist now.

—Come on, admit it, you like him because he smokes a pipe.

—No, because he's the gentle type, and understanding.

—His mother castrated him, plain and simple.

—I like him and that's enough for me. And you, you like the assistant, some urban guerrilla that one!

—I like her, sure, more than the panther woman.

—Ciao, you tell me why tomorrow. Let me get some sleep.

—Ciao.

—We were just where she's going to marry the pipe-smoker. I'm all ears.

—What's the little sneer for?

—Nothing, tell it to me, go ahead, Molina.

—No, you go ahead, you tell me about the pipe-smoker, since you know him so much better than me, I only saw the film.

—The pipe-smoker's no good for you.

—Why not?

—Because what you have in mind's not strictly platonic, right? Admit it.

—Obviously.

—Okay, the reason he likes Irena is because she's frigid and he doesn't have to make her, that's why he looks after her and takes her home where the mother's all over the place. Even if she's dead she's there, in every stick of furniture, and the curtains and all that junk, didn't you say so yourself?

—Go on.

—If he's left all his mother's stuff in the house just the way it was, it's because he still wants to be a little boy, back in his mama's house, and what he brings home with him isn't a woman, it's a little playmate.

—But that's all your own concoction. How do I know if the house was the mother's? I told you that because I liked the apartment a lot, and since it was decorated with antiques I said it could be the mother's, but that's all. Maybe he rents the place furnished.

—Then you're inventing half the picture.

—No, I'm not inventing, I swear, but some things, to round them out for you, so you can see them the way I'm seeing them . . . well, to some extent I have to embroider a little. Like with the house, for example.

—Admit that it's the house you'd like to live in yourself.

—Yes, obviously. And now I have to put up with you while you tell me the same old thing everybody tells me.

—Is that so . . . What is it exactly I'm supposed to tell you?

—You're all alike, always coming to me with the same business, always!

—What?

—How they spoiled me too much as a kid, and that's why I'm the way I am, how I was tied to my mother's apron strings and now I'm this way, and how a person can always straighten out though, and what I really need is a woman, because a woman's the best there is.

—That's what they tell you?

—Yes, and my answer is this . . . great! I agree! And since a woman's the best there is . . . I want to be one. That way I save listening to all kinds of advice, because I know what the score is myself and I've got it all clear in my head.

—I don't see it so clear, at least not the way you just worked it out.

—Okay, I don't need you to clear up anything for me, and now if you want I'll go on with the film for you, and if you don't, so much the better, I'll tell it to myself in a whisper, and *saluti tanti, arrivederci, Sparafucile.*

—Sparafucile?

—Obviously you don't know anything about opera. He's the villain in *Rigoletto.*

—Tell me the picture and then ciao, because now I want to know what happens.

—Where were we?

—The wedding night. When he doesn't touch her.

—That's right, he's sleeping on the living-room sofa, and oh, what I didn't tell you is they've arranged, they've come to an agreement, that she'll go see a psychiatrist. And she starts going, and she gets there the first time and finds that the guy's incredibly good-looking, a fantastic flirt.

—What's your definition of incredibly good-looking? I'd like to hear.

—Well, he's tall, dark, wears a mustache, very distinguished-looking, broad forehead, but with a pencil-line mustache a little bit like a pimp's . . . I don't know if I'm making it very clear . . . a wise-guy's mustache, which gives him away. Anyhow, since we're on the subject, the guy who plays the psychiatrist's definitely not my type.

—What actor was it?

—I don't remember, just a supporting role. He's good-looking but too thin for my taste, if you want to know the truth, the type that looks good in a double-breasted suit, or if it's a regular suit they have to wear a vest. He's the type women find attractive. But with this little hotshot something shows, I don't know, how he's so positive women find him attractive. But the minute he comes on . . . you have to dislike him. And so does Irena, who's over on the couch beginning to talk about her problems, but she doesn't feel comfortable, doesn't feel like she's with a doctor, but with some guy, and she's afraid.

—This picture's really something.

—Really what? Silly?

—No, coherent, it's fantastic, go on. But don't get so uptight.

—She begins to talk about how afraid she is of not being a good wife and they decide next time she ought to tell him something about her dreams, or nightmares, and how in one dream she turned into a panther. So that's okay, they end the session at that point, but the next time she has her appointment she doesn't show up, she lies to her husband, and instead of going to the doctor she goes to the zoo, to look at the panther. And she stands there as if she's fascinated, she's wearing that thick plush coat, it's black but glistens almost iridescent in the light, and the panther's fur is iridescent black too. The panther is pacing back and forth in the huge cage, never taking his eyes off the girl. And here the keeper comes along, and opens the door on one side of the cage . . . opens it for just a second, tosses the meat in and shuts it again, only he's so busy with the hook the meat was slung on, he forgets and leaves the key in the lock of the cage. Irena sees all that, keeps quiet, the keeper picks up a broom and sets to work sweeping up the scraps of paper and cigarette butts strewn all over the place near the cages. Irena moves a little closer, stealthily, toward the lock. She removes the key and looks at it, a large key, covered with rust, she stands there pensively, a few seconds go by . . .

—What's she going to do?

— . . . but she goes over to the keeper and hands him the key. The old man, who seems like a good-natured guy, thanks her for it. Irena returns home, waits there for her husband to arrive, it's already the time when he usually gets back from the office. And I forgot to add to all this how every morning she tenderly feeds the canary, and always changes the water, and the canary sings to her. And finally the husband arrives and she hugs him and almost kisses him, she has such a strong desire to kiss him, on the mouth, and he gets all excited, and he thinks maybe the psychoanalytic treatment is doing some good, and the moment's finally approaching to really become husband and wife. But he makes the mistake of asking her how the session went that afternoon. That makes her feel really bad, since she didn't even go, and really guilty, so she slips out of his arms and lies to him, that she went and everything was fine. But she's already slipped away and there's nothing more to do about it. He just has to grin and bear it. And another day he's back once more at work with the other architects. And the assistant, who's always looking at him, because she still cares for him, sees he's troubled and asks him to go have a drink after work, it'll lift up his spirits, and he says no, he has a lot to do, he'll probably work overtime and finally the assistant who's never cared for anyone but him says she can stay and help him out for a while.

—I go for that chick. It's the strangest thing, you haven't said anything about her but she strikes me as okay. Funny thing, imagination.

—She stays late with him, but it's not that she's on the make or anything, she's already given him up for lost after the marriage, but she wants to help him as a friend now. And there they are working away after hours. It's a big studio, with different tables to work at, to draw on, each architect has his own, but now they've all gone home and everything is swallowed up in darkness, except his table, which has a glass top, with light coming from underneath the glass, so their faces catch the light from below, and their bodies cast a rather sinister shadow on the walls, gigantic-looking, and the drawing rule looks more like a sword whenever he or the assistant picks it up for a minute to draw a line. But they work silently. She peeks at him now and then, and even though she's dying to know, she never asks what's bothering him.

—She's okay. Considerate, discreet. Maybe that's why I like her.

—Meanwhile, Irena is waiting and waiting and finally she decides to call his office. The assistant answers and hands the phone to him. Irena is jealous, she tries to hide it. He tells her he called earlier to let her know but she wasn't in then. Obviously, she'd been to the zoo again. So since he catches her in the wrong she has to keep quiet, she can't object about him. And from then on he begins to come home late, because something makes him put off going home.

—It's all so logical, it's fantastic.

—Then you're contradicting yourself . . . You can see he's normal, he just wants to sleep with her, that's all.

—No, listen. Before, he went home willingly because he knew she wasn't about to sleep with him, but now with analysis there's a chance, and that upsets him. As long as she was just a baby, like at first, they didn't do anything more than play around a little, like kids. And maybe by playing around that way they began to get somewhere sexually.

—Playing around like kids, God, how insipid!

—Doesn't sound wrong to me, see, as far as your architect goes. Sorry if it sounds like I'm contradicting myself.

—What doesn't sound wrong to you?

—That they began by playing around, without all the usual fireworks.

—Okay, so back to the film. But one thing—why's he so willing to stay out with the assistant?

—Well, because he figures being married, nothing can happen. The assistant's no sexual possibility anymore, because the wife's apparently got him all served up already.

—That's all in your head.

—If you embroider, why can't I too?

—Just let me go on. One night Irena has dinner all prepared, and he doesn't come home. Table's all set, with the candles lit. She doesn't know one thing though, that since it's their wedding anniversary he'd left early that afternoon to pick her up outside her psychiatrist's, and obviously, he doesn't meet her because she never goes anymore. And he finds out how long it's been since she's been there and telephones Irena, who's not at home, of course, she's gone out like every other afternoon, drawn irresistibly toward the zoo. So then he goes back to his office in desperation, he needs to tell the whole thing to the assistant. And they go off to a nearby bar for a drink together, but it's not so much a drink they want, but a chance to talk privately, away from the studio. When she sees it's getting so late, Irena begins to pace back and forth in the room like a caged animal, and she calls up the office. No one answers. She tries to do something to pass the time, she's terribly nervous, she goes over to the canary's cage and notices how the canary flutters desperately, sensing her nearness, and blindly flits from one side of its little cage to the other, smashing its little wings. She doesn't resist the impulse to open the cage and stick her hand in. The bird drops dead, as if struck down, sensing the closeness of her hand. Now Irena is desperate. All her hallucinations come back to her, she runs out, going off in search of her husband, he's the only one she can ask to help her, the only person who's going to understand her. But heading toward the office she unavoidably passes the bar and spots them. She stands still, she can't take another step, she's trembling with rage, with jealousy. The couple get up to leave, Irena hides behind a tree. She watches them say goodbye and separate.

—How do they say goodbye?

—He gives her a kiss on the cheek. She's wearing an elegant hat with the brim pulled down. Irena isn't wearing any hat, her curly hair shines under the street lights along the deserted street, because she's following the other one. The other one takes the direct route home, which means cutting through the park, Central Park, which is across from the office building, and by a street that sometimes is like a tunnel, because the park's got like little hills, and the road's straight, and at times it's cut right through the hills, it's like a regular street, with traffic but not much, like a shortcut, and a bus that cuts across there. And sometimes the assistant takes the bus so as not to walk so far, and other times she walks, because the bus only runs once in a while. And this time she decides to walk it, to air her thoughts a little, because her head is pounding after her talk with the guy. He's told her everything, about how Irena doesn't sleep with him, about the nightmares she keeps having of panther women. And the poor thing, who's so in love with the guy, she really feels all confused, because she's already resigned herself to losing him, and now, well, she's hopeful again. And on the one hand she feels glad, now that all's not lost, and on the other she's afraid of deluding herself all over again and having to suffer for it later, coming out empty-handed every time. And she goes on thinking about all this, walking a little faster because it's getting so cold. No one's around, the park's lost in shadows off to the side of the road, no wind, not a leaf stirring, so the only thing you hear is footsteps behind the assistant, a woman's high heels clicking. The assistant turns around and sees a silhouette, but at some distance, and with so little light she can't make out who's there. But by now the clicking can be heard getting faster. So she begins to get alarmed, because you know how it is when you've been talking about something scary, like about corpses or a crime, you're more impressionable, and you jump at every little thing, and this woman's got her mind on panther women and all that and begins to panic and starts to hurry, but she's just halfway through, with like about four blocks to go, where some buildings begin because the park comes to an end. So she almost begins to run, which is worse.

—Can I interrupt, Molina?

—Mmm-hmm, but there's not much more to go now, for tonight I mean.

—Only one question, which intrigues me a little.

—What?

—You won't get annoyed?

—Depends.

—It'd be interesting to know. And afterwards you ask me if you want.

—Let's have it then.

—Who do you identify with? Irena or the other one?

—With Irena, what do you think? She's the heroine, dummy. Always with the heroine.

—Okay, go on.

—And you, Valentin, with who? You're in trouble because the architect seems like a moron to you.

—Go ahead and laugh. With the psychiatrist. But no making jokes now, I respected your choice, with no remarks. Go on.

—We can discuss it later if you want, or tomorrow.

—Okay, but go on a little more.

—A little bit, no more, I like to leave you hanging, that way you enjoy the film more. You have to do it that way with the public, otherwise they're not satisfied. On the radio they always used to do that to you. And now on the TV soaps.

—Come on.

—Okay, we were just where this poor girl doesn't know whether to break into a run or not, when at this point the footsteps almost can't be heard anymore, the high heels on the other one I mean, because the steps sound different, almost inaudible. The ones the assistant hears now sound like the tread of a cat, or something worse. And she spins around and doesn't see the woman—how could she disappear so suddenly? But she thinks she sees some other shadow, it slips by and immediately disappears too. And what she hears now is the sound of feet trampling the bushes in the park, the sound of an animal, approaching.

—And?

—Tomorrow we'll go on. Ciao, sleep tight.

—You'll pay for this.

—See you in the morning.

—Ciao.

—You're a good cook.

—Thank you, Valentin.

—But you're getting me into bad habits. That could hurt me.

—You're crazy, live for the moment! Enjoy life a little! Are you going to spoil our dinner thinking about what's going to happen tomorrow?

—I don't believe in that business of living for the moment, Molina, nobody lives for the moment. That's Garden of Eden stuff.

—You believe in Heaven and Hell?

—Wait a minute, Molina, if we're going to discuss things let's have some ground rules, because if we don't stick to the point it's just kid stuff, strictly sophomoric.

—I'm sticking to the point.

—Great, then let me state my position first, so you'll have some idea of it.

—I'm listening.

—There's no way I can live for the moment, because my life is dedicated to political struggle, or, you know, political action, let's call it. Follow me? I can put up with everything in here, which is quite a lot . . . but it's nothing if you think about torture . . . because you have *no* idea what that's like . . .

—But I can imagine.

—No, you can't imagine . . . Anyway, I put up with all of it . . . because there's a purpose behind it. Social revolution, that's what's important, and gratifying the senses is only secondary. While the struggle goes on, and it'll probably go on for the rest of my life, it's not right for me to cultivate any kind of sensual gratification, do you get my point? because, really, that takes second place for me. The great pleasure's something else, it's knowing I've put myself in the service of what's truly noble, I mean . . . well . . . a certain ideology . . .

—What do you mean, a certain ideology?

—My ideals . . . Marxism, if you want me to spell it out in only one word. And I can get that pleasure anywhere, right here in this cell, and even in torture. And that's my real strength.

—And your girl?

—That's also secondary. I'm secondary to her, too, because she also knows what's most important.

—You taught her that?

—No, I think the two of us actually discovered it together. Make any sense, what I just explained to you?

—Mmm-hmm . . .

—You don't sound too convinced, Molina.

—No, don't pay any attention to me. And now I think I'll just get some sleep.

—You've got to be kidding! And the panther woman? You left me hanging in suspense last night.

—Tomorrow, okay?

—Come on, what's up?

—Nothing . . .

—Say something . . .

—No, I'm being silly, that's all.

—Give me some idea, at least.

—Look, it's just the way I am, I'm easily hurt by some things. And I cooked you this dinner, with my own provisions, and worst of all, mad as I am about avocados I gave you half, when I could just as easily have had the other half for myself tomorrow. And for what? . . . For you to throw it right back in my face about how I'm teaching you bad habits.

—But don't act like that, you're oversensitive . . .

—So what am I supposed to do about it? That's how I am, very sentimental.

—I'll say. It sounds just like a . . .

—What are you stopping for?

—Nothing.

—Say it, I know what you were going to say, Valentin.

—Don't be silly.

—Say it, like a woman, that's what you were going to say.

—Yes.

—And what's so bad about being soft like a woman? Why is it men or whoever, some poor bastard, some queen, can't be sensitive, too, if he's got a mind to?

—I don't know, but sometimes that kind of behavior can get in a man's way.

—When? When it comes to torturing?

—No, when it comes to being finished with the torturers.

—But if men acted like women there wouldn't be any more torturers.

—And you, what would you do without men?

—You're right. They're mostly brutes, but I like them.

—Molina . . . But you did say if they all acted like women then there wouldn't be any torturers. You've got a point there, a flimsy one, but still, it's a point.

—Nice of you to say so.

—What do you mean nice?

—Nice and uppity: "Still, it's a point."

—Okay, I'm sorry if I hurt your feelings.

—Nothing to be sorry about.

—Fine, then relax and don't try to punish me.

—Punish you? You're out of your mind.

—Act as if nothing happened, then.

—Want me to go on with the film?

—Sure, man.

—Man? Where's a man? Don't let him go.

—Okay, cut the jokes and get on with the story.

—Where were we . . . ?

—Where my girlfriend the assistant didn't hear the woman's footsteps anymore.

—Right, at this point she begins really shaking with terror, she has no idea what to do, doesn't dare turn around for fear of seeing the panther woman, stops a minute to see if she can hear the human footsteps anymore, but nothing, total silence, only the rustling of leaves moved by the wind . . . or by something else. Then she lets out a long, desperate wail somewhere between a sob and a moan, but the wail is drowned out by the noise of automatic doors on the bus that's just stopped in front of her; those hydraulic doors that sound like some kind of air pump, and she's safe. The driver saw her standing there and opened the doors; he asks her what's the matter, but she says it's nothing, she just doesn't feel well, that's all. And she gets on . . . All right, and when Irena gets back home she's totally disheveled, shoes filthy with mud. The architect's completely at a loss; doesn't know what to say, what to do with this weirdo he's married to. She walks in, looks at him strangely, goes into the bathroom to take off her muddy shoes, and he finally has the guts to talk to her because she's not looking at him, and she hears what he's saying to her, about how he went to meet her at the doctor's office and found out she hadn't been there in a long time. Then she starts crying and says how everything's ruined, that she's what she's always been afraid of being, an insane person, suffering from hallucinations, or worse even—a panther woman. Then he calms her down all over again, and takes her in his arms, and you're right, to him she's just like a baby, because when he sees her that way, so defenseless, so lost, he feels all over again how he loves her with all his heart, and lets her head rest on one shoulder, his shoulder I mean, and strokes her hair and tells her she's got to have faith, everything's going to work out okay.

—It makes sense, this film.

—But there's more, it's not finished.

—I hope so, it can't just stop there. But you know what I like about it? That it's just like an allegory, and really clear too, of the woman's fear of giving in to a man, because by completely giving in to sex she reverts a little to an animal, you know?

—We'll see . . .

—There's that type of woman, very sensitive, way too spiritual, who's been brought up on the idea that sex is dirty, that it's sinful, and this type of chick is screwed up, completely screwed up, most likely she turns out frigid when she gets married, because inside she's got this barrier, they've made her put up a kind of barrier, or wall, and not even bullets get through.

—Not to mention other things.

—Now that I'm serious, you're the one who's making jokes, see how it is, you too?

—Go ahead, O voice of wisdom.

—That's all. Go on with the panther woman.

—Okay, the problem is how's he going to convince her she's got to have faith and go back and see the doctor again.

—Me, you mean.

—Right, but then she tells him there's something about the doctor she doesn't like.

—Sure, because if he cures her, she'll have to give in to marital life, to sex.

—But her husband convinces her to go back. And she does, even though she's afraid to.

—Know what scares her most of all?

—What?

—Doctor's the sensual type—you said so yourself.

—Mmm-hmm.

—And that's just the problem, because he turns her on, and on account of that she won't give in to any treatment.

—Fine, so she goes to the doctor's office. And she confides to him in all sincerity, tells him her greatest fear is of kissing a man and turning into a panther. And here's where the doctor makes a mistake and tries to remove her fear by showing how unafraid he is himself, how sure he is she's an enchanting woman, an adorable woman and that's all. I mean the guy chooses a somewhat dubious treatment, letting his desires get the best of him because he's actually looking for some way to kiss her, that's what he's looking for. But she doesn't fall for it; she has just the opposite response, that yes, the doctor's right and she's normal and so she leaves his office right then and goes away satisfied, goes straight to the architect's studio, as if with the intention, the decision already made, of giving herself to her husband that very night. She's happy, and runs all the way, and gets there almost out of breath. But in the doorway she's suddenly paralyzed. It's late already and everyone's gone home, except her husband and the assistant, and they seem to be talking, holding hands, but you can't tell if it's a friendly gesture or what. He's talking, with his eyes lowered, while the assistant listens to him knowingly. They have no idea someone's walked in. And here my memory's foggy.

—Wait a second, it'll come back to you.

—I remember there's a scene in a swimming pool, and another right there in the architect's studio, and still another, the last, with the psychiatrist.

—Don't tell me that at the end the panther woman winds up with me.

—No. Don't rush. Anyway, I can tell you this whole last part in a very sketchy way if you want, as much as I remember of it.

—Sure.

—So, he and the other one are busy talking there in the studio, and they stop talking because they hear a door creak. They look up and nobody's there; it's dark in the studio, there's no other light than the table they're at, with that slightly sinister glare coming from below. And you hear an animal's footsteps, rustling papers underfoot and, yes, now I remember, there's a wastepaper basket in a dark corner and the basket tumbles over and the footsteps crumple some papers. The assistant screams out and hides behind him. He yells, "Who's there? Who is it?" and now, for the first time, you hear an animal's heavy breathing, like a snarl with the teeth clenched, you see? The architect has no idea what to defend himself with and grabs one of those big rulers. And you realize that unconsciously or whatever, he remembers what Irena's told him, how the sign of the cross can frighten both the Devil and the panther woman, and the light from under the table casts gigantic shadows on the wall, of him with the assistant hanging onto him, and a few feet away the shadow of a beast with a long tail, and it looks like the architect's holding up a cross in his hands—which is nothing but two drafting rulers he's put together like a cross. But suddenly you hear a horrible growl and footsteps of a frightened animal escaping into the darkness. Anyway, I don't remember if what happens now is that same night, I think so, the other one goes home again, which is like a very big hotel for women, some kind of women's club, where they live, with a big swimming pool in the basement. The assistant's so nervous, on account of everything that's happened, and returning to her hotel tonight, where they don't allow male visitors, she thinks the best thing might be to go down and take a swim for a little while to calm her nerves, because she's so on edge. It's already very late at night and there's absolutely no one in the pool. They have changing rooms down there and she's got her own locker where she hangs her clothes and puts on her bathing suit and bathrobe. Meanwhile, upstairs in the hotel the front door opens and in comes Irena! She asks the woman at the desk about the other one, and, without suspecting anything, the woman tells her the other one just went down to the pool. And because she's a woman, Irena has no problem getting in, they just let her by and that's that. Down below the pool's totally dark; the other one comes out of the changing room and switches on some lights inside the pool, below the surface of the water. She's fixing her hair to fit inside her bathing cap when she hears footsteps. She asks, kind of alarmed, if it's the attendant. No answer. Then she gets really terrified, throws off her bathrobe and dives in. From the middle of the water she peers toward the sides of the pool, still in darkness, and now you hear the snarling of some wild black beast pacing furiously, you can barely make it out, but a shadow's moving, sort of slipping along the edges of the pool. The snarls can hardly be heard, they're always snarls like with the teeth clenched, and those green eyes glitter watching the other one in the pool who now really starts screaming like crazy. At this the attendant comes running downstairs and turns on all the lights, asking her what's the matter. No one else is there, why all the screaming? The other one's completely embarrassed, doesn't know how to explain why she's so frightened; imagine what'll happen if she says some panther woman got in down there. And so she says she thought somebody was there, an animal prowling around. And the woman on duty looks at her as if to say listen to this dope talking, some friend comes to see her so she's shaking all over, just because she hears some footsteps, and there the two of them are when they notice the bathrobe on the floor, ripped to shreds, and the tracks of an animal, from having stepped in the puddles . . . Are you listening to me?

—Yeah, but I don't know why I can't get something out of my head tonight.

—What?

—Nothing, I can't concentrate . . .

—But come on, open up a little.

—I'm just thinking about my girl.

—What's her name?

—That's not the point. Look, I never talk to you about her, but I'm always thinking about her.

—How come she doesn't write to you?

—How do you know if she writes or not! I could say I'm getting letters from somebody else and they're hers. Or are you going through my stuff when I'm taking a shower?

—You're crazy, Valentin. But you never showed me a letter from her.

—Well, I don't like to talk about this ever, but, I don't know, just now I felt like discussing something with you . . . When you started talking about the panther woman's following the assistant around, I got scared.

—What scared you?

—I wasn't afraid for myself but for my girl.

—Ah . . .

—I must be nuts, bringing this subject up.

—Why? Talk if you feel like it . . .

—When you started telling how the girl was being followed by the panther woman, I pictured that it was my girl who was in danger. And I feel so helpless here, about warning her to be careful, about not taking too many risks.

—I understand.

—Well, you can imagine, if she's my woman, it's because she's in the struggle too. Although I shouldn't be telling you, Molina.

—Don't worry.

—It's just that I don't want to saddle you with any information you're better off not having. It's a burden, and you've already got enough of your own.

—Me too, you know, I have that sensation, from being in here, of not being able to do anything; but in my case it's not a woman—not a girl I mean, it's my mother.

—Your mother's not all alone, or is she?

—Well, she's with an aunt of mine, my father's sister. But it's just that she's so sick. She's got high blood pressure and her heart's weak.

—But, you know, with that kind of thing you can still go on, sometimes for years and years . . .

—But you still have to avoid upsetting them, Valentin.

—Why do you say that?

—Imagine, the shame of having a son in prison. And the reason.

—Don't think about it. The worst's over, right? Now she's got to accept it, that's all.

—But she misses me so much. We've always been very close.

—Try not to think about it. Or if not . . . accept the fact that she's not in any danger, like the person I love.

—But she's got the danger inside, she carries the enemy around inside, it's that weak heart of hers.

—She's waiting for you, she knows you're going to get out of here, eight years do go by, and there's always the hope of time off for good conduct and all. That will give her the strength to wait for you, think of it that way.

–Mmm-hmm, you're right.

–Otherwise, you'll go crazy.

—Tell me more about your girlfriend, if you feel like it . . .

—What can I tell you? Nothing in common with the assistant; I don't know why I put the two together.

—Is she pretty?

—Yeah, sure.

—She could be ugly—what are you laughing at, Valentin?

—Nothing, I don't know why I'm laughing.

—But what strikes you so funny?

—I don't know . . .

—Must be something . . . something to laugh at.

—At you, and me.

—Why?

—I don't know; let me think about it, because I couldn't explain it to you anyway.

—Okay, just stop laughing.

—Better I tell you when I really know why I was laughing.

—How about if I finish the film?

—Yes, please.

—Where were we?

—Where the girl saves herself in the swimming pool.

—Right, so how did it go? . . . Now comes the confrontation between the psychiatrist and the panther woman.

—Can I interrupt? . . . You won't get annoyed?

—What's the matter?

—Better if we go on tomorrow, Molina.

—Not much left to finish.

—I can't concentrate on what you're saying. Sorry.

—Bored?

—No, not that. My head's a mess. I want to just keep quiet and see if the hysterics will pass. Because that's what my laughing's all about, a fit of hysterics, nothing else.

—Whatever you want.

—I want to think about my woman, there's something I'm not understanding, and I want to think about it. I don't know if that's happened to you, you feel like you're about to understand something, you're on the point of untangling the knot and if you don't begin pulling the right thread . . . you'll lose it.

—Fine, tomorrow then.

—Okay, tomorrow.

—Tomorrow we'll be all finished with the film.

—You don't know how sorry that makes me.

—You too?

—Yes, I'd like it to last a little longer. And the worst thing's that it's going to end sadly, Molina.

—But did you really like it?

—Well, it made our time go by faster, right?

—But you didn't really really like it then.

—Yes I did, and it's a shame to see it ending.

—But don't be silly, I can tell you another one.

—Honestly?

—Sure, I remember lots of lovely, lovely films.

—Then great, you start thinking about one you liked a lot, and meanwhile I'll think about what I have to think about, it's a deal?

—Don't lose that thread.

—Right.

—But if you drop the ball of yarn, I'll give you zero in housekeeping, Miss Valentina.

—You just don't worry yourself about me.

—All right, I won't meddle anymore.

—And don't call me Valentina, I'm no woman.

—How can I tell?

—Sorry, Molina, but I don't give demonstrations.

—Don't worry, I'm not asking for any.

—Good night, have a good sleep.

—Night, you too.

—I'm listening.

—Well, as I was telling you yesterday, I don't remember this last part so well. That very night the husband calls her psychiatrist to get him to come to the house. They're there waiting for her, for Irena, who hasn't arrived yet.

—At whose house?

—The architect's. But then the assistant calls up the architect to get him to go to the women's hotel and from there to the police station, because the incident in the pool just happened, so the architect leaves the psychiatrist by himself for just a little while, no more, and, zap! Irena comes home, and finds herself face to face with the psychiatrist. It's nighttime, obviously; the room's lit with only a table lamp. The psychiatrist, who's been reading, takes off his glasses, looks at her. Irena feels that same mixture of repulsion and desire for him, because he's good-looking, like I told you, a sexy guy. And here something strange happens. She throws herself into his arms, because she feels so abandoned, nobody wants her, her husband's forsaken her. And the psychiatrist interprets this as a sign that she's interested in him sexually, and to top it off he thinks if he kisses her and even manages to go all the way, he'll be able to rid her of those strange ideas about being a panther woman. And he kisses her, and they press up against each other, embracing and kissing, until all of a sudden she . . . she kind of slips out of his arms, looking at him through half-closed eyes, green eyes glittering with something like desire and hatred at the same time. And she breaks away from him and goes to the other end of that room filled with lovely turn-of-the-century furniture, all beautiful velvet armchairs and tables with crochet doilies on them. But she goes into that corner because the light from the table lamp doesn't reach there. And she drops down to the floor, and the psychiatrist tries to defend himself, but it's too late, because now over in that dark corner everything turns blurry for an instant, and before you know it she's transformed into a panther, and he just manages to grab the poker from the fireplace to defend himself, but the panther's already pounced on him, and he tries to strike with the poker, but she's already ripped his throat open with her claws and the man's already fallen to the floor with his blood gushing out. The panther snarls and bares a set of perfect white fangs and sinks her claws in again, this time into his face, to tear it to pieces, those cheeks and mouth she'd kissed a few moments ago. By then the assistant's already with Irena's husband who'd gone to meet her at the hotel and there at the front desk they try to call the psychiatrist to warn him he's in danger, because now there's no way around it, it's not just Irena's imagination, she really is a panther woman.

—No, she's a psychopathic killer.

—Okay, but the telephone rings and rings and no one answers; the psychiatrist is lying dead, all his blood drained. Then the husband, the assistant and the police who'd already been called to the house, climb the stairs slowly, find the door open and inside the guy's dead. Irena, she's not there.

—And then?

—The husband knows where to find her, it's the only place she'd go, and even though it's midnight already, they go over to the park . . . more specifically, to the zoo. Oh, but I forgot to tell you something!

—What?

—That afternoon Irena went to the zoo the same as every afternoon to see the panther that had her hypnotized. And she was right there when the keeper came along with his keys to give the meat to the beasts. The keeper's that absent-minded old guy I told you about. Irena kept at a distance but watched everything. The keeper came up with the keys, opened the lock on the cage, slid back the bolt, opened the door and tossed in a couple of gigantic chunks of meat, and afterwards shot the bolt back through the latch on the door again, but forgot the key in the lock. When he wasn't looking, Irena approached the cage and took the key. Anyway, all that was in the afternoon but now it's night already and the psychiatrist's dead already, when the husband with the other one and the police rush toward the zoo, just a few blocks away. But Irena's just getting there, at the very cage the panther's in. Walking like a sleep-walker. Holding the keys in her hand. The panther's asleep, but Irena's odor wakes him up. Irena looks at him through the bars. Slowly she goes up to the door, puts the key in the lock, opens it. Meantime, the others are arriving; you hear police cars approaching with sirens going to clear a way through the traffic, even though at that hour the place is almost deserted. Irena slides back the bolt and opens the door, setting the panther free. Irena's almost transported into another world; her expression's strange, tragic and yet excited sort of, her eyes misty. The panther escapes from the cage in a single leap; for a split second he looks suspended in midair, with nothing in front of him but Irena. Only the force of his leap and Irena's knocked down. Cars are pulling up. The panther runs through the park and across the road, just as a police car races by at full speed. The car hits him. They get out and find the dead panther. The architect goes toward the cages and finds Irena stretched out on the cobblestone, right where they met for the first time. Irena's face is disfigured from the swipe of the claw. She's dead. The young assistant comes over to where he's standing and they walk off together arm in arm, trying to forget the terrible spectacle they've just seen, and, The End.

— . . .

—Did you like it?

—Yes . . .

—A lot or a little?

—I'm sorry it's over.

—We had a good time, didn't we?

—Yeah, for sure.

—I'm glad.

—I must be crazy.

—What's wrong with you?

—I'm sorry it's over.

—So what, I'll tell you another one.

—No, it's not that. You're going to laugh at what I'm going to tell you.

—Let's have it.

—I'm sorry because I've become attached to the characters. And now it's all over, and it's just like they died.

—So, Valentin, you too have a little bit of a heart.

—It has to come out some place . . . weakness, I mean.

—It's not weakness, listen.

—Funny how you can't get along without becoming attached to something . . . It's . . . as if the mind had to secrete affection without stopping . . .

—You think so?

— . . . same way your stomach secretes juices for digestion.

—You really think so?

—Sure, like a leaky faucet. And those drops continue dripping on anything, they can't be turned off.

—Why?

—Who knows . . . because they're spilling over the top of their container.

—And you don't want to think about your girl.

—But it's like I can't avoid it . . . because I get attached to anything that reminds me of her.

—Tell me a little what she's like.

—I'd give . . . absolutely anything to be able to hold her, even for just a second.

—That day'll come.

—Sometimes I think it's never going to come.

—But you're not a lifer.

—Something could happen to her.

—Write her, tell her not to take any chances, that you need her.

—Never. If you're going to think like that, you'll never change anything in this world.

—And you think you're going to change the world?

—Yes, and I don't care if you laugh . . . It makes people laugh to say it, but what's got to be done more than anything . . . is change the world.

—But you can't change it just like that, and you can't do it all alone.

—But that's just it, I'm not alone! . . . you get me? . . . There's the truth, that's what's important! . . . That's just it, right at this minute I'm not alone! I'm with her and with everybody who thinks like her and me . . . and I can't let myself forget it. That's the piece of thread that sometimes slips out of my fingers. But luckily I've got a good grip on it now. And I'm not about to let go . . . I'm not far from any of my comrades, I'm with them! Now, at this very moment! . . . It doesn't matter if I can't see them.

—If you can swallow something like that, great.

—What an idiot you are!

—Such names . . .

—Don't be so annoying then . . . Don't say things like that, as if I were some dreamer who kids himself about everything, because that's not how it is! I'm not some loudmouth playing at cafe politics, understand? The proof's that I'm here in this place, not in a cafe!

—Sorry.

—It's all right.

—You started to tell me something about your girl and you never told me anything.

—No, better we forget the whole thing.

—Whatever you want.

—Even though there's no reason not to talk. It shouldn't upset me to talk about her.

—If it upsets you, don't . . .

—It doesn't upset me . . . Only it's better for me not to tell you her name.

—I just remembered the name of the actress who played the assistant.

—What is it?

—Jane Randolph.

—Never heard of her.

—She goes back a ways, to the forties, around then. For your girl's name we can simply say Jane Randolph.

—Jane Randolph.

—Jane Randolph in . . . *The Mystery of Cellblock Seven.*

—One of the initials actually fits . . .

—Which?

—What do you want me to tell you about her?

—Whatever you want to say, what kind of girl she is.

—She's twenty-four, Molina. Two years younger than me.

—Thirteen less than me.

—She always was a revolutionary. At first in terms of . . . well, I won't hesitate with you . . . in terms of the sexual revolution.

—Please, tell me about it.

—She comes from a bourgeois family, people who aren't very rich, but, you know, comfortable enough, two-story house in Caballito. But she spent her whole childhood and adolescence tormented by watching her parents destroying one another. With a father who deceived the mother, but you know what I mean . . .

—No, what?

—Deceived her by not telling her how he needed outside relationships. And the mother devoted herself to criticizing him in front of the daughter, devoted herself to being the martyr. I don't believe in marriage—or in monogamy, to be more precise.

—But how marvelous when a couple loves each other for a lifetime.

—You'd really go for that?

—It's my dream.

—So why do you like men then?

—What's that got to do with it? . . . I'd like to marry a man for the rest of my life.

—So you're a regular bourgeois gentleman at heart, eh, Molina?

—Bourgeois lady, thank you.

—But don't you see how all that's nothing but a deception? If you were a woman, you wouldn't want that.

—I'm in love with a wonderful guy and all I ask is to live by his side for the rest of my life.

—And since that's impossible, because if he's a guy he wants a woman, well, you're never going to undeceive yourself.

—Go on about your girl, I don't feel like talking about me.

—Well okay, as I was telling you, they . . . what's the name?

—Jane. Jane Randolph.

—They raised Jane Randolph to be a proper lady. Piano lessons, French, and painting, and after the lycée the Catholic University.

—Architecture! That's why you connected the two.

—No, sociology. And that was when the mess began at home. She wanted to go to the state university but they made her register at Catholic. There, she got to know some college kid, they fell in love and had an affair. The boy was also living with his parents but he left home, got a night job as a telephone operator and rented a small apartment, and they started spending days there.

—And didn't study anymore.

—That year they did less studying, at first, but then later on she began to study more.

—But not him.

—Exactly, because he was working. And a year later Jane moved in with him. There was friction at home in th . beginning, but afterwards they accepted it. They hoped that since the kids were so much in love they'd eventually get married. And the student wanted to marry her. But Jane didn't want to repeat any part of the same old story, so she had her doubts.

—Abortions?

—Yes, one. But that strengthened her determination instead of depressing her. She saw clearly that if she had a child she'd never mature, never be able to pursue her own development. Her freedom would be limited. She took a reporting job on some magazine, snooping really.

—Snooping?

—Right.

—What an ugly word.

—Well, it's an easier job than reporting; mostly you're out in the street picking up whatever information's needed for articles. And that's how she got to know some kid in the political division. She felt immediately drawn to him, that her relationship with the other one was stagnating.

—Why stagnating?

—They'd already given all they had to give. They were very attached, yes, but they were too young to settle just for that, they still hadn't any idea yet . . . what they really wanted, neither one of them. And . . . Jane, she proposed to the student a kind of opening up of the relationship. And the student accepted it, and she started seeing the boyfriend from the magazine at the same time.

—Still sleeping at the student's place?

—Yes, and sometimes no. Until she went to live permanently with the reporter.

—Where did the reporter stand politically?

—Leftist.

—And he taught her that?

—No, she'd always felt the need for change. Anyway, you know it's getting kind of late, isn't it?

—It's about two A.M. now.

—I'll go on tomorrow, Molina.

—Revenge, eh?

—No, clown. I'm tired.

—Not me. I'm not sleepy at all.

—Good night.

—Good night.

—Sleep any?

—No, I told you I wasn't tired.

—I'm feeling a little restless, too.

—You said you were sleepy.

—Yes, but then I kept thinking, I left you hanging.

—Left me hanging?

—Yes, I didn't go on with our conversation.

—Don't worry about it.

—You feeling okay?

—Mmm-hmm.

—So why not go to sleep?

—I don't know, Valentin.

—Look, I really am a little sleepy, and I'm about to drop off any minute now. And I've got a way for you to get some sleep too.

—What?

—Think about the picture you're going to tell me next.

—Great idea.

—But it better be a good one, like the panther woman. Choose carefully, Molina.

—And you, you'll tell me more about Jane.

—No, I don't know about that . . . Let's do something; whenever I feel I can tell you something I'll go ahead and do it gladly. But don't you ask me about it, I'll bring it up when it's right for me. A deal?

—A deal.

—And now think about the picture.

—Okay.

—Ciao.

—Ciao.

CHAPTER 3

—It takes place in Paris, a couple of months after the start of the German occupation. Nazi troops are filing through the Arch of Triumph. Flags with German swastikas, fluttering all over the place, on the Eiffel Tower and everywhere else. Soldiers parading past, totally blond, marvelous to look at, and the French women all applaud as they march by. Not far from there, one small group of soldiers make their way along a typical little side street and go into a butcher shop, where there's an old butcher, with a pointy head, and one of those tiny caps sitting on the back of his scalp.

—Like a rabbi.

—His face looks so ugly. And a horrible fear overtakes him the moment he sees the soldiers come into the shop and start to search the premises.

—What are they searching for?

—Anything, and they discover a hidden cellar stocked with hoarded provisions, which evidently come from the black market. And a mob collects just outside the store, mostly housewives, and Frenchmen with berets, very lower-class looking, and they're all talking about the old buzzard getting arrested, and that Europe's not going to be hungry anymore, because the Germans are putting an end to people taking advantage of the poor. And just as the soldiers are leaving, the officer in charge, who's a youngish lieutenant with a very nice face, gets hugged by this old woman, who says thank you my son, or something like that. But while all this is going on there's a pickup truck coming down the same side street, but whoever's sitting next to the driver, when he sees the soldiers, or maybe the huge crowd, he tells the driver to pull over. The driver's got a face like a murderer's, kind of cross-eyed looking, a criminal's face, but retarded too. And the other one—you can tell he gives the orders—he looks in the back of the truck and tries to fix the tarpaulin a little to hide the load they've got back there; it's more hoarded provisions of food. And they shift the car into reverse and get away, until finally the one giving the orders gets out of the truck and walks into some typically Parisian-type bar. He's a clubfoot; one of his shoes has a giant block under it, almost like a hoof, made out of silver. He talks on the phone, reports how the black-marketeer butcher just got caught, and as he's about to hang up he gives their salute: long live the maquis, because they're all in the maquis together.

—Where did you see this picture?

—Right here in Buenos Aires, at some movie house in the Belgrano district, over where they had all those big houses and gardens, not the section that goes toward the river, the one in the other direction, toward Villa Urquiza, you remember? They tore it down a few years ago. My house is just near there, but over in the crummy section.

—Go on with the film.

—Sure. Suddenly you're inside this fantastic theater in the heart of Paris, gorgeous, all upholstered in dark velvet, with heavy chrome balustrades up the boxes and staircases, and railings out of chrome too. It's a famous music hall, and there's a number starting with just chorus girls, nothing else, such divine figures on every one of them, unforgettable, because down one side they're all made up black and when they kick they hold onto each other around the waist and as the camera focuses on them they look like a line of African girls, with skirts all made out of bananas, and nothing else, but then the cymbals clang and they turn to the other side, and suddenly they're blonde, and instead of bananas they're wearing little strips, all in strass, and nothing else, an arabesque of strass.

—What's strass?

—I can't believe you don't know.

—I don't.

—It's back in fashion again, it looks like diamonds, only it's not worth anything, it's like little pieces of glass that sparkle, and out of them they make up those little strips, or any kind of costume jewelry.

—Don't waste so much time, tell me what happens.

—And when the chorus number's finished, the stage gets left in total darkness until, up above, a light begins to rise like mist and the silhouette of some divine-looking woman, who's very tall, absolutely perfect, but still just a hazy outline, slowly emerges sharper and sharper, because she steps forward through layers and layers of hanging tulle, and you obviously get to see her more and more clearly, wrapped in a silver lamé gown that fits her like a glove. The most divine woman you can imagine. And she sings a song, first in French and afterwards in German. She's way high up over the stage, and then all of a sudden some lightning flashes under her feet and she makes her way downwards and with each step, zap! another streak of lightning, and finally the whole stage is left crossed by horizontal lines, because actually each line of light is on the edge of a step, and takes the form of a staircase all in lights without your realizing it. And in one of the box seats is this young German officer, not as young as the young lieutenant back at the beginning, but every bit as handsome.

—Blond?

—Yes, but she's a brunette, with incredibly white skin, but her hair's pitch black.

—How is her figure? Does she have a good build, or is she more on the flat side?

—Not at all, she's very tall, with a good build, but not stack stacked, because what was in fashion back then was the long slinky profile. And while taking her bows she exchanges a few quick looks with the German officer. Then back in her dressing room she finds a beautiful bouquet of flowers, but with no card. And at this point one of the blond chorus girls, very French-looking, knocks on the door. Oh, but the one thing I didn't tell you is whatever it was she sang was really strange, and it scares me each time I remember that song she sings, because when she sings it, she stares straight out into black space, and it's not a very happy expression she's got on her face at that moment; you can't believe it, how frightened she looks, but at the same time like she's not doing a thing to defend herself, but just surrendering to whatever has to happen.

—And what does she sing?

—I don't have any idea, a love song, I'm sure. But it really got to me. Anyway, so one of the blond chorus girls comes into her dressing room, all excited, and tells her about what's happened to her, because she wants her—the artist she admires the most—to be the first to know about it. She's going to have a baby. And obviously the singer, whose name is, I'll never forget, Leni, the singer is disturbed because she knows the girl's single. But the other one says not to worry, the baby's father is a German officer, a boy who really loves her and they're just in the process of arranging everything so they can get married. But at this point the chorus girl's expression clouds over, and she tells Leni that she's afraid something else might happen. Leni asks her what, but the girl tells her, Oh, it's really nothing, just some foolishness, and she leaves. Then Leni's there all alone, thinking about whether she could ever love an invader of her country, and she stays like that, thinking . . . And at a certain point she finally notices the flowers that were sent to her, and asks her personal maid what kind they are, and it turns out that they come all the way from the German Alps, shipped to Paris specially, at an incredible expense. By then the blond chorus girl's on her way through the streets of Paris, dark streets during the night because of wartime, but she looks up and sees, way up on the top floor, in an old apartment building, a light on, and her face glows with a smile. She has an antique watch, the chorus girl does, like a brooch on the front of her dress, and she looks at it and sees that it's just about midnight. Then a window opens way up, there where the light is, and the same boy as back in the beginning leans out, the young German lieutenant, and smiles at her with the face of someone head-over-heels in love, and he throws down the key, which falls in the middle of the street. And she goes over to pick it up. Oh, but when you first see the street, before all this, like a shadow passes by. Or no, a car's parked nearby, and in the darkness you barely make out some-one who's hiding in the car. No! Now I remember, while the girl's busy walking through this neighborhood it seems like someone's following her, and it's a strange kind of footstep you hear, first a step and then something that drags behind it.

—The clubfoot.

—Right, the clubfoot guy appears, and he sees a coupe pulling up, and the one who's driving the coupe is the cross-eyed guy, the one with the murderer's face. The clubfoot gets into the car and gives the signal so the car screeches off, the accelerator floored. And now when the girl's in the middle of the narrow street and stoops down to pick up the key, the car goes by with the accelerator floored, it runs her down. And they keep on going until finally they vanish into the dark streets, empty of all traffic. The young German, who's watched it all, now runs down the stairs desperately. The girl is still moaning, he takes her up in his arms, she wants to tell him something, you can hardly make it out, she tells him not to be scared, the baby's going to be born healthy and make his father proud. And her eyes stay open, lost, she's dead. You like the film?

—I don't know yet. But go on, will you?

—Sure. Then it turns out next morning, the German police call on Leni, to get her to confess whatever she knows, because they found out she was a friend of the dead girl. But Leni doesn't know anything, just that the girl was in love with a German lieutenant, that's all. But they don't believe her, and they detain her for a couple of hours, but since she's a well-known singer, a voice on the telephone orders her release, in custody, so she can still perform that evening like every other night. Leni's scared, but she sings that night and, when she gets back to her dressing room, again she finds more flowers from the Alps, and just as she's looking for the card, a man's voice tells her not to look any further, because this time he has brought them to her personally. She spins around, startled. It's a high-ranking German officer, but rather young; the guy's more handsome than you can imagine. She asks who he is, but obviously, she already sees he's the one that was in the box seat. He says he's in charge of German counterespionage operations here in Paris, and he's come personally to offer his apologies for the trouble she had to put up with that morning. She asks if the flowers come from his country, and he answers yes, they come from the Upper Palatinate, where he was born, near a marvelous lake set between snow-capped mountain peaks. But I forgot to tell you one other thing: he's not in uniform, he's wearing tails, and he invites her for supper after the show, at the tiniest and most fabulous cabaret in all of Paris. It's got an orchestra with black musicians, and you can hardly see the people it's so dark, and one dim spotlight falls on the orchestra through the smoke-filled air. They're playing an old jazz piece, heavy black jazz, and he asks her why her first name's Leni, that's German, while the last one's French, but I don't remember what it was. And she says she comes from Alsace, on the border, where the German flag has also flown in times past. But she insists she's been taught to love only her France, and wants nothing but the good of her own country, and wonders how the German occupation is going to be of any help in this. He says he hasn't any doubts about that, because Germany's now committed to the task of ridding Europe once and for all of the true enemies of all peoples, who sometimes even disguise their crimes behind the masks of patriotism. He orders some kind of German brandy, and for a minute it seems like she wants to irritate him, because she orders a Scotch whiskey. The fact is that she can't really accept him, she barely touches the drink to her lips, says she's tired, and lets him take her home, in a fantastic-looking limousine, with chauffeur and all. They stop in front of her place, a lovely town house, and she asks him ironically whether he has plans for any further interrogation some other day. He denies he ever had any such idea, or even would have in the future. She gets out of the limousine, he kisses her on the hand, her glove's still on. She seems impervious, cold as ice. He asks her whether she lives alone, whether she's not afraid. She says no, there's a couple of elderly caretakers at the back of the garden. But as she turns to walk into the house she notices a shadow in the window up on the top floor, which immediately disappears. She shivers, but he doesn't notice anything, dazed as he is by her loveliness, so she, all she can say is yes, she does feel a little bit frightened tonight, about being alone, and, please, will he take her away from here. And they go to his apartment, what a place he's got, but really very strange, absolutely white walls with no pictures and very high ceilings, and not much furniture, all of it dark, like packing crates, but you can see it's all incredibly expensive, just very stark. The window curtains are in white chiffon, and there are several statues in white marble, very modern, not exactly Greek, mostly male figures, like out of a dream. He orders the guest room prepared by the majordomo, who gives her a rather strange look. But first he asks her, won't she have a glass of champagne, the very best from her own France, like the nation's blood streaming up from its very soil. Some marvelous music is playing, and she says how the only thing she loves from his country is its music. And a breeze comes through the open window, a very tall casement window, with the white chiffon curtain billowing in the wind like a ghost, and the candles blow out, the only lighting. And now there's nothing but the moonlight coming in, and shining upon her, and she too looks like a statue so tall, with that white gown of hers that fits so tightly, looks like an ancient Greek amphora, with obviously the hips not too heavy, and a white scarf almost reaching the floor draped around her head, but without crushing her hairdo in the slightest, just framing it perfectly. And he says what a marvelous creature she is, with an unearthly beauty and most assuredly a noble destiny. His words make her sort of shiver, she's totally enveloped by some premonition, somehow sensing that in her own lifetime, terribly important events are about to unfold, and almost surely with tragic consequences. Her hand trembles, her glass falls to the floor, Baccarat splintering into a thousand pieces. She's like a goddess, and at the same time incredibly fragile, a woman trembling with fear. He takes her hand, he asks if she's not too cold. She answers no. At this point the music turns fortissimo, violins play sublimely, and she wonders aloud what the melody is trying to suggest. He confesses it's his very favorite piece of music and says the waves of the violins are like the waters of a German river, navigated by some man-god who actually is just a man, but whose love of country makes him invincible, like a god, because now he knows no fear whatsoever. The music moves him so completely, his eyes fill with tears. And that's what's so marvelous about the scene now, because seeing how moved he is, she realizes how much he too has his emotions like any man, even though he seems as invincible as a god. He tries to conceal his feelings by going over to the window. A full moon's over the city of Paris, the grounds around the house seem silvery, black trees set against the gray sky, not blue, because the film's in black and white. The white fountain bordered by jasmine, flowers in silvery-white too, and the camera on her face then with a close-up, all in divine grays, with perfect shadowing, and a tear rolling down her cheek. When it's just about to fall it's not so shiny, but when it starts to run down along her high cheekbone the tear begins to shine

as much as the diamonds in her necklace. And the camera
again shows you the silvery garden, and there you are in the
movies but it's more as if you were a bird taking off because
now you see the garden from above, smaller and smaller, and
the white fountain seems . . . like meringue and the casement
windows too, a white palace all out of meringue, like in certain
fairy tales, where they eat the houses, and what a shame they
don't show the two of them right then, because they'd look like
two dolls. Do you like the picture?

—I don't know yet. And you, why do you like it so much?
You seem transported.

—If I had the chance to choose one film to see all over again,
it would have to be this one.

—But why? It's a piece of Nazi junk, or don't you realize?

—Look . . . it'd be better if I shut up.

—Now don't stop talking. Say what you were going to say,
Molina.

—No more. I'm going to sleep.

—What's the matter?

—Luckily there's no light on and I don't have to look you
in the face.

—That's what you had to say to me?

—No, it's that if there's any junk around here it might be
you and not the film. So don't speak to me anymore.

—I'm sorry.

— . . .

—Really, I'm sorry. I didn't think I was being offensive.

—Of course you're offensive the way you . . . you think I
don't even . . . realize what Nazi propa- . . . ganda is, but even
if I . . . if I do like it, well, that's be- . . . because it's well made,
and besides it's a work of art, you don't under- . . . understand
because you never even saw it.

—But you must be crazy, crying over that!

—I can cry how- . . . however much I feel like . . . !

—Whatever you want . . . I'm sorry.

—And don't think you're what's making me cry now. It's just that I was thinking of . . . of him, of what it'd be like to . . . to be with him, and to . . . to talk to him about all the fi- . . . films I like so much, instead of being here with you. Today I was thinking about him all day. It's three . . . years ago today I met him. That's . . . why I'm cry- . . . ing.

—I tell you, really, it wasn't my intention to hurt you. Why don't you tell me about your friend, it'll do you good to talk about him a little.

—What for? So you can tell me he's . . . a piece of junk too?

—Come on, please, what kind of work does he do?

—He's a waiter, in a restaurant . . .

—Is he a nice person?

—Mmm-hmm, but he has his moments . . . like you wouldn't believe.

—What makes you like him so much?

—Lots of things.

—For example . . .

—Well, I'll be totally honest with you. First, because he's so marvelous-looking. And after that because I think he's very intelligent, but he had none of the opportunities in life, and here he is still working at that shitty job, but he deserves much more. Which makes me feel like I want to help him out.

—And he wants your help?

—What do you mean?

—Does he let you help, or not?

—I think you must be psychic or something. Why did you ask me that question?

—I don't know.

—Well, you put your finger right on it.

—So he doesn't want your help?

—He didn't back then. Now I don't know, it's anybody's guess how he feels now . . .

—Isn't he the friend who came to visit you, the one you told me about?

—No, that one's a girlfriend, about as much of a man as I am. Because this other one, my waiter friend, has to work during visiting hours here.

—He never comes to see you?

—No.

—Poor guy, he has to work.

—Listen, Valentin, don't you think he could trade shifts with someone else?

—They probably don't allow that.

—You're all so good when it comes to defending each other . . .

—Who all?

—You men, all a bunch of . . .

—A bunch of what?

—Sons of bitches, no reflection on your mother, who certainly isn't to blame.

—Look, you're a man just as much as I am, so cut it out . . . Don't go setting us apart.

—Want me to come closer?

—Not close, and not apart.

—Listen, Valentin, I remember very well one time, he traded shifts with another guy to take his wife to the theater.

—So he's married?

—Mmm-hmm, he's completely straight. I was the one who started it all, he wasn't to blame for anything. I butted into his life, but I just wanted to help him.

—How did it all begin?

—One day I went to a restaurant and saw him there. I was crazy about him right off. But it's a long story, I'll tell you some other time, or maybe, no I won't, I'm not saying anything to you anymore, who knows what you'll come out with.

—Just a minute, Molina, you're really wrong. If I ask about him it's because I feel somehow . . . how can I explain it?

—Curiosity, that's all you feel.

—That's not true. I think I have to know more about you,

that's what, in order to understand you better. If we're going
to be in this cell together like this, we ought to understand one
another better, and I know very little about people with your
type of inclination.*

—I'll tell you how it happened then, quickly though, so as
not to bore you.

—What's his name?

—No, his name no, that's for me. No one else.

—Whatever you like.

—That's the only thing of his that I have all to myself, inside
me, it's in my throat, and I keep it down there just for me. I'll
never let it out . . .

—Have you known him a long time?

—Three years today, the twelfth of September, the first day
I went to the restaurant. But I feel so funny talking about this.

—Never mind. If you want to talk about it sometime, talk.
If not, don't.

—Somehow I feel embarrassed.

—That's . . . that's how it is when it comes to really deep
feelings, at least I think so.

—I was just with some friends of mine. Well, actually a
couple of harlots, unbearable, the two of them. But cute, and
sharp too.

---

*The English researcher D. J. West suggests there are three principal
theories with respect to the physical origins of homosexuality, and then
proceeds to refute all three.

The first of these theories tries to establish the fact that abnormal sexual
behavior stems from an imbalance, proportionally speaking, in male and
female hormones, both being present in the bloodstream of either sex. But
tests performed directly on homosexuals have not yielded results which
would confirm such a theory, that is to say, have not demonstrated a
deficiency in hormonal distribution. As Doctor Swyer explains it in his
study, "Homosexuality: The Endocrinologic Aspects," the charting of hormonal levels in homosexuals and heterosexuals has not revealed such
differences. Moreover, were homosexuality to presuppose a hormonal origin
(the hormones are secreted by the endocrine glands), it could be cured by
means of injections to restore the hormonal balance. But this has not been

—Two girls?

—No, dummy, when I say harlots I mean queens. And so one of them was rather bitchy to the waiter, which was him. I saw from the beginning how handsome he was, but nothing more. Then when my friend got really snotty with him, the guy, without losing his self-control at all, he put her right in her place. I was surprised. Because waiters, poor guys, they always have this complex about being servants, which makes it difficult for them to answer any rudeness, without coming across like the injured servant bit, you get what I mean? Anyway, this guy, nothing doing, he explains to my slutty friend just why the food isn't up to what it ought to be, but with such finesse, she winds up looking like a complete dope. But don't get the idea he acted very haughty—not at all, perfectly detached, handled the whole situation. So immediately my nose tells me there's something unusual, a real man. So the next week this woman heads straight to the same restaurant, but this time alone.

—What woman?

—Listen, I'm sorry, but when it comes to him I can't talk about myself like a man, because I don't feel like one.

—Go on.

—The second time I saw him he looked even cuter, in a

the case, and in his study, "Testosterone in Psychotic Male Homosexuals," the investigations of Barahal suggest that with such administering of masculine hormones to male homosexuals, the only identifiable result has been a marked increment in the desire which the individual experiences for that form of sexual activity to which he has been accustomed. As for experiments conducted on women, Doctor Foss, in "The Influence of Urinary Androgens on Sexuality in Women," states that administering large doses of masculine hormones to women has in fact produced a noticeable change, and in the masculine direction, but only concerning the physical aspect: voice noticeably deeper, beard, reduction in the breast size, clitoral expansion, etc. As for sexual appetite, it is in fact stimulated, but normally remains feminine, that is to say that the object of the urge continues to be men, but clearly only if one is not dealing with a woman of lesbian tendencies. In addition, with the male heterosexual, the administering of large

white uniform with a Mao collar, it fitted him divinely. Like some movie star or something. Everything about him was perfect, the way he walked, the husky voice, but sometimes a slight lilt to it, kind of tender, I don't know how to put it. And the way he served! I'm telling you, it was poetry, one time I saw him do a salad, I couldn't believe! First he sat the customer at a table, because it was a woman, a real dog, and he sets up a little side table next to hers, to put the salad tray down right there, then he asks her, some oil? some vinegar? some of this? some of that? until finally he picks up the wooden fork and spoon and gets right down to mixing the salad, but I don't know how to explain it, like he caressed the lettuce leaves, and the tomatoes, but nothing softy about it—how can I put it? They were such powerful movements, and so elegant, and soft, and masculine at the same time.

—And what's masculine in your terms?

—It's lots of things, but for me . . . well, the nicest thing about a man is just that, to be marvelous-looking, and strong, but without making any fuss about it, and also walking very tall. Walking absolutely straight, like my waiter, who's not afraid to say anything. And it's knowing what you want, where you're going.

—That's pure fantasy, that type doesn't exist.

---

quantities of feminine hormones does not awaken homosexual urges, but it does contribute to a lessening of sexual energy. All of which indicates that the furnishing of masculine hormones to women and of feminine hormones to men reveals no necessary relationship between the percentage of masculine and feminine hormones in the bloodstream and corresponding sexual urge. One can therefore assert that sexual preference in a particular subject bears no demonstrable relationship to endocrinal activity, that is to say, to hormonal secretion.

The second important theory on the possible physical origin of homosexuality is, according to D. J. West, one referring to intersexuality. Intersexuals, or hermaphrodites, are those individuals who pertain physically to neither one of the sexes completely, although they still present certain features of both. The sex to which an individual will belong is determined at the moment of conception, and depends upon genetic variety of the

—Yes it does so exist, and it's him.

—Okay, so he gives you that impression, but inside, at least as far as this culture goes, without power behind you no one walks tall, not the way you say.

—Don't be so jealous, there's just no talking to a guy about some other guy without getting into a fuss, you're all like women that way.

—Don't be stupid.

—See how you react, even insulting me. You men are just as competitive as women.

—Please, let's stick to a certain level, or let's not talk at all.

—What's with this level bit . . .

—With you there's simply no talking, unless it's when you're spouting off about some film.

—No talking to me? I'd like to know why.

—Because you can't carry on a discussion, there's no line of thought to it, you come out with any nonsense at all.

—That isn't true, Valentin.

—Whatever you say.

—You're so damn pedantic.

—If you think so.

—Show me. I'd like to see how I don't come up to your level.

—I didn't say you don't come up to my level; I just meant

---

corresponding spermatozoid that fertilizes the ovule. The physical causes of intersexuality have still not been properly determined; commonly it is produced by a malfunction of the endocrine system during the fetal state. The degree of intersexuality varies greatly; in some cases the internal sexual glands (ovaries or testicles) and physical appearance are contradictory, in others the internal sexual glands result in a varying mixture of testicle and ovary, and in still others the outer genitals may present all intermediate phases between masculine and feminine, up to and including the presence of penis and uterus simultaneously. The researcher T. Lang in his "Studies in the Genetic Determination of Homosexuality," for example, adduces that male homosexuals might actually be, genetically speaking, women whose bodies have suffered a complete sexual inversion, in a masculine direction. To demonstrate this hypothesis he conducted several surveys and in the end concluded that male homosexuals are the result of families which contain

you don't stick to the point when we carry on a discussion.

—You'll see, I do so.

—Why go on talking, Molina?

—Just go on talking, and I'll show you.

—What do we talk about?

—Well . . . Why don't you tell me what it means to you, being a man?

—You got me, that time.

—Let's hear then . . . Give me your answer, what makes a man in your terms?

—Mmm . . . his not taking any crap . . . from anyone, not even the powers that be . . . But no, it's more than that. Not taking any crap is one thing, but not the most important. What really makes a man is a lot more, it has to do with not humiliating someone else with an order, or a tip. Even more, it's . . . not letting the person next to you feel degraded, feel bad.

—That sounds like a saint.

—No, it's not as impossible as you think.

—I still don't get you . . . explain a little more.

—I don't know, I don't quite know myself, right this minute. You've caught me off guard. I can't seem to find the right words. Some other time, when my ideas are a little clearer on the subject, we can go back to it. Tell me more about your

---

an excessive number of brothers and an insufficient quantity of sisters, with the resulting male homosexual thus viewed as a form of intermediary product, of unsuccessful compensation. If in fact the data prove to be of interest, the theory thereby formulated by Lang is marred by a failure to account for the normal physical characteristics of a large majority—99 percent—of homosexuals. This last consideration has led to G. M. B. Pare's researches, presented in "Homosexuality and Chromosomal Sex," where Lang's hypothesis is refuted; according to Pare, by resorting to modern microscopical technology, he was able to identify as equally masculine, biologically speaking, every male homosexual examined during the course of his extensive investigations, which included male heterosexual subjects. In addition, Lang's theory is also rejected by J. Money in his study, "Imprinting and the Establishment of Gender Role," where Money affirms that intersexuals, despite their apparent bisexuality, do not seem to operate

waiter at that restaurant.

—Where were we?

—The business of the salad.

—Who knows what he's doing now ... Makes me sad. Poor baby, there in that place ...

—This place is a lot worse, Molina.

—But we won't be in here forever, right? But him, that's it, he doesn't have any other future. He's condemned. And I told you already what a strong character he's got, he isn't afraid of anything; but you can't imagine, sometimes, the sadness you see in him.

—How can you tell?

—It's in his eyes. Because he's got those fair eyes, greenish, somewhere between brown and green, incredibly big, swallowing up his face it seems like, and it's that look in his eyes that gives him away. That look that makes you see sometimes how bad he feels, how sad. And it's what attracted me, and made me feel more and more like talking to him. Especially when things in the restaurant got a little slow and I'd notice that melancholy look on him, he'd go to the back of the dining room, where they kept a table so the waiters could sit sometimes, and he'd stay quiet there, lighting up a cigarette, and his eyes would slowly get strange, sort of misty. I started going there more and more often, but in the beginning he barely said anything unless it was absolutely necessary. And I always ordered the cold meat salad, the soup, the main course, dessert and coffee, so he'd come back and forth to my table a whole

---

bisexually when selecting the object of their individual sexual preference; the sexual drive of such individuals, Money states, does not follow the direction of their inner sexual glands, whether it be ovaries, testicles, or a glandular mix. The urge of the intersexual is, on the contrary, adapted to that of the sex to which he has been educated, even when the chromosomes and dominant characteristics of his outer and inner sexual organs may be from the other sex. From all of the above, one can surmise that heterosexuality and homosexuality, in all cases, whether the individual has a physically normal constitution or not, are roles acquired

lot of times, and little by little we began to have a bit of conversation. Obviously, he had me pegged right off, because with me it's easy to tell.

—To tell what?

—That my real name is Carmen, like the one in Bizet.

—And because of that he started talking more to you.

—Christ! you don't know very much, do you? It was because I'm gay that he didn't want to let me come near him. Because he's an absolutely straight guy. But little by little, dropping a few words here, a few there, I made him see I respected him, and he started telling me little things about his life.

—All this was while he waited on you?

—For the first few weeks yes, until one day I managed to have a cup of coffee with him, one time when he was on day shift, which he hated the most.

—What were his regular hours?

—Well, either he came in at seven in the morning and left about four in the afternoon, or he'd show up about six in the evening, and stay until roughly three in the morning. And then one day he told me he liked the night shift best. So that aroused my curiosity, because he'd already said he was married, although he didn't wear any ring, also fishy. And his wife worked a normal nine-to-five job in some office, so what was going on with the wife? You have no idea how much trouble I went through to convince him to come have coffee with me, he always had excuses about things he had to do, first the brother-in-law, then the car. Until finally he gave in and went with me.

---

through psychological conditioning, and not predetermined by endocrinal factors.

The third and last theory on the physical origin of homosexuality with which West occupies himself is one that proposes a hereditary determinant. West points out that in spite of the seriousness of the studies carried out, among which he cites "Comparative Twin Study of the Genetic Aspects of Male Homosexuality," by F.J. Kallman, the vagueness of the data available still does not allow us to determine that homosexuality is a constitutional characteristic of the hereditary type.

—And what had to happen finally happened.

—Are you out of your mind? Don't you understand anything at all? To begin with, I already told you he's straight. Nothing at all happened. Ever!

—What did you talk about, in the cafe?

—Well, I don't remember anymore, because afterwards we met lots of times. But first thing I wanted to ask him was why anybody as intelligent as he was had to do that kind of work. And now you can begin to see what a terrible story it was. Like, well, the story of so many kids from poor families who don't have the cash to study, or maybe don't have the incentive.

—If people want to study, some way they find the means. Listen . . . in Argentina an education's not the most difficult thing in the world, you know, the university's free.

—Yes, but . . .

—Lack of incentive, now that's something else, there I agree with you, yes, it's the inferior-class complex, the brainwashing society subjects everyone to.

—Wait, let me tell you about it, and you'll understand what class of person he is, the best! He admits himself how, for a moment in life, he gave in, but he's been paying for it too ever since. He says he was around seventeen, anyway I forgot to tell you, he had to work from the time he was a kid, even in elementary school, like all those poor families from certain neighborhoods in Buenos Aires, and after elementary school he started working in a mechanics shop, and he learned the trade, and like I said, at about seventeen, more or less, already in the flower of his youth, he started in with the chicks, making it like crazy, and then yes, even worse: soccer. From when he was a kid he could play really well, and at eighteen, more or less, he started in as a professional. And now comes the key to it all: why he didn't make himself a career out of professional soccer. The way he tells me, he was only at it a short time when he saw all that crap that goes on, the sport is riddled with favoritism, injustice of every kind, and here comes the key, the key to the key, about what happens with him: he can never keep his mouth shut; whenever he smells a rat, the guy yells. He's not two-faced, and doesn't know when to keep his mouth shut. Because the guy's straight that way, too. And that's what my nose told me from the very beginning, see?

—But he never got involved in politics?

—No, he's got strange ideas about that, very off-the-wall, don't even mention the union to him.

—Go on.

—And after a few years, two or three, he quit soccer.

—And the chicks?

—Sometimes I think you're psychic.

—Why?

—Because he also quit soccer on account of the chicks. Lots of them, because he was in training, but the chicks grabbed him more than the training.

—He wasn't very disciplined after all, it seems.

—Sure, but there's also something I didn't tell you yet: his fiancée, the one he was serious with, and got married to eventually, she didn't want him to keep on with the soccer. So he took a job in a factory, as a mechanic, but the work was fairly soft, because his fiancée arranged it for him. And then they got married, and there he was at the factory, almost immediately he'd become a foreman, or chief of some division. And he had two kids. And he was nuts about his baby girl, the oldest of two, and at six she ups and dies. And at the same time he was having a row at the factory, because they started laying off people, favoring those who had connections.

—Like him.

—Yes, he did start off on the wrong foot there, I admit it. But now comes the part that's so great about him, to me, and makes me forgive anything, listen. He took sides with some poor old guys at the factory who'd been working part-time but non-union, so the boss gave him the choice of getting tossed out on his ass or toeing the line . . . and so *he quits*. And you know how it is when you quit on your own—you don't get a red cent in severance pay, not a fucking thing, and he wound up out on the street, more than ten years he'd put in at that factory.

—By then he must have been over thirty.

—Obviously, thirty plus. So he began, imagine, at that age, looking for work. In the beginning he was able to manage without just taking anything, but eventually he got offered that job as waiter and had to take it, naturally.

—He was the one who told you all that?

—Mmm-hmm, basically, little by little. I think it was a relief for him, to be able to tell somebody everything, and get it off his chest. That's why he started to open up to me.

—And you?

—I adored him all the more, but he wouldn't let me do anything for him.

—And what were you going to do for him?

—I wanted to convince him there was still a chance for him to go back to school and get a degree or something. Because there's another thing I forgot to tell you: the wife made more than he did. She was secretary in some company and slowly got to be sort of an executive, and he didn't go for that too much.

—Did you ever meet his wife?

—No, he wanted to introduce me, but deep down I hated everything about her. Just the thought of him sleeping beside her every night made me die of jealousy.

—And now?

—It's strange, but now it doesn't matter.

—Really?

—Mmm-hmm. Look, I don't know . . . Now I'm glad she's with him, so he's not all alone, since I can't pal around with him any longer, those times at the restaurant when not too much is going on and he gets bored, and smokes so much.

—And does he know how you feel about him?

—Obviously he does, I told him everything, when I still had some hope of convincing him that, with us two . . . something might really . . . happen . . . But nothing, nothing ever happened, no convincing him on that score. I said to him, even just one time in his whole life . . . but he never wanted to. And after a while I was too embarrassed to insist on anything, and satisfied myself with friendship.

—But according to what you said, he wasn't doing so well with his wife.

—There was a period, it's true, when they were fighting, but deep down he always loved her, and what's worse, he admired her for making more than he did. And one day he told me something that I nearly strangled him for. Father's Day was coming up, and I wanted to give him something, because he's so much of a father to that kid of his, and it seemed like a marvelous excuse to get him a present, and I asked him if he'd like a pair of pajamas, and then, complete disaster . . .

—Don't leave me hanging . . .

—He said he didn't wear pajamas, he always slept in the raw. And he and his wife had a double bed. It killed me. But for a while, it did seem like they were on the verge of splitting up, and that's how I kidded myself, such illusions I had! You have no idea . . .

—What kind of illusions?

—That he might come to live with me, with my mom and me. And I'd help him, and make him study. And not bother about anything but him, the whole blessed day, getting everything all set for him, his clothes, buying his books, registering him for courses, and little by little I'd convince him that what he had to do was just one thing: never work again. And I'd pass along whatever small amount of money was needed to give the wife for child support, and make him not worry about anything at all, nothing except himself, until he got what he wanted and lost all that sadness of his for good, wouldn't that be marvelous?

—Yes, but unreal. Look, there is one thing, you know, he could also go right on being a waiter but not feel humiliated about it, or anything like that. Because however humble his work is, there's always the option: joining the union movement.

—You think so?

—Of course! There's no doubt about it . . .

—But he doesn't understand any of that.

—He doesn't have any ideas about politics?

—No, he's rather ignorant. And he even says some foul things about his union, and probably he's right.

—Right? If the union's no good he should fight to change it, so it gets to be better.

—You know, I'm a little tired, how about you?

—No, not me. Aren't you going to tell me a little more of the film?

—We'll see . . . But you don't know, it all seemed so nice, to think I could do something good to help him. You understand, being a windowdresser all day, enjoyable as it is, when the day's finished, sometimes you begin to ask yourself what's it all about, and you feel kind of empty inside. Whereas if I could do something for him it'd be so marvelous . . . Give him a little bit of happiness, you see what I mean? What do you think?

—I don't know, I'll have to analyze it some more; right now I couldn't really say. Why don't you tell me a little more of the film now and tomorrow I'll talk about your waiter.

—Okay . . .

—They shut the lights off in here so early, and those candles give off such a foul smell, and they ruin your eyes too.

—And they burn up the oxygen, Valentin.

—And I can't sleep when I don't read something.

—If you want I'll tell you a little bit more. But the stupid thing is that I'm the one who'll be up later on then.

—Just a little more, Molina.

—Ohh-h . . . kay. Where were we?

—Don't start yawning at me, sleepyhead.

—What can I do? I'm sleepy.

— . . . Now you've got . . . me . . . doing it.

—So you're sleepy too, eh?

—Maybe I could get . . . some sleep.

—Mmm-hmm, and if you wake up, think about this Gabriel business.

—Gabriel, who's Gabriel?

—My waiter. It slipped out.

—Okay, in the morning then.

—Mmm, see you in the morning.

—See how life is, Molina, here I am staying up at night, thinking about your boyfriend . . .

—Tomorrow you can tell me about it.

—Good night.

—Good night.

CHAPTER **4**

—And that was the beginning of the romance between Leni
and her German officer. They were soon mad about each other.
Every night on stage she dedicates her songs to him, especially
one in particular. A beautiful habanera. The curtain goes up
and behind are palm trees made out of silver paper, like the
inside of cigarette packs, you know? Anyway, right above the
palm trees you have this full moon embroidered in sequins and
reflected in a sea made out of some kind of silk fabric, with
the reflection of the moon in sequins too. It looks like a small
tropical harbor, a little dock on an island, and all you hear is
waves breaking, simulated by the maracas in the orchestra.
And there's a yacht, luxurious as can be, faked up in cardboard
but looking very real, and a handsome man with silver-gray
temples at the helm, wearing a captain's hat and smoking a
pipe. Suddenly this incredible bright spotlight shows a little
open doorway going down into the cabin and there she is,
gloomy, and staring at the sky. He tries to fondle her but she
backs away. Her hair's loose, parted down the middle; she has
a long black lace dress on, not sheer, but sleeveless, two
spaghetti straps and that's all, the skirt billowy. That's when
the orchestra does a sort of introduction, and she's watching
an islander down on the beach picking a flower from a clump
of wild orchids; he's smiling and sort of winks at the native girl
who comes up to him. He places the orchid in her hair and
embraces her, they walk off together and vanish into the jungle

darkness, not realizing that the flower's fallen from the girl's hair. And then there's a close-up of the wild orchid, it's delicate though, fallen in the sand, and over the orchid the image of Leni's smoky face begins to fade in, as if the flower was changing into a woman. Then a wind comes up like it's about to storm, but the sailors shout it's a favorable wind, and now the boat's ready to weigh anchor, but she goes down the ramp and onto the sand, and picks up the flower that looks so beautiful, faked in velvet. And she sings.

—What are the words?

—Who knows? . . . because they didn't translate those songs. But it was sad, as if someone had lost a true love and just wanted to give up now but she can't, and she leaves it all in the hands of fate. It must be like that, because when they tell her the wind's favorable she smiles a very sad smile, like whatever way the wind takes her it's all the same. And singing that way she walks back to the boat, which little by little sails off toward one side of the stage, with her at the stern, still gazing back with that lost look across the palm trees, where the darkest part of the jungle starts.

—She always finishes with that lost look of hers.

—But you can't imagine the eyes that woman has, so black against the white white skin. And I'm forgetting the best part: when at the end you see her in the stern of the boat, she's got the velvet flower in her hair, and you can't tell what's softer, the velvet orchid or her skin, like the petals of some flower, like a magnolia I guess. And afterwards the applause, and then some short scenes with the two of them very happy: an afternoon at the horse races, with her all in white, wearing a sheer picture-hat and with him in a top hat; and next a toast together on some yacht sailing down the River Seine; and then in a private room of a Russian nightclub, he's in tails, blowing out the candelabra and he opens a jewel case and takes out a necklace of pearls, and you don't know how but even in the darkness they shine so fantastically, through some movie trick.

Anyway, next comes a scene where she's having breakfast in bed, and the maid comes in to announce some relative that's waiting downstairs and just arrived from Alsace. And some gentleman's with him. She goes downstairs, in a satin negligee with black and white stripes, the scene's set at her place. The visitor is this young cousin of hers, dressed in simple clothing, but the one who's with him . . . it's the clubfoot.

—The clubfoot?

—The one who ran over the chorus girl with his car. And they begin talking, and her cousin says they've asked him to do an important favor, which is to come and talk to her, a Frenchwoman, about helping them on a mission. She asks what mission, and he says the one the blond chorus girl began but refused to finish for them. Because it's for the maquis. She's scared to death but manages to pretend otherwise. They ask her to uncover a very important secret, which is to find out the location of a huge ammunition dump which the Germans have somewhere in France so the enemies of the German forces can wipe it out. And the blond chorus girl was actually on that same mission, because she belonged to the maquis, but after she began her affair with the lieutenant she fell in love with him and refused to cooperate, which is why she had to be bumped off, before she denounced all of them to the authorities of the German occupation forces. Then the clubfoot says she has to help them, and she says she wants to think about it, because she knows nothing about things like that. Then the clubfoot says "That's a lie," because the head of German counterintelligence is in love with her, so it won't cost her anything to get the documents. But she gets up her courage and tells the clubfoot absolutely no, because she hasn't got the guts for that kind of thing. Then the clubfoot says that she better do it . . . or they'll have to resort to certain reprisals. Then she sees the cousin lower his eyes, his chin quivering, and his forehead beaded with sweat. He's actually a hostage! Then the clubfoot explains how the poor kid has nothing to do with this,

his only mistake's in being a relative of hers. Because the dirty rats went all the way to some town in Alsace where the poor kid was from and brought him back with them, I don't know, under false pretenses. But the point's just this: if she doesn't help them, they'll just, the maquis that is, they'll just go and kill the kid who's totally innocent. So she promises to do whatever she can. And they leave it at that. So the next time she's together with the German officer, at his house, she begins to search in all the drawers, but she's fantastically frightened all the same because the majordomo's always hanging around her, from the first moment always eyeing her suspiciously, and looking like he doesn't miss a trick. But then comes the scene where she's in the garden having lunch with her officer and some other ones too, and the majordomo, who's obviously German, the officer asks him to go down into the wine cellar to find this incredibly rare wine, oh! I forgot, she's the one who asks for it, a particular vintage that only the majordomo himself can find. Then when the guy goes to get the wine, she sits down at a white grand piano which is in one of those rooms I told you about, and you see her through a white lacy curtain. She's accompanying herself on the piano because he asked her to sing for them, the officer, that is. But she manages to prepare a little bit of a ruse, and puts on a recording of herself that's accompanied by piano too, and meanwhile she goes into his private study and starts rummaging through his papers. But it turns out the majordomo has forgotten his keys, so when he gets to the door of the cellar where the wines are kept he has to go back to look for them, and as he's walking along the balustrade facing the garden he looks through the casement window and he can't tell through that lacy curtain if she's sitting at the piano or not. During all this the officer is still in the garden, where he's been busy talking with the other brass. The garden is French, without any flowers in places, and instead there's just hedges cut into all different shapes, like obelisks and so on.

—Then it's a German garden . . . Saxon, to be exact.

—How do you know?

—Because the French gardens use lots of flowers, and even though the arrangements are geometrical they tend to be much more casual-looking. That garden sounds German, plus the film was obviously made in Germany . . .

—And you, how do you know all that? That's women's stuff . . .

—From courses in architecture.

—And you studied architecture?

—Yes.

—And you just decide to tell me that now?

—It never came up.

—But didn't you major in political government or something?

—Yes, political science. But go on with the film, I'll tell you some other time. And by the way, art's not just something for women.

—One of these days they'll realize who's the fag around here.

—Sure. But what about the film?

—Okay, so then the majordomo hears the singing but not at the piano, and he goes off to look for her, she's right there in the study, ransacking through all the papers, oh! because earlier she managed to get the key to the desk, and actually took it off the officer, and now she finds the map of the zone where all the ammunition is hidden, the German arsenal itself, but at this point she hears footsteps and just manages to hide out on the balcony off the study, but in plain view of all the brass right there in the garden! So she's caught smack in the middle, because if anyone in the garden so much as glances up they'll see her. The majordomo goes into the study and looks around, she holds her breath, fantastically nervous because the record's just about to finish, and at that time, you see, recordings just had one song on them, that's all, they didn't have long-playing albums yet. But the majordomo goes back out of the room then, and in the same instant she flies out too, the song just about to end. And all the brass are listening outside, enchanted, and as the record finishes they get up to applaud her and she's already seated at the piano once again and everyone believes it was actually her, live, and not a record. And next comes another rendezvous with the clubfoot and the cousin, in order for her to turn over the secret of the German arsenal. The place they meet is in some museum, unbelievably gigantic, with tremendous dinosaurs on exhibition, and in place of walls it has these enormous panes of glass, looking over the River Seine, and when they meet she tells the clubfoot yes, she's managed to get hold of the necessary information, and then the clubfoot who's feeling pleased with himself begins to tell her how this is only the beginning of the jobs she'll be expected to do for the maquis, because once you get involved with spying, there's no backing out. Then she's about to decide not to give him the location, but she sees the poor kid trembling there, so she says it, the name of some region in France and the exact village where the ammunition lies hidden. Then the clubfoot who's actually kind of a sadist begins to tell her how much the German officer will loathe her with his whole being when he discovers her treachery. And I don't remember what else he says. Then the kid sees Leni turning livid with impotent rage, and he looks out the window, and since they're right up next to the glass, on the fifth or sixth floor of that huge museum they're in, before the clubfoot can even realize what's happening the kid tries to push him through the glass, out the window, but the clubfoot puts up a wild struggle and the kid sacrifices himself, hurling both of them into space, paying the price with his own life. She mixes into the crowd that gathers to see what's happened, and since she's wearing a hat with a veil no one recognizes her. Wasn't that kid good to do that, really?

—Good to her, but a traitor to his own country.

—But he understood the maquis were all a bunch of mafiosos; just wait and listen to what you find out later on in the film.

—Do you know what the maquis were?

—Yes, I already know they were patriotic, but in this film they're not. Let me finish, okay? So . . . let's see, what happened next?

—I don't understand you at all.

—Well, it's just that the film was divine, and for me that's what counts, because I'm locked up in this cell and I'm better off thinking about nice things, so I don't go nuts, see? . . . Well?

—What do you want me to say?

—That you'll let me escape from reality once in a while, because why should I let myself get more depressed than I am? Otherwise I'll go nuts, like Charlotte of Mexico. Though I'd rather be Christina of Sweden, since I'll end up a queen, no matter what.

—No, be serious, it's true you can end up going nuts in this place, but you can drive yourself crazy here in other ways, not just out of despair . . . but from alienating yourself the way you do. Because that business of only thinking about nice things, as you put it, well, that can be dangerous too.

—How? I don't think so.

—It can become a vice, always trying to escape from reality like that, it's like taking drugs or something. Because, listen to me, reality, I mean *your reality*, isn't restricted by this cell we live in. If you read something, if you study something, you transcend any cell you're inside of, do you understand what I'm saying? That's why I read and why I study every day.

—But politics . . . What's the world coming to, with all your politicians . . .

—Don't talk like a nineteenth-century housewife, because this isn't the nineteenth century . . . and you're not a housewife. And tell me some more of the film, or is there much more left to go?

—Why, bored?

—I don't like it, but somehow I'm intrigued.

—If you don't like it, then I'll stop.

—Whatever you want, Molina.

—One thing is for sure, there's no way to finish it tonight, there's still lots left, like almost half.

—It interests me as propaganda, that's all. In a certain sense it serves as a document.

—Yes or no, once and for all?

—Maybe just a little more.

—Now it sounds like you're the one doing me the favor. Remember, you asked me because you couldn't get to sleep, that's why I started telling it.

—And I appreciate that, Molina.

—But now I'm the one who's awake, so you pulled a fast one on me.

—Then tell me a little bit more and maybe we'll both get sleepy at the same time, thank God.

—You atheists never stop mentioning God.

—It's an expression. Come on, tell me some more.

—Okay. So she, without telling him anything about what just happened, she asks the officer to put her up at his place, she's so afraid of the maquis. Now, this scene is really fantastic, because I didn't tell you he plays the piano too, and this time he's in a brocaded robe, I couldn't begin to describe it to you, the way he looks! With this white silk ascot around his neck. And by the light of a few candelabras, he plays something rather sad, because I forgot to tell you she's very late getting back to his place. And he thinks she's somehow never coming back again. Oh, because I didn't tell you either how she leaves the museum when nobody notices her and walks insanely through all the streets of Paris, she's so confused, with the death of that poor kid, her cousin, she loved him so much.

And it's already getting dark, and she continues just to walk, all over Paris, past the Eiffel Tower, up and down through all the bohemian quarters, and past the artists that paint in the streets there, and they all stare at her, and so do the couples under the streetlamps on the edge of the River Seine, because she's walking along like a poor lost soul, like a sleepwalker with the veil of her hat pushed back, and not caring any longer whether anyone recognizes her or not. In the meantime, the officer is giving orders for a candlelight dinner for two, and afterwards you see the candles all look twice as short as they did before, but he's still playing the piano, a sort of very slow, very sad waltz. And that's when she walks in. He doesn't get up to say hello; he keeps on playing that marvelous waltz on the piano, which seemed so sad a minute ago but now it's turning faster and happier, more romantic than you could believe, but so, so joyful. And at that point the scene ends, without him saying a word, you just see his smile, his relief, and you hear the music. Listen . . . you can't imagine how great that scene was.

—And then?

—Then she wakes up in a marvelous bed, all upholstered in pure satin, I think it must have been in like faded pink or pale green, with satin sheets. It's a shame some films aren't made in color, isn't it? And tulle curtains on the sides of the canopy, wonderful, and she wakes up so in love and looks out the window and a slight drizzle is falling. She goes to the telephone, lifts the receiver and without meaning to she hears him talking to someone. He's advising what form of punishment should be dealt out to a couple of mafiosos from the black market. And she can't believe her ears when he says execute them, but she waits for the conversation to end and when they hang up, she hangs up the receiver, too, so he doesn't realize she's been listening. Next thing he comes into the bedroom, and says, does she feel like breakfast now? She's so divine-looking, reflected in the windowpane where the drizzle falls, and she asks him, is he truly unafraid of anyone, the way they say the soldiers of the new Germany are, like that hero he talked about. He answers, if it's for his own country, then he's ready to accept any challenge. So then she says, she wonders if it's not just fear that makes someone kill a defenseless enemy, the fear that sometime in the future the tables might be turned and you might have to face him that way, too, with nothing but your bare hands. He says he doesn't understand what she's getting at. But she changes the subject. Then later that day when she's by herself, she dials the number she got from the clubfoot to contact someone from the maquis, in order to hand over the secret of the arsenal. Because, having heard how ready he is to condemn someone to death, he now seems less of a man to her. So she goes off to meet one of the maquis, and they decide to rendezvous at the theater, as a cover, because she's busy there with rehearsals. And she sees the man approaching and gives the agreed-upon signal, when all of a sudden someone comes down the center aisle of the empty theater and calls for Miss Leni, Miss Leni. It's that they've sent her a telegram from Berlin to invite her to star in an important film, with one of the best studios in Germany, and right there with the invitation is an official connected with the government of the occupation and so she can't say anything to the maquis now, and she has to start packing immediately to go off to Berlin. Like it?

—No, and now I am sleepy. Let's wait for tomorrow to go on, all right?

—No, Valentin, if you don't like it I don't want to go on.

—I'd like to know how it ends.

—No, if you don't like it, why bother? . . . So now it's settled. Good night.

—Tomorrow we'll talk.

—But not about that.

—Whatever you want, Molina.

—Night.
—Good night.*

—Why are they taking so long to bring dinner? I think they already brought it to the next cell a while ago.
—Mmm, I heard it too. You stop studying?
—Not yet. What time is it?
—After eight. I'm not very hungry today, luckily.
—That's strange for you, Molina. Are you sick?
—No, it's just nerves.
—Here they come, I think.
—No, Valentin, that's just the last of the prisoners coming back to their cells from the showers.
—You never told me what they said to you in the warden's office.
—Nothing. It was just to sign some papers with the new lawyer.
—Power of attorney?
—Mmm-hmm. Since I changed lawyers I had to sign a few things.
—How did they treat you?
—No way special. Like a faggot, same as always.

---

*Press-book from Tobis-Berlin Studios, for their international distributors of Tobis-Berlin releases, regarding the superproduction entitled *Her Real Glory* (middle pages):

The unexpected arrival of the foreign vedette had not been announced with the usual fanfare; on the contrary, it was decided for Leni Lamaison to arrive incognito at the capital city of the Reich. Only after makeup and wardrobe tests were the press summoned. The foremost diva of French song was to be introduced, that afternoon, finally, to prominent representatives of the free press, there at Berlin's Grand Hotel. Soft echoings of the orchestra in the tea garden reached the Imperial Room, located on the mezzanine floor and reserved for the occasion. Leni had already been identified with the latest rages in Parisian fashion, her beauty having so often served to embody the same. Everyone therefore expected to see a mechanical doll adorned with the tightest of permanent

—Listen, here comes somebody, I think.

—Mmm, here they are. Stash the magazines, quick; if they see them, they'll get stolen for sure.

—I'm dying of hunger.

—Please, Valentin, no complaining to the guard.

—Okay . . .

— . . .

— . . .

—Take it . . .

—Rice . . .

—Right . . .

—Thanks.

—Eh, so much . . .

—That's to keep you guys happy.

—Okay, but what about this other plate . . . Why so much less?

—What's your problem, bud? Ain't no use griping about it anyway . . .

— . . .

— . . .

—I didn't answer back for your sake, Molina, if it weren't for you, I think I would have thrown it right back in his face, this shitpile of glue they call rice.

---

waves, her two cheekbones heavily rouged over a foundation of white lacquer. It was likewise taken for granted that she would scarcely be able to keep her eyes open, given the thick layering of black mascara and the imposing set of false eyelashes. But the greatest curiosity was centered on her attire, inasmuch as it could be assumed to include, inevitably, the useless profusion of draperies dictated by the decadent couturiers of the Ultra-Rhine, aspiring as they do to a distortion of the female figure. But when one eventually caught the sudden murmurings of profound admiration voiced among the gathering, it was an altogether different woman who in fact emerged among all those who now so rapidly made way for her. No, her tiny waist and rounded hips were not buried beneath any sort of superfluous trappings, her firm bust was not flattened by some extravagant design: on the contrary the girl—right out of Sparta, one might well have imagined—stepped forth girded in the simplest sort of

—But what's the good of complaining.

—One plate has twice as much as the other, the guard must be crazy, that fat son of a bitch.

—Look, Valentin, I'll keep the smaller plate.

—No, you always eat the rice anyway, take the big one.

—No, I told you I'm not hungry. You keep the big one for yourself.

—Don't stand on formalities, take it.

—No, I tell you. Why should I get the bigger dish?

—Because I know you like rice.

—I'm not hungry, Valentin.

—Take some, and then you'll feel like the rest.

—No.

—Look, it's not so bad today.

—I don't want any. I'm not hungry.

—Afraid of getting fat?

—No . . .

—Eat it then, Molina. The glue's not so bad today anyway, it almost tastes like rice. The smaller portion's more than enough for me.

—Ahg . . . aghhh . . .

— . . .

---

white tunic which amply expressed the perfect fullness of her figure, and the bright, clean face could have belonged to a healthy shepherdess. Her hair, in turn, was parted in the middle and fixed into a long braid completely encircling the crown of her erect head. And the gymnast's arms were unencumbered by sleeves, just a short cape of the same white fabric to cover her shoulders. "Our ideal of beauty must forever be one of healthy fitness," so our Leader has stated, and more specifically as applied to women, "Her single mission is to be beautiful and bear the sons of the world. A woman who bequeaths five sons to the *Volk* has made a greater contribution than that of the finest woman jurist in the world. Because there is no place for women in politics within the ideological context of National Socialism, inasmuch as to drag women into the parliamentary sphere, where they pale, is to rob them of their dignity.

—Aghhh . . .

—What's wrong?

—Nothing, agh . . . this girl is in a bad way, that's all.

—What girl?

—Me, stupid.

—What are you moaning like that for?

—My stomach . . .

—Want to throw up?

—No . . .

—I'll get the bag out just in case.

—No, leave it . . . The pain's lower down, in my gut.

—It's not diarrhea?

—No . . . It's a really sharp pain, but up further.

—I'll call the guard . . .

—No, Valentin. It feels like it's going away . . .

—How does it feel when it hurts?

—Like stabbing pains . . . but really sharp . . .

—On one side?

—No, all over my stomach . . .

—Could it be appendicitis?

—No, I already had mine out.

—The meal didn't bother me . . .

—Has to be my nerves. I was so nervous today . . . But it feels like it's letting up . . .

The German renaissance is a masculine undertaking, but the Third Reich, which presently numbers upwards of 80 million subjects, within a century —in the glorious year of 2040—will have need of 250 million patriots to govern the destinies of the entire world, from the Fatherland itself and from our countless colonies. And that will be a feminine undertaking, after having learned the lesson of so many other peoples, concerning the grave problem of racial degeneration, which can and will be halted by means of concerted nationalism on the part of the populace itself, synthesis of State and People." These same words are repeated to the lovely foreigner, there in the so-called Imperial Room, by the representative of the Berlin studios—words which make a lasting impression upon Leni, just as her pure beauty makes its own impression upon the many members of the international press gathered together there.

—Try to relax yourself as much as possible. Loosen up your arms and legs.

—Mmm, it feels like it's letting up a bit.

—Has it been hurting you long?

—Mmm-hmm, a while now. I'm sorry I woke you up.

—No: at all . . . You should have gotten me up earlier, Molina.

—I didn't want to bother you with . . . aghhh . . .

—It hurts a lot, huh?

—Just these sharp stabs . . . now it feels like it's going away again.

—Want to sleep a little? Or can't you?

—I don't know . . . Ugh, how awful . . .

—If we talk a little, maybe it would help to take your mind off the pain.

—No, you get back to sleep, or you won't be able to.

—Oh, I'm already up.

—Sorry.

—No, most of the time I wake up by myself, and can't fall back to sleep anyway.

—Feels like it's letting up a bit. Aghhh, no, ugh, it's awful . . .

—Maybe I better call the guard.

The following day, her new image adorns the front pages of all the newspapers of the free world, but Leni wastes no time reading hymns of praise to her loveliness; instead, she picks up the telephone and—overcoming her strong mistrust—calls up Werner. She asks him if, during those few days he plans to spend in the capital before returning to Paris, he would perhaps help her to discover some of the marvels of the new German world. Werner begins by driving her to a gigantic assembly of German youth, taking place in an enormous stadium. However, he prefers to disregard the usual amenities of an official limousine, and instead to take Leni there in his dashing white coupe; his intention being that she might thus experience herself as only one of thousands among that zealous multitude—and what is more, he succeeds. All those who pass close by to Leni of course admire her, but not for the eccentricities of some diva precieuse, but rather because of her majestic poise,

—No, it's letting up . . .

—You know something?

—What?

—I'm still curious about the end of that film, the Nazi one.

—Didn't you hate it?

—Yes, but all the same I want to know how it turns out, just to understand the mentality of whoever made the film, the kind of propaganda they were into.

—You can't imagine how marvelous it is to see it.

—Well, if it helps to distract you, why don't you tell me a little more of it, briefly? The ending just.

—Ow! Damn it!

—Hurting a lot again?

—No, it comes and goes, but whenever those stabbing pains do come back they feel incredibly sharp, but once they're over with it hardly hurts at all.

—How does the film end?

—Where did we leave off?

—When she was about to help the maquis, but then along came the offer to make films in Germany.

—So it got to you after all, eh?

—Well, it's not just an ordinary film. Tell me quickly, that way you can get to the ending faster.

---

her example of healthy womanhood, undefiled by cosmetics. In short, Leni makes her appearance in a simple two-piece outfit, reminiscent of our stark military uniforms. The fabric, a typical cloth of the Alpine region, reflects something of the ruggedness of all mountain folk, but nevertheless highlights her comely feminine shape, and only the square shoulder padding departs from the contours of her lovely silhouette, and then only to strengthen them. Werner is contemplating her ecstatically, because he has of course anticipated Leni's astonishment at the monumental façade of the stadium, and in fact she has not escaped its impact. Leni then asks Werner why his nation proves capable of creating something so purely inspired, while in the rest of Europe an art all too frivolous and ephemeral has been imposed, as much in painting and sculpture as in architecture, a merely decorative and abstract art destined to perish as quickly as any expendable haute couture concocted in the

—Okay, so what happened after that? Uhmm . . . ugh, this is awful, hurts so damn much . . .

—Tell me about the film so you don't think about the pain, it hurts you less if you try not to pay so much attention . . .

—Afraid I'll kick the bucket before you hear the ending?

—No, just telling you something to try and help a little.

—Okay, so she goes to Germany to make films, and she's absolutely crazy about Germany, and the young people who exercise all the time. And she forgives her officer for everything because she found out the guy he put to death was a horrible criminal, and had done all kinds of evil things. And they show her a photo of another criminal they still haven't been able to catch up with, some accomplice of the one the officer sentenced to death . . . Aghhh, it's still there . . .

—Then stop, better try to sleep.

—Forget it . . . no way . . . it still hurts too much.

—You get them often, those pains?

—Christ Almighty! I never felt this kind of sharp . . . Ugh . . . You see, now it's gone . . .

—I'm going to try to go back to sleep.

—No, wait.

—You'll fall asleep too.

—No, no way for that . . . I'll go on with the film.

---

capital of the Ultra-Rhine. He knows very well what to answer her, but chooses not to do so immediately, and asks her to wait one more instant. And now the two find themselves before the unforgettable spectacle that the flower of German youth offers them: across the green field spread rows of straight lines which then dissolve and suddenly recompose, to give way to curves which undulate momentarily and in their turn reassert the virility of rectilinear composition. These are the young gymnasts of both sexes, dressed in black and white for their gymnastic exhibition. And then Werner says, as if to comment upon this truly olympic vision at which Leni cannot help but stare in awe: "Yes, heroism emerges as the only future model for all political destinies, and it is up to art to lend expression to this, the spirit of our age. Communist futuristic art is retrograde, anarchical. Ours is Nordic culture in opposition to the fool-hardiness of just so many Mongolian communists, and to the Catholic

—Okay.

—What then? Oh, she thinks she recognizes the other criminal but doesn't have any idea where she's seen him before. And then she goes back to Paris, which is the place where she thinks she actually came across the guy. But she's hardly back there when she tries to make contact with the maquis again, only this time to see if she can net the real head of the whole organization that's secretly behind all the black market, and responsible for everything being so scarce. And she leads them on with the promise of the secret location of the German arsenal, which is what the clubfoot was after, you remember?

—Yes, but you know the maquis were actually heroes, don't you?

—Hey, what do you take me for, an even dumber broad than I am?

—If you're into that girl stuff again you must be feeling better.

—So, whatever . . . But just try and remember that when it came to the love scenes the film was divine, an absolute dream. The political stuff, well, it was probably foisted onto the director by the government, or maybe you don't know how those things work?

---

farce, a product of Assyrian corruption. Love must be replaced by Honor. And Christ will become the Athlete who with a proud fist forcibly ejects the merchants from the Temple." And as if to echo his very words the youth—veritable torch of National Socialism—now together intone their martial chorale, vibrant with patriotism: ". . . wave on high, O majestic banner of yore, the young revolutionary must spew forth volcanic passions, incite all wrath, directing all suspicion and righteous anger with a cold and steady hand, and thus do we enlist the mass of humanity," paraphrasing the motto of our Supreme Commandant for Propaganda, Field Marshal Goebbels. And Leni, in spite of the conflict which her mind has fed upon since that day when she heard Werner pronounce the death sentence, she feels suddenly transported with jubilation. Werner grasps her hand, drawing her closer to him, but not daring to kiss her, afraid that her lips might still be cold. That same

—If the director made the film, then he's certainly guilty of complicity with the regime.

—Okay, just let me finish it once and for all. Aghhh . . . you start one of your discussions and the pain comes right back . . . Ugh . . .

—Tell some more, distract yourself.

—What happens now is that she insists that, in order to be persuaded to turn over the secret arsenal, she must be allowed to meet the high command of the maquis. And so one day they drive her out of Paris, to some castle or other. But first she arranges to be followed by her officer, with some of his soldiers, so they can round up all the maquis from the black market. But the driver who takes her, and happens to be that same murderer who was always driving the clubfoot around, he realizes that he's being followed and changes his direction, suddenly, to make them lose the trail, the Germans following right behind him, with the boyfriend in the lead. Anyhow, then he drives up to the castle and makes Leni go inside, and to settle things quickly they present her to the head of the maquis, and it's the majordomo! the one who was spying on her all the time!

—Who?

—The one who worked in the boyfriend's house. Then she

---

evening they dine together in complete silence. Werner, unable to further divine the truth, senses only how distant she has in effect become, lost in her own secret thoughts. Neither of the two so much as tastes their food. Leni just drains her fine goblet of sweet Moselle wine and hurls the crystal into the blazing fireplace with all her might; it shatters to bits. Without further preamble Leni finally poses the question burning inside of her for so long: "How is it possible that you, a superior being, can have allowed yourself to order a human being to be put to death?" Werner, realizing at once, replies in astonishment: "Is this what has kept you so aloof from me?" When Leni responds in the affirmative, Werner without more ado orders her to proceed with him to the Ministry of Political Affairs. Leni obeys. In spite of that late hour, the government offices are still bustling with activity, because the new Germany will not rest, neither day nor night. At the mere sight of his arrogant uniform,

looks more closely and suddenly realizes it's the same horrible guy with the beard, the one from the film about the two criminals that she saw back in Berlin. And she tells him the secret, because she's so sure her officer is about to arrive with all the soldiers to save her. But since he lost the trail, it gets later and later and they still don't arrive. Then she overhears that sleazy driver talking secretly to the boss, about how he has a hunch they were being followed. But at this point she remembers how the majordomo was always peeping in her window back at the house, to catch her in the nude, etc., so she plays her last trump, which is to try and seduce the guy. During all this, the young officer and his patrol are still trying to follow the tracks left by the other car in the rain. And after a lot of searching, but I don't remember how they actually did it, they find the way. And she's there all alone with that monster, the major-domo, who is actually the boss of everybody, a worldwide figure in crime, and when he throws himself at her, there in that curtained back room where an intimate dinner's already set out for them, she grabs the carving fork and stabs him to death. And now the officer and the others arrive, she opens a window to escape and right there down below stands the driver assassin, and her boyfriend sees him in time and fires a shot, but the clubfoot, no, I mean the driver, because the clubfoot's

---

all doors open to make way for Werner. A few minutes later access is given to a basement corner which serves as a screening room. Werner orders an immediate projection. The screen lights up ... with atrocities —actually, a long documentary on famine, world famine. Hunger in North Africa, hunger in Spain, hunger in Dalmatia, in the Yang-Tse-Kiang Valley, in Anatolia. And just prior to each of these agonies, the punctual appearance in these same areas of two or three implacable beings, always the same ones, wandering Jews bearing death's fateful tiding. All of it accurately registered by the unmistakable camera eye. Yes, funereal merchants, vultures, visiting their feast upon droughts, floods, every type of propitious catastrophe, in order to assemble their satanic banquet: the hoarding of goods, usury itself. And behind them, their retinue, all of them cursed children of Abraham, repeating with mathematical precision the very same operations: first the wheat crops

alreaαy dead back at the museum, then the driver, while he's dying there, manages to get off one shot at the girl. She grabs onto the curtain and manages not to fall, so her boyfriend and the young officer still find her on her feet, but just as he gets to her and takes her in his arms, she loses whatever strength she has left and says how much she loves him, and how they'll soon be together in Berlin again. And now he sees that she's really wounded because his hands are red with her blood, from the bullet wound, in her shoulder, or in the chest, I don't remember. He kisses her, and when he takes his lips away from her mouth she's already dead. And the last scene takes place in this Pantheon, in Berlin, for heroes, and it's an incredibly beautiful monument, like a Greek temple, with huge statues of each hero. And she's there, too, like an enormous statue, or life-size I mean, incredibly beautiful in like a Greek tunic, but I think it was herself standing there just like a statue, with her face powdered white, and he places flowers on her arms, which are reaching out, as if to hug him. And he's leaving now, and there's a light that seems to come from way up in heaven, and he goes off with his eyes full of tears and the statue of her remains there with the arms extended. But all alone, and there's an inscription on the temple, which says something like how the fatherland will never forget them. And he walks all alone, but the road is bathed in sunlight. The End.

---

disappear, then step by step the other grains, down to the coarsest of cereals, fit only to feed the cattle. And then the meats, and the sugar, together with the many oleaginous by-products, and fruits and vegetables, fresh and canned. Thus famine runs its dreadful course throughout the cities, and inhabitants flee to the countryside, only to find there as well the vandalistic spectacle which these locusts of Jehovah have left in their wake. And the faces of peoples begin to shrivel up, now no one manages to stand erect, along the horizons of holocaust are etched the vanished silhouettes of the hungry who take a few last steps toward the mirage of a stale piece of bread ... that they will not manage to grasp, ever.

Leni's blood runs cold as she witnesses the projection, but even more, she feels anxious to have the lights back on, in order to dispel a mystery.

In short, she wants to find out from Werner the identity of one of those two infamous physiognomies. Thus Leni refers to the two heads of the lethal organization, while Werner glows with excitement, inasmuch as he thinks that Leni has somehow recognized in one of the two faces the very same criminal that he himself had condemned to death, much to the consternation of his beloved. But no, Leni refers to the other one. Werner therefore becomes even more agitated; has Leni somehow succeeded in what the entire staff of Intelligence has come to think of as sheer impossibility? Because Jacob Levy is the most hounded anti-Nazi agent still at large. Leni however offers no clear-cut answer, only that she is sure of having seen that depraved face somewhere before, with its greasy bald head and its long pawnbroker's beard. They run the film backwards and stop the projector wherever the image of that same master criminal appears. Leni makes a superhuman effort but is unable to ascertain where, how and when she has seen the monster. Finally they leave the projection room, deciding to walk for a few blocks down an avenue dotted with linden trees. Leni continues to be absorbed in the labyrinth of her recollection, certain to have come across this Jacob Levy once before, her only fear being that she might have seen, or better said, imagined him in some nightmare. Werner for his part remains silent, his intention in showing the film to Leni was only to demonstrate what a vile insect he had ordered to be executed, after managing to corner him in a small village near the Swiss border. But with a single gesture, Leni dispels any such cloud in the amorous heaven of Werner, for she has just now taken his rugged right palm with her soft white hands and holds it close to her woman's heart. Everything is explained then, once and for all, how the death of one Hebraic Moloch has meant the salvation of millions of innocent souls. A light drizzle is coming down over the Imperial City. Leni asks Werner to shelter her with his embrace, tells him it is rest that she needs. When aided by the light of the coming day they will undertake to hunt down the other beast who still runs rampant. But at that instant no snarls are to be heard echoing from the jungles of the world, none at all, because they find themselves in a land chosen by the gods to house their golden mansion, there where the merchants have already lost a first battle against the morality of the Hero.

A sunny Sunday morning now, and Leni has asked Werner to spend this last weekend with her, before his return to Paris, so that they might dedicate some little time to visit the bewitching valleys of the Bavarian Alps. Those same enchanted mountains where the Leader has his vacation home, precisely where during his clandestine period a humble family of peasants had once given him shelter. The grass is green and fragrant, the sun mild, the breeze carries the refreshing coolness of perpetual snows which forever top the huge peaks like sentinels. On the grass a simple peasant tablecloth. On the tablecloth the frugal diet of a small picnic. But now Leni finds no limit to her curiosity, and asks Werner everything concerning the Leader. At the beginning his words sound difficult to fathom for the girl: ". . . the socioeconomic stalemate in the liberal-democratic states has led to problems which can in essence be solved more effectively, and to everybody's satisfaction, by a form of authoritarian government rooted solidly in the people itself and not in abusive international elites . . ." and so she asks him to speak more plainly about the Leader's own personality and, if appropriate, of his rise to power. Werner relates: ". . . the Marxist rags and Jewish gazettes were announcing only chaos and humiliations for the German people. From time to time they would also publish a false account of the arrest of Adolf Hitler. But this was not possible, inasmuch as no one could recognize him: he had never permitted himself to be photographed. He would crisscross our territory to attend countless secret meetings. At times I myself accompanied him, in precariously small aircraft. I remember all that so well, the motor roared and there we were taking off from the ground and into the night, even in the very midst of storms. But he would pay no attention to the lightning, and would speak to me all wrapped in his sorrow at the tragedy of a people routed by Marxist absurdities, by the poison of pacifism, by every sort of imported idea. . . . And how many times we traversed this our itinerary of yesterday by auto, and that we shall repeat again tonight, you and I . . . from the Alps to Berlin. All the roads were familiar to him, arteries along his route to the hearts of the people. We would halt no more than once, that was all, like you see here now . . . we would open up a tablecloth on the lawn, under trees, and partake of our frugal luncheon. A slice of bread, a hard-boiled egg and some fruit was all the Leader would have. In rainy weather we would just have a little pick-me-up right inside the car. And finally we would reach our destination, and at the meeting this very simple man would become a giant, and over rebel broadcasts the ether waves would transmit his hammers of persuasion. He risked his life once and again, because the roads ran red with the bloodthirsty Marxist mania . . ." A fascinated Leni listens, but wants to learn even more, as a woman, interested in the innermost secret of the Leader's personal strength. Werner answers: ". . . the Leader manifests himself completely in every one of his words. He believes in himself and in everything he says. He is just what is so difficult to find these days: authenticity. And the people recognize the authentic and grasp it to themselves. The true Why, however, of the personality of the Leader . . . will forever remain a mystery, even for those of us most intimately connected with him. Only a belief in miracles can explain it. God has blessed this man, and faith can indeed move mountains, the faith of the Leader and faith in the Leader . . ."

Leni leans back in the clover and looks into Werner's limpid blue eyes, eyes of a peacefully confident gaze, inasmuch as they are fixed upon Truth. Leni throws her arms around his neck and can only utter emotionally: ". . . now I understand how much you welcomed his message. You have captured the essence of National Socialism . . ."

There follow, for Leni, weeks of exhausting work in the Berlin studios. And after the last roll of the camera she rushes to the nearest telephone to call her beloved, now engulfed in his Paris assignment. He has a marvelous surprise in store for her, however: he has arranged for a brief furlough with her before their eventual reunion in Paris, and those days they can spend in some gorgeous corner of the nation which now acclaims her: the National Socialist Republic. But Leni has an even greater surprise in store for him: from that very day at the screening of the documentary she has not ceased for one instant to ponder the face of that criminal still at large, and day by day she grows more and more certain of having seen the beast in Paris. She wishes, therefore, to return without delay to that very city and begin their search.

Werner accepts—in spite of the fear it causes him—the entry of his Leni into an espionage cadre. But Leni gets off the train fully confident of her mission, even though the sight of her France causes her grief. In effect, accustomed already to the sun which shines upon the faces of the National Socialist Fatherland, Leni is now disgusted to see her France debased as it is by racial contamination. A France which looks to her undeniably negrified and Jewish. *(continues)*

—You should have had something for lunch.

—It's just I didn't want anything at all.

—Molina, why not ask to go to the infirmary? Maybe they could give you something, so you would get better.

—I'm already getting better.

—But then don't look at me that way, as if I were the one to blame.

—What do you mean look at you "that way"?

—Staring at me like that.

—You're crazy, Valentin, just because I look at you doesn't mean I'm blaming you. For what? You crazy or something?

—Well, you're arguing again so you must be feeling better.

—No, I'm not any better, it's left me feeling awfully weak.

—Your blood pressure must be way down.

— . . .

—Well, I think I'll study a little.

—Talk to me a bit, Valentin, come on.

—No, it's time to do some studying. I have to keep up with my reading schedule, you know that.

—Just one day, what can that do . . .

—No, if you skip a day, that's just the beginning.

—An idle mind is the devil's workshop, my mother always told me.

—Ciao, Molina.

—How much I'd love to see my mom today. What I wouldn't give to see her for a little while.

—Hey, how about a little quiet, I have a lot to read.

—You're such a pisser.

—Don't you have a magazine to look at, or something?

—No, and it bothers me if I read, just looking at the print makes me dizzy. I'm not well, so there.

—Excuse me, but if you're not well you should go to the infirmary.

—Fine, Valentin. You study, you're perfectly right.

—Don't be unfair, don't talk to me in that tone.

—Sorry. Enjoy your studying.

—We can rap a little bit tonight, Molina.

—You'll tell me a film.

—I don't know any, you can tell me another one.

—Boy, how I'd like you to tell one, right now. Some film I never got to see.*

—In the first place I don't remember any films, and in the second place I have to study.

—Someday this could happen to you, then you'll see how it feels . . . Oh, I'm just kidding. You know what I think I'll do?

—What?

---

*After having classified the various theories on the physical origins of homosexuality into three groups, and having refuted them one by one, the above-mentioned English researcher D. J. West, in his work *Homosexuality*, suggests that the most popular non-scientific interpretations for the causes of homosexuality are also three in number. Before he goes on to list them, West again stresses the absence of perspective on the part of those theoreticians who would consider homosexual tendencies as unnatural, alleging— without proof of the fact—glandular or hereditary causes. Oddly enough, West considers to be somewhat more advanced—in comparison to the attitudes of those theoreticians—the view espoused by the Church with respect to the problem. The Church has catalogued the homosexual impulse as simply one among several "wicked" although natural urges which happen to scourge mankind.

On the other hand modern psychiatry concurs in reducing the causes of

—Think about some film to myself, one you wouldn't like, totally romantic. That way I'll keep myself busy.

—Fine, that's a good idea.

—And tonight you'll tell me about something, like what you're reading.

—Great.

—Because I'm half out of it, anyway. Right now, I couldn't even remember any film enough to tell you in detail.

—Mmm, think about something nice.

—And you, you study and no nonsense . . . because remember, an idle mind is the devil's workshop.

—Right.

—*forest, lovely little houses, all in stone, roofs of straw? no, slate, misty winter, no snow on the ground so it has to be autumn, guests arriving in comfortable cars, headlights illuminating the cobblestone drive. Elegant palisades, windows open so it has to be summer, gorgeous chalet, the air suffused with the scent of pines. Living room lit with candles, no logs burning—such a sultry evening—in the fireplace highlighted by the English furnishings. So not looking onto a fire, instead, the armchairs turned the other way around facing a grand piano, finished in pine? or mahogany? no, sandalwood! A blind pianist, surrounded by the guests, his eyes—almost no pupils*

---

homosexuality to the realm of the psychological. In spite of this, however, as West points out, a number of theories still persist which, although devoid of scientific support, lend themselves to the popular imagination. The first of them might be called the theory of perversion, according to which the individual would tend to adopt homosexuality just as he would any one of a number of vices. But its fundamental error lies in the fact that such a miscreant deliberately adopts the form of deviant behavior which most appeals to him, whereas the homosexual cannot develop a normal sexual pattern of conduct even if he sets out to do so, since whenever he might actually perform heterosexual acts he will find himself hard put to eliminate his more profound homosexual drives.

The second popularization is the theory of seduction. In his study, "The Sexual Behavior of Young Criminals," T. C. N. Gibbons investigates this matter, and he agrees with West and other researchers that while an

left—don't see what's in front of them, appearances that is, they see other things, the ones that really count. Debut for a sonata, composed by the blind man, to be played tonight in front of his friends: women in lovely long dresses, not too formal, just right for a country supper. Or maybe some rustic furniture, Colonial-American? atmospheric lighting provided by oil lamps. Happy-looking couples, young, middle-aged, and some of them old, all turning toward the blind man, who's ready to begin. Silence, the blind man's explanation of the actual events that inspired the composition, a story of love transpired in this very same forest. The tale itself, prior to the performance, so as to allow the guests a better insight into the music, "It all began one autumn morning while strolling through the forest," gnarled wooden cane and seeing-eye dog, so many fallen leaves providing a carpet, acute sound of foot-steps, crack-crack of leaves splitting like laughter, is the forest laughing? nearby an old chalet, probing with his cane, making his way along the palisade, certainty of witnessing a rare phe-nomenon, a house enveloped by something strange, enveloped by what? nothing visible, given his blindness. House en-veloped by something strange, it isn't music, resounding in its walls, its stones, its beams, its roughcast of cement, the ivy vines clinging to the stones: it's a heartbeat, they are alive, the

individual might well have—consciously, for the first time—come to feel homoerotic impulses when stimulated by someone of the same sex who has set out to seduce him, the said seduction—which almost always occurs in adolescence—can simply explain the initiation into homosexual behavior; it cannot, on the other hand, justify the arrest in the individual's flow of heterosexual urges. Thus, an isolated incident of that order cannot explain persistent homosexuality, which in the majority of cases is found to be exclusive, which is to say, incompatible with heterosexual acts.

The third theory alluded to is the one called segregation theory, accord-ing to which adolescents raised among males alone, without contact with women, or vice versa, women raised without contact with men, would tend to initiate sexual practices among themselves that might actually mark them forever. C. S. Lewis, in his study "Surprised by Joy," asserts that some boarding-school pupils, for example, probably have their first sexual experi-

blind man for just a moment standing so still, but the beating ceases, from off in the forest the slow approach of timid footsteps, in our direction. A girl it is. "I do not know whether you, sir, and your dog might perhaps be the masters of the house, or perchance you two are lost?" and the girl's voice sounds so sweet, so polite a manner, lovely like a sunrise, I'm sure she must be, and though I shan't manage to look at her in the eyes let me at least doff my hat to greet her. Poor sweet old blind man, doesn't even know I'm just a servant, so he takes off his hat to me, he's the only human being without the need to conceal his shock at my ugliness, "Do you live in this cottage, sir?" "No, I was out walking and had to tarry a moment," "Isn't it that you've lost your way? In that case I could show you, for I was born in the county," or do they say hamlet? county and hamlet are both of ancient times, and in Argentina we say townships, so what could be the name for villages in those lovely forests up in the United States? my mama, just like me, was once a serving maid and—a babe in her arms— she took me to Boston, and since she passed away I've been left all alone in the world, so I came back to the forest, and I'm looking for the house of a woman, who's living all alone and needing a maid. Squeaking of a door on its hinges, embittered voice of an old spinster, "Might there be something you're looking for?" giving the impression of being annoyed. Farewell from the blind old man, entrance of the ugly girl into

---

ences among other males, but the frequency of homosexual practices in boarding schools has more to do with the imperative demands for sexual discharge than with any willful choice of sexual partner. West adds that simply the lack of psychological contact with the feminine sex, caused by the total segregation which boarding-school life occasions or by the mere spiritual segregation within certain family structures, can in fact become a much more serious determinant of homosexuality than any incidence of sexual play among boarding-school pupils.

Psychoanalysis, whose principal characteristic is a probing of the mind in order to awaken infantile recollection, precisely maintains that sexual peculiarities have their origin in infancy. In *The Interpretation of Dreams,*

the quaint old house. To the spinster a letter of recommenda-
tion, agreement to stay as a maid, spinster's curt remarks, news
of the imminent arrival of tenants, "Seems impossible, I know
it, but nevertheless happy people do exist in this world, though
it's difficult to believe somehow, but when they arrive you'll
have to admit yourself what a handsome pair of sweethearts
they make. Anyway what do I want with such a big house? I
can make do with a cozy little room on the first floor, and you,
you'll have a maid's room in the back." Beautiful country-style
living room, varnished wood and stone, sputtering logs on the
hearth, windowsill invaded with ivy. Windowpanes not large,
little casement panels all a little warped and no two alike, so
rustic, stairway of dark and polished wood leading up to the
bedroom, the bride and groom's, and for the young man's work
a study, an architect perhaps? Such rushing to ready every-
thing by this afternoon, house-cleaning under the spinster's
supervision, unkind look of the old lady, apologies with every
complaint of how the maid doesn't know her job, "I'm sorry
I'm so bossy, it's just I'm nervous and can't control myself."
But with that voice, better no apologies at all. And nothing left
for me to do but wash out the spinster's favorite vase and fill
it with flowers, a car is pulling up! A couple getting out of the
car, a blonde divinely dressed, a fur coat, mink? little maid
looking out the window, at the young man with his back
turned, closing the car door, maid's rush to arrange the flowers,

---

Freud postulates that sexual and amorous conflicts are at the center of all
personal neuroses: once nourishment and bodily protection—food and shelter—have been accounted for, man has to deal with the urgency of his
sexual and emotional needs. This combined urge has been termed *libido*,
and its presence would be felt from infancy. Freud and his followers
maintain that manifestations of the libido are quite varied, but that the
rules established by society impose a constant vigilance on such manifestations, above all in order to preserve the basic unit of social conglom-
eration: the family. Therefore, the two most inappropriate manifestations
of the libido would have to be the incestuous and the homosexual
drive.

*messy splat on the floor of the water in the vase, it's falling!
. . . But there! thank goodness I managed to catch it in my
clumsy hands and save it from getting smashed, dying to catch
a glimpse of the couple, maid bent over, mopping up the floor,
words of the spinster showing them the house, voice of the
young man unable to contain his excitement, voice of his
fiancée not altogether pleased with the house, or rather, its
feeling of isolation out in the woods, dare I lift my head to look
at them? is it correct, or not, for a maid to greet them? voice
of the fiancée fairly curt, so demanding, quick glance of the
maid over in the young man's direction, no one could ever be
more handsome, but not even a greeting from him. Complaints
on the part of his fiancée over the loneliness of a house lost
in the forest, such sadness must invade the place at dusk.
Impossibility of dissuading him, final decision to take the
house, word of honor given, promise to write and mail the
lease, along with a certified check, arrival more or less planned
for just after the wedding. Young man's request for the maid
to leave the room, her nervous hands trying to arrange the
flowers in the vase, young man's desire to be alone with his
fiancée, "Let me just take a minute more to finish arranging
these lovely flowers," "That's okay like that, now please go."
Desire to sit with his fiancée over by the window and look out
on the forest while taking hold of those soft hands, with long,
lacquered fingernails, hands of a woman worlds apart from
domestic chores. Timeworn inscription roughly cut into one of
the thick little windowpanes, coarsely beveled lettering: a couple's names and the date just below, 1914. Young man's suggestion to his fiancée that she take off her engagement ring and
give it to him, fat stone cut rhomboidally, wish to carve their
own names as well, with the stone, into one of the windowpanes. But while trying to inscribe the name of his fiancée the
stone slips out of the setting and onto the floor. Both of them
silent, unspoken fear of a bad premonition, ominous music,
spinster's shadow falling on the leafless garden, down below.
Departure of the couple shortly thereafter, promise to be back*

soon, growing fear of fated consequences, impossible to quell.
How sad autumn can be at times! with sunny afternoons cut
short, and long twilights, spinster's own story confided to the
little maid, "I too was once on the verge of getting married."
Outbreak of the war in 1914, death of her fiancé at the front,
and everything prepared for him: little stone house in the
forest, lovely-looking trousseau, tablecloths and sheets, curtains all embroidered by the spinster's very hand, "Each stitch
I put into those fine clothes was like one more declaration of
love." Almost thirty years gone by, a love still intact, an inscription on a casement window the very day of his departure.
"I go on wanting him just as if it were only yesterday, and
worse still, go on missing him as much as that same afternoon
he departed and left me here all alone." And how sad, more
than ever this autumn afternoon, an ill-fated broadcast on the
radio, the nation's entry into still another war, the second
worthless world war. Yesterday is once again today, inconsola-
ble weeping of the spinster, locked in her bedroom, little maid
shivering from the cold, only a couple of dying coals, no right
to add logs to the fire just for herself all alone and forgotten
by the world there in the living room, with a shovel carefully
removing ashes of a last flickering ember. Days later arrival of
a letter, from that young man so taken by the house, virtually
its tenant already, but news of his enlistment in the air force,
for the time being postponing any wedding, and apologies for
not keeping his word, history repeating itself? Unnecessary
presence of a maid now in the empty house, lack of daily
chores, no tenants, all day long just to look out the window,
at the rain, nothing to do anymore, talking to herself . . . Aren't
you tired of reading yet?

—No. How do you feel?

—I think I'm becoming horribly depressed.

—Come, come, old buddy, no getting soft now.

—Don't you get tired of reading in this miserable light?

—No, I'm used to it by now. But what about your stomach,
how is it feeling?

—A little better. Tell me something about what you're reading.

—What can I tell you? It's philosophy, a book concerning political power.

—But it must say something, doesn't it?

—It says that honest men cannot deal with political power, because their concept of responsibility prevents them.

—And that's true, because politicians are all a bunch of crooks.

—To me it's just the opposite. Only a flawed conception of responsibility makes one stay away from political involvement. Rather, my responsibility is precisely to stop people from dying of hunger, and that's why I go on with the struggle.

—Cannon fodder, that's what you are.

—If you can't understand, then shut your mouth . . .

—You don't like my saying the truth . . .

—What an ignoramus! When you know nothing, then say nothing.

—It's no accident you're so angry . . .

—Enough! I'm reading!

—You'll see. One of these days you'll be the sick one and I'll get even.

—Molina, once and for all, shut up!

—You wait and see. Sometime I'll tell you a thing or two.

—Fine. Ciao.

—Ciao.

—*explanation on the part of the spinster, permission granted to the maid to stay on at the house since she has no other place to go, spinster's sadness and the maid's too, sum of two sadnesses, better each one alone than one mirrored by the other, no matter if sometimes it's better together, at least to share one can of soup that makes two servings. Bitter winter, nothing but snow, total silence, white blanket deadening the noise of a running motor in front of the house, windowpanes all misted on the insides and frosted over outside, maid's hand rubbing in a circle to clean the glass, young man outside with his back turned, closing the car door, joy of the maid, why? hurried footsteps to the front door, I'll fly to open the door to the young man so spirited and handsome coming here finally with his nasty fiancée! . . . "Ahhh!!! forgive me!" shame of the maid, unable to contain her own gesture of disgust, black look of the poor young man, his once fearless pilot's face crossed now with a horrible scar. Young man's conversation with the spinster, relating the battle, his injury and eventual nervous collapse, impossibility of returning to the front, proposal to rent the house for himself, spinster's actual sorrow at seeing him thus, young man's bitterness, his sharp words to the maid, sharp commands, "Bring me what I tell you and leave me alone, and don't make any noise, because I'm very tense," memory of the young man's happy lovely face still in the mind's eye of the little maid and I ask myself: what is it that makes a face so lovely? why such an urge to caress a lovely face? why do I feel the urge to always have a lovely face close to mine, to touch, and to kiss? a lovely face should have a petite nose, but sometimes big noses can be appealing, and big eyes, or even little eyes if they smile a lot, little eyes sparkling with goodness . . . A scar from the tip of the forehead cutting down across one of the eyebrows, down across the same eyelid, furrowing into the nose until it sinks into the opposite cheek, a face xed out, a black look, an evil look, reading a work of philosophy and just because I ask a question he gives me that black look, it feels so bad when somebody gives you a black look, what's worse? when they give you a black look or when they refuse to look at you altogether? mom never gave me that black look, they condemned me to eight years for fooling around with a minor but mom never gave me that black look, but because of me my mom could die, tired heart of a woman suffering so much, tired heart, from forgiving too much? so many hardships her whole life beside a husband that never understood her, and later on the hardship of having a son steeped in vice, and the judge wouldn't pardon me a single day, and there in front of my mom said that of all things I was the* worst, a revolting fag, and in order to keep me away from any other kids, he wouldn't allow me one single day less than the full weight of what the law permitted, and after him saying all that, my mom still kept her eyes fixed on him, eyes full of tears as if someone had just died, but when she turned from the judge to look at me she gave me a smile, "The years go by quickly and, God willing, I'll still be alive to see it," and everything will be like nothing ever happened, and each passing minute her heart beats on, weaker and weaker? so terribly easy for her heart to get tired and not be able to beat anymore, but I never said a word to this son of a bitch, not a word about my mother ever, because if he dared to say one stupid word about her I'd kill the son of a bitch, what does he know about feelings? what does he know about dying of grief? how does he know what you feel when you're to blame for a sickly mother getting worse and worse? is mom worse? is mom dying? can she wait those seven years until I get out? will the warden keep his promise? is it true what he promised? a pardon? a reduction in my sentence? one day a visit by the parents of the wounded flyer, the flyer locked in his room way up on the top floor, "Tell my parents I don't want to see them," insistence on the part of the parents, a couple of rich stuffed shirts cold as ice, parents departing, arrival of his fiancée, "Tell my fiancée I don't want to see her," his fiancée begging at the bottom of the steps, "Let me come up and see you, my love, because I swear to you nothing matters about your accident," fiancée's hypocritical voice, insincerity of every word she speaks, fiancée's brusque departure, the days passing, the drawings done by the young man while locked up in his study, view of the snow-covered forest from up in the window, first notes of spring, buds so tender and green, some drawings of trees and clouds done out in the open air, arrival of the maid carrying hot coffee and a couple of doughnuts into the forest, maid's observation with respect to the drawing set upon a cute little easel, surprise on the part of the wounded flier, what did the girl say exactly about that drawing? why did the young man *realize at just that moment that the maid actually possessed a refined soul? how does it happen that sometimes someone says something and wins someone else over forever? what was it the poor maid said about that drawing? how did she get him to see she was something more than just an ugly little maid? How I'd like to remember those words, what would she have said? nothing at all can I remember about that scene, and the other important scene, his encounter with the blind man, the blind man's own story of how little by little he resigned himself to the loss of his eyesight, and one night the flyer's proposition to the girl, "The two of us are all alone and expecting nothing more out of life, neither love nor joy, and so perhaps it's possible to help one another, for I have some money that could be your security, and you too might take care of me a little, since my health's no longer improving, and I don't want to be near anyone who feels sorry for me but you can't feel sorry for me, because you're as sad and lonely as I am, and so perhaps we could join together, but with nothing more to it than a contract, an arrangement between just friends." Could it be the blind man's idea? what would he have said to him which I can't remember now? at times a single word can work miracles. A wooden church, the blind man and the spinster as witnesses, a couple of candles burning on the altar, no flowers, empty benches, somber faces, organist's bench empty and the choir loft empty too, words of the priest, his blessing, footsteps resounding through the empty nave as the couple leaves, after-noon coming to its end, return to the silent house, windows open to catch the pleasant summer air, young man's bed shifted to his study, maid's bedroom shifted to his bedroom, to his ex-bedroom, wedding supper already prepared by the spinster, table set for two in the living room close to the window, candelabra between both plates, spinster's goodnight, her own skepticism before their simulacrum of love, embit-tered grimace on her lips, the couple in absolute silence, a bottle of vintage wine, a toast without so much as a word, impossibility of looking at one another, crick-crick of crickets out there in the garden, slight murmur—not heard until then —of forest foliage swayed by the breeze, strange radiance— not noticed until then—of candelabras, stranger and stranger radiance, hazier contours of everything in sight, of her face so ugly, of his face so disfigured, sound of music almost impercep- tible and so very sweet you don't know where it comes from, her face and all her features enveloped in a misty white light, only the glow of the eyes at all perceptible, mistiness fading little by little, agreeable face of a woman, same as the little maid's face but beautified, the coarse eyebrows transformed into light penciled lines, eyes illuminated from within, eyelashes elongated with curling, skin like porcelain, mouth widened in a smile of perfect white teeth, hair waved in silky ringlets, and her simple percale dress? an elegant lace evening gown, and what of him? impossible to determine his features, only an image distorted by the glare from candelabras or even like through eyes filled with tears, his face seen through eyes filled with tears, tears drying up, face seen with absolute clar- ity, face of as spirited and handsome a young man as ever could be, but with trembling hands, no, hers are the trembling hands, one hand of his moving closer to one hand of hers, whistling wind in the forest's foliage or violins and harps? gazing into one another's eyes, conviction they are both hearing violins and harps carried by the breeze perfumed with evergreens, coupling of hands, lips approaching lips, first and moist kiss, beating of two hearts . . . in perfect time, night crowded with stars, both no longer at the table . . . empty tables at the restaurant, waiters waiting for customers, slow calm after-mid- night hours, cigarette barely lit hanging from one side of his mouth, left or right corner of his lips, his saliva the taste of tobacco, black tobacco, sad eyes lost in the distance, looking through the windowpanes, cars passing all wet from the rain, one car after another, does he remember me? why is it he's never come to see me? couldn't he change shifts with one of his buddies? did he ever go to the doctor's office for that* earache? putting it off from one day to the next, terrible pains at night sometimes, he said, swearing next day he'd go have it looked at, then next day the pain gone and he forgets about the doctor, and after midnight while he's waiting in the restaurant for his last customers he must remember and think about me and say tomorrow he'll certainly come and see me, looking through the windowpane at all the passing automobiles, and the saddest thing of all is when the windowpanes in front of the restaurant get wet from the rain, as if the restaurant had been crying, because he never weakens, he holds up because he's a man and never cries, and when I think very hard about someone I can see their face pictured in my memory, on a clear glass pane wet with the rain, a hazy face I see in my memory, my mom's face and his face, he must remember, and I wish he'd come, I wish so much he'd come, first on a Sunday, for everything in life is just a question of habit, and he comes another day, and another, and when my pardon comes through he's waiting there on the corner for me outside the penitentiary, we take a taxi, coupling of hands, the first kiss timid and dry, closed lips are dry, half-parted lips are a bit moist, his saliva the taste of tobacco? and if I die before getting out of this prison I'll never find out how his saliva tastes, what happened that night? waking up and fearing it all a dream, infinitely afraid to glance at one another in the light of day, in that house where lives as lovely a girl and as handsome a young man as could ever be. And they hide themselves from the spinster, so she never sees them, both afraid of her saying something and spoiling it all, and they go out into the forest just before dawn, when no one is around, watching the sunrise as it lights upon their faces so lovely and always so close to each other, close enough to give all those kisses each to each, but let nobody see them! because strange things can happen, and suddenly footsteps this morning in the forest! impossible to hide since the tree trunks aren't big enough, slow footsteps of a man who's trampling over the dewy grass, and behind him *a dog . . . oh, it's only the blind man, thank heavens! since he can't see them, but still he gives them a greeting because of the sound of their breathing, so cordial and sincere a greeting, the blind man's intuition of a change, the three of them back now to the house of enchantment, appetite of an early morning, breakfast like in American films, girl taking charge of preparing things, blind man and young flyer alone together for a moment, blind man asking what has happened, the whole story, blind man's joy, suddenly a black bolt of fear across the blind man's white retina when hearing the simple statement: "Know what I think I'll do? I'll contact my parents so that they come visit me and my darling wife," effort on the part of the blind man to hide his great apprehension, announcement of the arrival of the parents who have accepted his invitation, young man and his girl hiding in their bedroom awaiting the parents without courage to go downstairs, spinster waiting by the window, car pulling up, parents' chitchat with the spinster, happiness of the parents since he wrote them how he's all but better, appearance of the young man and his girl way up at the top of the stairs, parents' bitter disappointment, ferocious scar slashed across the young man's face, his bride a lowly servant with an ugly face and such clumsy manners, impossibility of pretending to be pleased, after a few short embarrassing minutes suspicion of the young man, has it all been nothing but a cruel deception? is it possible that we haven't changed? a look at the spinster hoping she'll regard him as handsome as ever, embittered grimace upon the spinster's lips, girl's flight to find a mirror, the cruel reality, young man standing beside her there in the mirror, the infamous scar, refuge in total darkness, horror of seeing one another, noise of the parents' car, noise of the motor already far off and bound for the city, girl taking refuge in her old room, from when as a maid, and his despair, destruction of his own self-portrait embraced with the girl, demented slashes reducing the canvas to tattered shreds, spinster's phone call to the blind man, visit by the blind man upon an autumn twilight, conversation with the sickly*

*young man and the ugly girl, lights turned off to avoid the sight
of each other, three blind beings thrown together at the saddest
hour of day, spinster listening behind the door, "Don't you two
realize what has happened? Please, after I finish this talk, go
back to looking at one another like before, as I know you have
not done in all these many days, hiding from one another, and
it's so simple to explain the very enchantment of this lovely
summer now gone by. To put it simply . . . you are beautiful
to one another, because you love each other so and thus see
nothing but your souls, is that perhaps so difficult to understand? I do not ask you to look at each other now, but once
I have left you . . . please do, without the slightest tremor of
doubt, because the love that beats within the stones of this old
house has caused a miracle: that of permitting yourselves, as
if blind, to see not the body but only the soul." Departure of
the blind man with the last reddening rays of sunset, young
man's ascent to his room to ready himself for suppertime, table
set by the girl herself, her fear of facing the mirror in order
to fix herself and comb her hair, spinster's firm footsteps as she
enters the little maid's quarters, spinster's eyes lost in the
distance, her words of encouragement, impossibility of the
girl's combing her own hair given the trembling of hands,
words of the spinster as she starts to comb the girl's hair for
her, "I heard all that the blind man said to you and I tell you
he's so very right, this house has been waiting to shelter two
such beings in love, ever since my fiancé couldn't come back
from the cruel trenches of France, and the two of you have
been chosen; and love is that, rendering beautiful whoever
manages to love without hoping for return. And I am certain
if my fiancé were to come back from the far beyond that even
today he would find me just as beautiful and just as young as
I was back then, yes, I'm absolutely sure, because he died
loving me," table set close to the window, young man standing
looking out the window at the forest sunk in darkness, her
footsteps, his fear of turning around and looking at her, his
hand taking her hand, removing her ring and inscribing their*

names in the glass, and then caressing her silky hair, caressing her porcelain skin, his smile as handsome as can be, her smile of perfect white teeth, their wet kiss of happiness, the end of the blind man's story, first chords of the sweet sonata, arrival on tiptoe of two additional guests, who are the young man and the girl? seen from behind, looking elegant, but from behind of course no way to tell if the faces are beautiful or not, and no one realizing that these two are the protagonists of the story that's just been told, and mom was crazy about it, and me too, and luckily I didn't tell this son of a bitch, and I'm certainly not going to tell him another word about anything I like, so he can't laugh anymore about how soft I am, we'll see if ever he weakens or not, but I won't tell him any more of the films I like the most, they're just for me, in my mind's eye, so no filthy words can touch them, this son of a bitch and his pissass of a revolution

—The meal is about to arrive, Molina.

—So, you do have a tongue.

—Yes, I do have a tongue.

—I thought maybe the rats ate it.

—No, the rats didn't eat it.

—Then bend over and see if you can reach there to shove it up your ass.

—Listen, I don't like your tone or the liberties you're taking.

—Well, we just won't say another word then, get me? Not another word.

— . . .

—No thanks.

—Take the bigger plate.

—Take it yourself.

—Thanks.

—Don't thank me.

—I swore I wouldn't tell you any more films. Now I'll go to hell for breaking my word.

—You don't know how it hurts. Like a terrible stabbing pain.

—Just what happened to me the day before yesterday.

—But they're getting stronger and stronger, Molina.

—Well then you should go to the infirmary.

—Don't be so stupid, please. I already said no.

—A little seconal won't do you any harm.

—Yes it will, you get habituated. You just don't know about it, so it's easy for you to talk.

—Okay, then I'll tell you a film . . . But what don't I know about seconal?

—Never mind . . .

—Come on, tell me, don't be that way. Besides, I can't exactly go telling anyone else.

—It's one of those things I can't talk about because I took an oath, everyone does in the movement.

—But just about the seconal, nothing else, so I can protect myself too, Valentin.

—Promise not to tell anyone.

—I promise.

—It happened to one of our comrades, they got him hooked on it, and that softened him up and completely broke his willpower. A political prisoner can't afford to end up in an infirmary, ever, you understand? Not ever. In your case it wouldn't do any harm. But with us our resistance would eventually break down until finally, when interrogated, we could be made to say anything . . . Agh, aghhh . . . See what I meant before . . . the pains become so sharp . . . as if they were punching holes in me . . . It's like having nails hammered right into my stomach . . .

—Well, let me tell you the film, to distract you a little and take your mind off the pain.

—What one are you going to tell?

—One I'm positive you'll really like.

—Aghhh . . . what a bitch . . .

— . . .

—Just begin, don't pay any attention if I complain, go right on with it.

—Okay, well it starts out, where was that place now? Because it moves around to a lot of different places . . . But first I should explain something: it's not my kind of film.

—And so?

—It's one of those films men usually go for, that's why I picked it . . . for you, since you don't feel so well.

—Thanks.

—Now how does it start? . . . Wait, oh right, at that auto racetrack, I don't remember the name of it, the one in the south of France.

—LeMans.

—How do men always remember all about auto races? Anyway, this South American kid is racing there, very rich, a playboy son of one of those wealthy landowners with the big banana plantations, and it's during the qualifying heats at LeMans. He's explaining to another driver how he doesn't race for any manufacturer's make of automobile because those companies all exploit the masses. So he races in an auto built with his own two hands, because he's that kind of guy, with a mind of his own. And it's the qualifying heats and they decide to have a soda while waiting their turn for the trials, and he's incredibly confident because, according to every calculation, he's going to qualify fantastically well—at least, that's what everyone is saying who has seen his machine perform on that same track during pretrials, and obviously, it's going to be a terrible blow to the famous makes of automobiles when this fellow wipes the floor with them. Anyway, while they're busy having their drink, you see someone go up to his auto; one of the marshals by the stand is watching the whole thing but plays dumb because they're all in on it together. So the one who goes up to the racing car, his face like a real s.o.b., he fools around with the motor somehow, loosening something, and then splits. The kid comes back and climbs into the shell and moves out to the starting line. He takes off like a shot, but on the third lap the motor catches fire and he barely manages to escape. He's safe and sound, but . . .

—Aghhh . . . fuck them . . . these fucking pains.

— . . . but the car's completely wrecked. He gets together with the team and says it's all over, there's no money left to even start building another racer, and so he goes off to Monte Carlo, nearby, where his father hangs out on a yacht with a chick; she's a lot younger, stunning looking. Actually the father gets a call from his son while he's on the yacht, then they meet out on the terrace of the father's suite at the hotel where he's staying. But the girlfriend isn't there because the father has a certain amount of scruples with his son; you can tell how much he likes the kid because he was so happy when he got the telephone call. As for the son, he's thinking of asking his father for more money, but he can't make up his mind, he's ashamed at being such a no-good loafer, yet when he meets with his father the old man embraces him so affectionately and tells him not to worry about the car being wrecked, he's already figured out what to do so his son can manage to get another one, even though it upsets him to see him racing and risking his neck like that. Then the son says they've been over all this before, and obviously, knowing it was the kid's one great passion, the father had pushed him into auto racing so he would drift away from those hotbeds of political activity among the leftist students, because the kid was studying political philosophies in Paris.

—Political science.

—That's it. And then the father asks him why he doesn't drive for some known make of automobile, hoping to steer his son back on the right track with something more secure for himself. But the son just gets pissed and tells his father, wasn't it enough that you kept me out of Paris all that time, because while he was involved in building his own racing car he'd forgotten about everything else, but to put himself to work for any of those international corporate bloodsuckers, never! Then the father says he's sorry he even brought it up, not to mention that whenever he hears him ranting on like that, all infuriated, it reminds him of his ex-wife, the kid's own mother. She was passionate and idealistic too, and all for what . . . to end up the way she did . . . Then his son half turns to go, and so the father, feeling remorse, tells him to wait, he'll give him whatever's needed to build a new car, and I forget what else, but the son, who you can see has a special weakness for the mother, he just keeps going, slamming the door behind him. Then the father stands there lost in thought, all upset, staring from his terrace at the divine harbor of Monte Carlo with all those yachts lit up, each one of them outlined with tiny lights on the masts and sails, like a vision. But at this point the phone rings and it's the young chick, and the old man apologizes and says he won't be going to the casino tonight, because a serious problem has come up and he wants to take care of it. So anyway, just as the kid is walking out of the hotel, he bumps into some old friends who drag him off to a party. And the kid is so depressed at the party that what he does is carry off a bottle of cognac with him to some remote room, only what I didn't say is that the scene is situated in this dreamy villa, on the outskirts of Monte Carlo, you know those houses along the Riviera, all incredibly luxurious, this one with sprawling stone steps out onto the gardens, and for decoration on the balustrades and on the steps, too, some huge stone pots, like urns, or giant vases, with a beautiful plant growing in each pot, and it's usually a gigantic cactus—you know what a century plant looks like?

—Yes.

—Well, like that. And the kid's made himself at home in some room off from the party, a library, and he's all alone there getting totally drunk. Suddenly he notices someone coming into the room, a woman, already in her forties but elegant-looking and kind of imperious, and with a bottle in her hand, too. But since he's in the dark—the only light comes from an open window—she doesn't see him right away and she sits down and pours a drink, but at this point fireworks suddenly illuminate the Bay of Monte Carlo, it's some national holiday, and he takes the opportunity to say cheers. She's caught by surprise, but when with a movement he shows her how they've both done the same thing, carrying off a bottle of Napoleon brandy to forget about the world, there's nothing left for her but to smile. He asks her what she's trying to forget, and she suggests he tell her first, then she'll do the same.

—I feel like I have to go to the bathroom again . . .

—Should I call the guard to open up?

—No, I'll try to stand it . . .

—You'll only make yourself worse.

—But they'll see how sick I am.

—Listen, they won't stick you into the infirmary because of a little diarrhea . . .

—Who knows, it's already the fourth time today, wait and see if I can stand it . . .

—You're white, it's more than just diarrhea. If I were you I'd go to the infirmary . . .

—Shut up, please.

—I'll go on with the film, but listen . . . stomach problems can't be contagious, right? because it seems like the same problem I had, exactly . . . You won't blame me, will you?

—It must be something to do with the food, for both of us to get sick . . . You turned white, the same way. But it's starting to subside now, so go on with the film . . .

—With me, how long did it last? . . . Two days, more or less.

—No, it was just one night, by the next day you were already feeling better.

—Then call the guard, because it won't matter if you're sick for just one night.

—Go on with the film.

—Sure. We were where he meets an elegant woman. I told you she was kind of middle-aged, a society type.

—But, physically, what was she like?

—Not too tall, some French actress, really stacked, but at the same time very slender, with a tiny waist, wearing a very fitted evening dress, really low-cut, and strapless, with those reinforced cups, you remember them . . .

—No.

—Sure you do, they used to look like they were serving their tits on a tray.

—Don't make me laugh, please.

—The undercups were really stiff, reinforced with wire on the inside of the fabric. And as casual as you please: would you care for a tit, sir?

—Come on, don't make me laugh.

—But that way you'll forget about the pain, silly.

—It's just that I'm afraid of going in my pants.

—No, please, or we'll die in this cell. I'll go on. So anyway, it ends up he's the one who is supposed to tell first why he wants to drink himself into oblivion. And he gets very serious and says that he's doing it to forget everything, absolutely everything. She asks him doesn't he have anything he wants to remember, and he says he'd like his life to begin at this very moment, starting when she walked into the room, the library. Then it was her turn to tell, and I imagined she was going to say the same thing too, that she wanted to forget everything. But not at all, she says how she's been given a lot of things in life, and she's very grateful for them, because she's the editor of a successful fashion magazine, and she's crazy about her work, and she has a couple of adorable children, not to mention her family inheritance, because it turns out she's the owner of that unbelievably beautiful villa, which looks just like a palace, but obviously, she has something to forget: the rough time men have given her. The kid tells her he envies her luck, whereas, on the other hand, he's had zero. Obviously the guy doesn't want to talk to her about his problem with the mother, because he's like obsessed by his parents' divorce, and he feels guilty about having abandoned his mother, who even though she was always very rich and still lives on a divine coffee plantation, after his father left her she went and married another guy, or was about to get married, and the kid thinks it was just her way of escaping her loneliness. Ah, yes, now I remember, the mother always writes saying exactly that, that she's going to marry someone, without loving him, because she's afraid of being left all alone. And the kid, he feels very bad about having left his country, where the workers are so mistreated, and he's got revolutionary ideas but it's just he's the son of a multimillionaire and no one wants to have anything to do with him, no one from the workers I mean. And he feels bad about having left his mother, too. And he tells all of that to this older woman. You know something . . . you never talk about your mother.

—Of course I do, what do you mean?

—I swear to God, never, never.

—Well, maybe I have nothing to tell.

—Thanks. I appreciate the trust.

—Why the nasty tone?

—Never mind, when you're better we'll talk about it.

—Agn . . . aghhh . . . I'm sorry . . . Ugh, what am I doing? . . .

—No no, don't wipe yourself on the sheet, wait . . .

—No, stop it, not your shirt . . .

—Yes, take it, wipe yourself. Keep away from the sheet; you'll need it so you don't catch a chill.

—But it's your change of clothes, you won't have any shirts left . . .

—Take it, wait, lift yourself, not that way, that's it, careful, wait, so it doesn't get on the sheet.

—It didn't, did it?

—No, just on your shorts. Come on, let's go, off with them.

—I feel embarrassed . . .

—There you are, slowly, careful . . . perfect. Now the difficult part, wipe yourself with the shirt.

—I'm ashamed . . .

—Weren't you the one who said you have to be a man? . . . So what's this business of being embarrassed?

—Roll them up good . . . the shorts, so it doesn't smell.

—Don't you worry, I know how to take care of things. See, like this, all wrapped up inside the shirt, which is easier to wash than a sheet. Take some more paper.

—No, that's yours, you won't have any left for yourself.

—You don't have any, come on, don't be proud . . .

—Thanks . . .

—Forget it, come on now, finish wiping yourself and relax a little, you're trembling.

—I'm enraged. I'm so enraged I could cry, enraged at my fucking self.

—Now, now, calm down, why do you have to keep picking on yourself, you're crazy . . .

—Yes, I'm crazy all right, with rage, for letting these bastards lock me up.

—Try and relax.

—Ah, that's smart . . . The newspaper around the shirt

so the smell won't escape . . . right?

—Good idea, isn't it?

—Uh-huh.

—Try and relax, and keep yourself covered.

—Mmm-hmm, tell me a little more now, about that film.

—I can't even remember where I was at.

—You were just asking me about my mother.

—Yes, but with the film I don't remember where I stopped.

—I don't know why I never talked to you about my mother. I don't know much about yours, but I can picture her somehow.

—As for me, I can't picture your mother one bit.

—My mother is the kind of woman who's very . . . very difficult, that's why I don't talk about her much. She's never liked my ideas, she believes she's entitled to everything she owns, her family has always had money, and a certain social position, you know what I mean?

—Upper-crust like.

—You might say that, not the very top, but upper-crust, yes. She eventually separated from my father, and now he died just two years ago.

—A little like the film I'm telling you.

—No . . . you're crazy.

—Well then, more or less.

—Not at all. Aghhh . . . hurts so much . . .

—You like the film?

—I can't concentrate. But go on, finish it quickly.

—Then you don't like it.

—What happens finally? Tell me in a few words, the gist of it, how it ends.

—Well, the kid latches onto this woman, a little older than him, and she thinks he's just interested in her money, to make himself a new racer, and at this point suddenly he has to return to his own country, because his father, who also went back himself in the meantime, has been kidnapped by guerrillas. And the kid makes contact with them, and convinces them how he's for the same cause, and when she finds out he's in real danger, the woman, the European one, goes to look for him, too, and they save the father in exchange for a lot of money, but when the moment arrives for the father to be freed, and the kid, too, because he's taken his father's place without the guerrillas realizing anything about it, anyway there's a mixup and they're about to kill the kid because they discover the trick, but the father intercedes and they kill the father. Then the kid prefers to remain there with the guerrillas, and the woman goes back all alone to her job in Paris, and the parting is really sad, because the two of them actually love one another, but each one belongs to a different world, and ciao, The End.

—And what way does it seem the same?

—The same as what?

—As my situation. What you said about my mother.

—Oh, nothing, just that the mother comes out very well dressed to meet him, when the kid returns home to where all those coffee plantations are, and she asks the kid to go back to Europe, oh, and I forgot to tell you how when at the end they free the father there's a shootout with the cops, and the father is mortally wounded by them, and the mother reappears, and they end up together, the son and the mother I mean, because the other woman doesn't stay, the one who loves him, she goes back to Paris.

—You know something, I'm beginning to feel sleepy.

—Then take advantage of it and get some sleep.

—Yes, let me try to sleep a little.

—And if you feel bad, no matter what time it is, wake me.

—Thank you, you've had a lot of patience with me.

—Nonsense, get some sleep. Forget it.

—Nightmares, all night long.

—What were you dreaming?

—I don't remember at all. It's that my system is still messed up, but it'll go away soon.

—Hey, you're eating too fast! On top of which you're still not well at all.

—I feel so ravenous, and my nerves are jumpy, too.

—Honestly, Valentin, you shouldn't eat. You should have a special diet today.

—But I feel like I have a gigantic hole in my stomach.

—At least stretch out a little now that you've finished eating all your rice glue, don't start to study.

—But I wasted all morning by sleeping.

—Whatever you want. I'm just telling you something for your own good . . . If you want, I'll talk to help pass the time.

—No thanks, I'm going to see if I can read.

—Know something? If you didn't tell your mom that she can actually bring food to you each week . . . then you're a fool.

—I don't want her to feel obligated, I'm here because I asked for it, and she's got nothing to do with it.

—My mother doesn't come because she's sick, you know?

—No, you didn't tell me.

—They told her she can't get out of bed for anything, on account of her heart.

—Oh, I didn't know, I'm terribly sorry.

—That's why I'm almost out of provisions, besides which she doesn't want anyone else to bring me things; she thinks the doctor is going to give her permission from one minute to the next. But in the meantime I'm screwed, because she doesn't want anyone except herself to bring me the food.

—And you think she's not going to get well?

—Oh, I don't give up hope, but it'll take months at least.

—If you were out of here, she'd get better, right?

—You've read my mind, Valentin.

—It's logical, that's all.

—But look, you've cleaned off your plate, you gobbled everything up, that's just crazy.

—You're right, now I feel so full I think I could explode.

—Stretch out awhile.

—I don't want to sleep; I had nightmares all last night and

then this morning too, every second.

—I told you the end of the picture already, so it's no fun now if I go on telling the rest.

—The pain's coming back, this is unbelievable . . .

—Where does it hurt?

—In the pit of my stomach, and lower down in my intestines, too . . . ugh . . . it's awful . . .

—Just relax, try to listen to me, it's probably all nerves.

—Agh, Molina my friend, it's just like having someone punching holes in your guts.

—Should I call to let us out to the john?

—No, the pain is higher up, as if something's burning my insides out, something in my stomach.

—Why don't you try to vomit?

—No, if I ask to go to the john they'll send me off to the infirmary.

—Vomit in my sheet then, wait, I'll fold it, and you can throw up into it, afterwards we'll wrap it up tight and there won't be any smell.

—Thank you.

—Forget it, come on, put your fingers down your throat.

—But you'll be cold later on, without a sheet.

—No, the blanket covers me okay. Come on, throw up.

—No, wait, it's subsiding a little now, I'm going to try to relax . . . like you told me, to see if it passes.

—a European woman, a bright woman, a beautiful woman, an educated woman, a woman with a knowledge of international politics, a woman with a knowledge of Marxism, a woman with whom it isn't necessary to explain it all from A to Z, a woman who knows how to stimulate a man's thinking with an intelligent question, a woman of unbribable integrity, a woman of impeccable taste, a woman of discreet but elegant dress, a woman who's young and at the same time mature, a

woman who knows a good drink, a woman who knows how to
order a meal, a woman who knows the right wine, a woman
who knows how to entertain at home, a woman who knows
how to give orders to her servants, a woman who knows how
to organize a reception for a hundred people, a woman of
poise and charm, a desirable woman, a woman who under-
stands the problems of a Latin American, a European woman
who admires a Latin American revolutionary, a woman more
preoccupied nonetheless with Paris automobile traffic than
with the problems of some colonized Latin American country,
an attractive woman, a woman who won't be shaken by the
news of someone's demise, a woman who is capable of hiding
a telegram for hours with the news of the death of her lover's
father, a woman who refuses to quit her job in Paris, a
woman who refuses to accompany her lover on a trip back to
the jungle coffee region, a woman who goes right back to the
daily routine of busy Parisian executive, a woman who nonetheless finds it difficult to forget true love, a woman who knows
what she wants, a woman who has no regrets about her final
decision, a dangerous woman, a woman who is capable of
quickly forgetting, a woman with the power to forget what
would have only become a burden, a woman who could even
forget the death of a fellow who returns to his own country, a
fellow who's flying back to his own country, a fellow who from
up in the sky observes the azure mountains of his country, a
fellow moved to tears, a fellow who knows what he wants, a
fellow who hates the colonialists in his country, a fellow ready
to sacrifice his life in defense of principles, a fellow who cannot
comprehend the exploitation of the workers, a fellow who's
seen old peons tossed out into the street because they're no
longer useful, a fellow who remembers peons imprisoned for
robbing the bread they couldn't afford and later turned to drink
to forget their own humiliation, a fellow with an unshakable
faith in the precepts of Marxism, a fellow with his mind made
up to enter in contact with guerrilla organizations, a fellow who

from up in the sky observes the mountains certain of his forthcoming meeting with the liberators of his country, a fellow who's afraid of being taken for an oligarch, a fellow who ironically enough could be kidnapped by the guerrillas in hopes of a ransom, a fellow who gets off the plane and embraces his widowed mother dressed there in strident colors, a mother without tears in her eyes, a mother respected by an entire nation, a mother of impeccable taste, a mother of discreet but elegant dress inasmuch as there in the tropics those strident colors are appropriate, a mother who knows how to give orders to her servants, a mother who finds it difficult to look her son in the face, a mother with some kind of problem on her mind, a mother who walks with her head held high, a mother whose straight back never touches the back of a chair, a mother who since her divorce has been living in the city, a mother who at the request of her son accompanies him to their old coffee plantation, a mother who now recalls in her son's presence various anecdotes of his childhood, a mother who manages to smile once again, a mother whose clenched hands manage to relax enough to caress her son's head, a mother who manages to relive for a moment the better years of her life, a mother who asks her son to have a walk with her through the old tropical park which she designed so long ago, a mother of exquisite taste, a mother who beneath palm trees relates how her husband was executed by guerrillas, a mother who in a flowery thicket of hibiscus relates how her ex-husband shot an insolent servant and in that way provoked the revenge of the guerrillas, a mother whose slender silhouette is outlined against a far-off blue sierra behind the coffee plantation, a mother who begs her son not to avenge the death of his father, a mother who begs her son to return to Europe even though it will mean their separation, a mother who fears for the life of her son, a mother who leaves unexpectedly to attend a charity event back in the city, a mother who from the comfort of her Rolls Royce pleads with her son to get out of the country, a mother who cannot conceal her nervous tension, a mother without apparent reason to be so tense, a mother who's hiding something from her son, a father who'd always been kind with his servants, a father who'd attempted to better the condition of his peons through charitable acts, a father who founded a country hospital for peons in the region, a father who constructed dwellings for those peons, a father who used to argue bitterly with his wife, a father who rarely talked to his son, a father who never came downstairs to eat with his family, a father who never pardoned the strikes by his peons, a father who never pardoned the burning down of hospital and dwellings by a faction of dissident peons, a father who'd permitted his wife to divorce him on condition that she go live in the city, a father who refused to deal with any guerrillas whom he'd never forgiven for the burnings, a father who leased his fields to foreign investors and took refuge on the Riviera, a father who later returned to his properties for reasons known only to himself, a father who sealed his fate with a shameful stamp, a father who was executed like a criminal, a father who perhaps was a criminal, a father who almost certainly was a criminal, a father who covered his son with ignominy, a father whose criminal blood runs in his son's veins, a peasant girl, a girl of Indian and white blood, a girl with all the freshness of youth, a girl with teeth yellowed by malnutrition, a girl of timid character, a girl who looks at the protagonist with rapture, a girl who delivers a secret message, a girl who notes with profound relief his favorable reaction, a girl who takes him that same night to rendezvous with an old friend, a girl who rides horseback admirably well, a girl who knows those mountain trails like the back of her hand, a girl who hardly speaks at all, a girl with whom he doesn't know quite how to talk, a girl who in less than two hours leads him to the guerrilla camp, a girl who gives a whistle to summon the head of the guerrillas, a classmate from the Sorbonne, a classmate with a militant political stance, a classmate whom he hasn't seen

since then, a classmate convinced of the honesty of the protagonist, a classmate who'd returned to his country to organize
subversive activities among the peasants, a classmate who'd
managed in just a few years to organize a guerrilla front, a
classmate who believes in the honesty of the protagonist, a
classmate prepared to make an incredible revelation,
a classmate who thinks he's caught wind of a governmental
conspiracy behind the dark episode which caused the death of
the father and the overseer, a classmate who asks him to return
to the plantation and unmask the guilty party, a classmate who
perhaps is mistaken, a classmate who's perhaps preparing an
ambush, a classmate who perhaps needs to sacrifice a friend
to continue the fight for liberation, a girl who takes him back
to his mansion, a girl who doesn't speak, a taciturn girl, a girl
merely exhausted perhaps after a long day's work and a long
night's ride, a girl who from time to time turns around and
observes him with mistrust, a girl who possibly detests him, a
girl who orders him to hold it, a girl who tells him to keep
quiet, a girl who hears the distant echoings of a reconnaissance
patrol, a girl who tells him to get down off his horse and wait
a few minutes hidden in the bushes, a girl who tells him to wait
for her quietly holding both horses by the reins while she
scrambles up a rocky crag and has a look, a girl who returns
and orders him to head back to a turn in the mountain trail,
a girl who a little while later points to a natural cave where they
can spend the night inasmuch as the soldiers won't break camp
until dawn, a girl who's shivering with the cold in the damp
cave, a girl of unfathomable intentions, a girl who's capable of
stabbing him in his sleep, a girl who without looking him in
the face asks with a choked voice if she can lie next to him to
keep herself warm, a girl who neither talks to him or looks up
at him, a shy girl or a cunning girl, a girl with nubile flesh, a
girl who lies there by his side, a girl whose breathing quickens,
a girl who lets herself be taken in silence, a girl treated like
a thing, a girl with whom you don't need to say nice things,

a girl with an acrid taste in her mouth, a girl with a strong odor of sweat about her, a girl who gets used up and then tossed aside, a girl to dump your semen into, a girl who's never heard of contraceptives, a girl who's exploited by her boss, a girl who can't make you forget a sophisticated Parisian, a girl with whom there isn't any desire to caress after the orgasm, a girl who relates how the ex-manager of the plantation raped her when she was just a kid, a girl who relates how the ex-manager of the plantation is currently very high up in government circles, a girl who asserts that this same man has something to do with the death of the fellow's father, a girl who dares to say that the one who perhaps knows the most about everything is the fellow's mother, a girl who reveals the cruelest fact of all, a girl who's actually seen the fellow's mother in the arms of the ex-manager, a girl with whom there's no desire to caress after the orgasm, a girl who gets slapped and insulted for saying such horrible things, a girl who gets used up and then tossed aside, a girl who's exploited by a cruel boss in whose veins runs the blood of an assassin

—You were crying out in your sleep.

—Really?

—Yes, you woke me up.

—Sorry.

—How do you feel?

—I'm all sweated up. Can you find the towel for me? without lighting the candle.

—Hold on, I'll give it a try . . .

—I don't remember where I left it . . . If you can't find it, Molina, it doesn't matter.

—Be quiet, I already found it, you think I'm some kind of nitwit?*

---

*Anna Freud, in *The Psychoanalysis of the Child*, indicates as the most generalized form of neurosis that of the individual who, in trying to gain complete control of his prohibited sexual desires, and in trying even to eliminate them—instead of classifying them as socially inconvenient, but

—I'm frozen.

—I'll fix you some tea right now, it's the only thing left.

—No, that's yours, forget it, I'm already feeling better.

—You're crazy.

—But you're using up all of your provisions, you're the one who's crazy.

—No, they'll be bringing me more.

—Remember that your mother's sick and can't come.

—Oh, I remember okay, but it doesn't matter.

—Thanks, really.

—Please.

—Yes, you don't know how much I appreciate what you've done. And I ask you to forgive me, because at times I tend to be rather brusque . . . and I hurt people for no real reason.

—Oh, stop it.

—Like when you weren't feeling well yourself. I didn't pay any attention, not a bit.

—Shut up for a while, will you.

—Seriously, and not just with you, I've hurt a lot of people plenty. I haven't told you, but instead of my telling you a film I'm going to let you in on something real. I was putting you on about my girlfriend. The one I told you about is someone else, whom I loved very much. As for my woman, I didn't tell

---

nevertheless natural enough—represses himself too far and becomes incapable of enjoying uninhibited relations under any circumstances. Thus an individual may lose control of his auto-repressive faculties and reach such extremes as impotence, frigidity, or obsessive guilt feelings. Psychoanalysis also indicates the following paradox: it is generally the precocious development of the intelligence and sensitivity of the child which can actually induce too strong a repressive activity in the same. It is a proven fact that the child possesses a libido from the very onset of life, and it is equally clear that he manifests it without the discrimination of an adult. He becomes fond of any person who may take care of him and takes pleasure in games with his own body and with the body of any other persons. But in our own culture —Anna Freud adds—these manifestations are promptly chastised, and the child acquires a sense of shame. From his first conscious acts until puberty sets in, the child passes through a period of latency.

you the truth, and what's more you'd really like her, because she's a very simple girl and very sweet and very brave.

—No, listen. Don't tell me about it, please. That's all just a lot of crazy business, and I don't want to know anything about your political goings-on, all those secrets and who knows what else. Please.

—Don't be idiotic, who would ask you something about me, about my goings-on?

—You never know with those things, they could interrogate me.

—I trust you. You trust me, right?

—Mmm-hmm . . .

—So everything should be fifty-fifty here, don't belittle yourself with me . . .

—It's not that . . .

—At times it's good to unburden oneself, because I really feel down now, I'm not kidding. There's nothing worse than feeling down about having done wrong by somebody. And that's just what I did with that nice kid . . .

—But not now, tell me some other time. Right now it's bad for you to go stirring things up out of the past, intimate things like that. Better you just take this tea I'm making, it'll do you good. Do as I tell you . . .

In *Three Essays on the Theory of Sexuality*, Sigmund Freud asserts that the incestuous fantasy of expelling the rival progenitor—which is to say the father for the boy, and the mother for the girl—and substituting oneself for the same is a recurrent fantasy among children, but such ideas tend to arouse intense feelings of guilt and fear of punishment. The consequence is that the boy or the girl suffers so greatly from the conflict that by means of a very painful but unconscious effort they manage to repress it, or to disguise it in the eyes of their consciousness. The conflict is resolved during adolescence, when the adolescent manages to transfer the emotional burden of the respective progenitor onto a boy or a girl of an appropriate age. But those who have developed a very close relationship with the progenitor of the opposite sex—and the correspondingly unavoidable feelings of guilt—will find themselves in danger of continuing with those sensations of discomfort for the rest of their lives in the face of any sexual experience, inasmuch as unconsciously they will associate it with those guilty incestu-ous desires from back in infancy. The outcome, once the neurosis takes hold, is not always the same: for a man it opens up the possibilities of impotence, or of exclusively depending upon prostitutes—women who in some way fail to represent the mother—or even more likely, the possibility of only being able to respond sexually to other men. For women the outcome of the unresolved conflict is primarily frigidity or lesbianism.

CHAPTER 7

"Dearest . . . I am writing you once more now, night . . . brings a silence that helps me talk to you, and I wonder . . . could you be remembering too, sad dreams . . . of this strange love affair . . ."

—What is that, Molina?

—A bolero called "My Letter."

—Only you'd come up with something like that.

—Like what? What's wrong with it?

—You're crazy. It's a lot of romantic nonsense.

—I happen to like boleros, and that one's really very pretty. I'm sorry if it wasn't very tactful, though.

—What do you mean?

—Well, today you got a letter and now you're really down.

—And what's that got to do with it?

—Well, next thing you know I start humming songs about sad letters. But I didn't do it on purpose . . . really I didn't, okay?

—No, I know.

—Why so sad?

—It was some bad news. You could tell?

—How should I know? . . . Well, yes, you look pretty depressed.

—It was some really bad news. You can read the letter if you want.

—No, better not . . .

—Don't start all over again like last night. You've got nothing to do with my problems, nobody's going to ask you anything. Anyway they already opened it and read it before they let me have it. You're really on the ball . . .

—Hey, that's right.

—If you want to read it you can read it. Here.

—The writing looks like chicken scratching to me. Why don't you read it to me if you feel like it?

—It's from a girl without much education, poor kid.

—I can't believe what a stupid girl I am, it never dawned on me that they open letters here if they want to. So, sure, it doesn't matter if you read it to me.

—"Dearest: I haven't written to you for a real long time because I didn't have the courage to tell you everything about what happened and you can understand why, can't you? Because you're the intelligent one, not me, that's for sure. I also didn't write to tell you the news about poor Uncle Pedro. Because they told me his wife already sent you a letter. I know how much you don't like to dwell on this type of thing. Because life has to go on somehow, and, well, we all need strength to continue the struggle to make our way through life and its trials. But as far as I'm concerned that's the worst part about growing old." It's all in code. Could you tell?

—Well, it's not very clear, that much I could tell.

—When she says "growing old," that means becoming part of the movement. And when she says "life and its trials," that's fighting for the cause. And Uncle Pedro, unfortunately . . . he's a fellow who was only twenty-five years old, one of our comrades in the movement. I didn't know anything about his getting killed. The other letter never reached me. They must have torn it or something when they opened it up here.

—Ah . . .

—Which is why this letter was such a shock to me. I had no idea.

—I'm very sorry.

—Well, what can you do . . .

— . . .

— . . .

—Tell me the rest of the letter.

—Let's see . . . ". . . growing old. Still, at least you've got lots of strength. I wish I was that way. So you're probably taking it okay. For me, the worst of it's how much I miss Uncle Pedro. Because he kind of left the family in my hands, and that's some responsibility. Listen, baldy, I heard they really gave you a good shaving. What a shame I can't get a load of you that way for a change. Too bad about those goldilocks of yours. But I always keep in mind the stuff we used to talk about. Above all about not letting ourselves get down in the dumps over personal stuff. So I try sticking to your advice by making the best of things, whatever way they fall." When she says that he left the family in her hands, that means that she's in charge of our group now.

—Ah . . .

—So . . . "I kept missing you more and more and that's why, especially after the death of Uncle Pedro, I finally had to take the responsibility on myself. Of letting my niece Mari start in having relations with a nice boy you never met. Who comes over to the house and seems decent enough about his plans to hold down a steady job. But I warned my niece not to get too serious. Because that just makes for more headaches. And not to try for anything more than a little nice companionship. Which, after all, everybody needs, to have the strength to get by with life and its trials." The niece named Mari is herself, and by saying some fellow is decent about holding down a steady job she means he's devoted to the cause, you get it? To the struggle.

—Mmm-hmm, but I don't understand the business about having relations.

—That means she's been missing me too much, and we, well, we commit ourselves, as comrades, to avoiding intense relationships of that kind because they can only be a hindrance when it comes time to act.

—Act how?

—Act decisively. Risk one's life.

—Ah . . .

—We can't get caught up in subjective feelings for one another, because naturally either person would want the other to stay alive. Then you both tend to be afraid of death. Well, not exactly afraid, but . . . it's painful if anyone suffers because you choose to risk your life. So to avoid that she's begun to have relations with another comrade . . . I'll go on. "I kept wondering whether I had better tell you or not. But I know you enough to realize you'd rather have me tell you all of it. Fortunately things are going well now. And we all feel optimistic that someday soon our house will turn out to prosper after all. It's night and I'm thinking maybe you're thinking about me too. Here's a big hug for you, Ines." When she says house, it means country.

—But I don't understand what you said last night then, about how your girlfriend isn't really like you described her.

—Damn! I'm dizzy again, just from reading a letter . . .

—You must be really weak . . .

—I feel slightly nauseous.

—Lie back and close your eyes.

—Damn! I swear, I was feeling so much better.

—Rest quietly, it's just from focusing your eyes too much. Keep them closed awhile.

—Mmm, it feels as if it's subsiding now . . .

—You shouldn't have eaten, Valentin. I told you not to.

—I was hungry, that's all.

—You were doing so well yesterday until you ate, and that screwed up your whole system. Now today you do it again, and this time the whole plate! Promise me you won't touch a bite tomorrow.

—Don't even talk about food, it makes me . . .

—I'm sorry.

—Know something? There I was laughing at your bolero, but the letter I got today says just wh t the bolero says.

—You think so?

—Mmm, I do . . . It seems to me I don't have any right to be laughing at your bolero.

—You were probably just laughing because it struck too close to the bone, and you laughed . . . so as not to cry. Like in another bolero I know. Or tango.

—How does it go? That one you were singing before?

—Which part of it?

—The whole thing.

—"Dearest . . . I am writing you once more now, night . . . brings a silence that helps me talk to you, and I wonder . . . could you be remembering too, sad dreams . . . of this strange love affair. My dear . . . although life may never let us meet again, and we—because of fate—must always live apart . . . I swear, this heart of mine will be always yours . . . my thoughts, my whole life, forever yours . . . just as this pain . . . belongs . . . to you . . ." "Pain" or "hurt," I don't remember which. It's one or the other.

—It's not the worst I've heard.

—To me it's divine.*

---

*In his *Psychoanalytic Theory of Neurosis*, O. Fenichel asserts that the probability of a homosexual orientation increases the more the male child identifies with his mother. This situation results especially when the maternal figure is more compelling than that of the father, or when the father is altogether absent from the family setting, as in cases of death or divorce, or whenever the figure of the father, if in fact present, is deemed repellent because of some serious defect, such as alcoholism, excessive strictness or extreme violence of character. The child has need of an adult hero to serve as a model for conduct: through identification, the child will go on to adopt characteristic parental traits of conduct, and even though, to a certain extent, he rebels against obeying their demands, unconsciously he will incorporate the habits and even the quirks of his progenitors, perpetuating the cultural traits of the society in which he lives. Once having identified with his father, Fenichel continues, the boy takes on a masculine view of the world, and in Occidental society that view includes a strong component

—What's the name of it?

—"My Letter," by Mario Clavel. He's from Argentina.

—Really? I would have thought he was Mexican, or Cuban.

—I also know lots by Agustin Lara, almost all of them.

—I don't feel quite as dizzy now, but the cramps are starting up again.

—Try to relax.

—It's not my fault for having eaten.

—Don't think about the pain if you can help it, and try to relax. It's when you get all tense . . . Just talk to me a little. About anything . . .

—What I was trying to explain last night was that the girl I talked about, the very liberated one, from the bourgeois family. She's really not my girl, not the one who wrote to me.

—So who's the one who wrote to you?

—No, see, the one I always talk about entered the movement at the same time that I did. But then later on she decided to quit, and she insisted I do the same.

—Why?

—She became too attached to life, too happy with me. Our relationship alone sufficed for her. And that's when all the trouble began. You see, she would get upset whenever I disappeared for a few days, and each time I came back there she was crying again. And that was nothing. She stopped telling me about phone calls from my comrades, and toward the end even intercepted letters. Well, that was the last straw.

---

of aggressivity—a vestige of his formerly indisputable condition of master —which helps the male child impose his new presence. On the other hand, the boy who is already adopting the maternal figure as a model and fails to encounter sufficiently early some masculine figure—to check his fascination for the maternal—will be socially ostracized because of his feminine traits, inasmuch as he fails to display the appropriate toughness of the normal male child.

With respect to the same matter, Freud states in *On the Transformation of Instincts* that within the male homosexual, the most complete masculine attitude can at times be combined with a total sexual inversion—understanding "masculine attitude" to include such traits as bravery, honor, and

—Has it been a long time since you've seen her?

—Almost two years. But I still think about her. If only she hadn't started acting that way . . . like some castrating mother . . . Anyway, I don't know . . . it seems like we were destined to be separated.

—Because you loved each other too much?

—That sounds like another bolero, Molina.

—Listen, big man, don't you know by now, boleros contain tremendous truths, which is why I like them.

—The healthy thing about her, though, was the way she stood up to me. We had a genuine relationship going for us. She never just . . . how can I explain it? She never let herself be manipulated, like the typical female . . .

—What do you mean?

—Aghhh, Molina, my friend . . . it feels like I'm getting sick all over again.

—Where does it hurt?

—Down in my gut . . .

—Don't tense up, Valentin, that'll make it worse; try to stay calm.

—Yes.

—Lie back.

—I just feel so sad, I can't tell you.

—What's the matter?

—That poor kid, if you only knew. What a wonderful person he was, poor guy . . .

---

the spirit of trial and adventure. But in his later work, *On Narcissism: an Introduction*, he elaborates a theory according to which the male homosexual would begin with a temporary maternal fixation, only to finally identify himself as a woman. If the object of his desire should happen to be a young boy, this is because his mother loved him, as a boy himself. Or because he would actually have wanted his mother to love him in the same way. In other words, the object of his desire is his own image. For Freud, then, the myths of Narcissus and Oedipus are both components of the original conflict which lies at the core of homosexuality. But of all of Freud's observations concerning homosexuality, this one has been most subject to attack, the principal objection being that homosexuals whose identification is

—Who?

—The one they killed.

—Well, he won his place in heaven, that's for sure . . .

—If only I could believe in that; it would be such a consolation sometimes, to believe that decent people ultimately find their reward. But I just can't buy it. Ugh . . . Molina, I'm going to have to pester you again—quick, call the guard to open up.

—Hold it just a second . . . I'm just . . .

—Aghhh . . . aghhh . . . no, don't call . . .

—Don't be upset, I'll get you something to wipe yourself right away.

—Aghh . . . aghh . . . the pains are so strong, as if my guts were about to burst . . .

—Loosen up your body, just let it come out and afterward I'll wash your sheet.

—Please, bundle up the sheet under me. Because it's coming out all liquid.

—Yes . . . sure, like this, there, you keep yourself calm now. Let it come out. Later on I'll just take the sheet in to the showers with me. It's Tuesday, remember?

—But that's your sheet . . .

—It doesn't matter, I'll be washing yours anyway, and luckily we still have plenty of soap.

—Thanks, Molina . . . I think I'm starting to feel a little better now . . .

---

deeply feminine seem to feel attracted to very masculine types, or to males of a much older age.

Again in the latter work, Freud talks about the development of erotic feelings and about still other aspects of the genesis of homosexuality. He asserts, for instance, that libido in babies is of a rather diffuse character, and has to pass through several stages until finally achieving the education of its impulse and managing to have it devolve upon a person of the opposite sex with whom pleasure can be attained through genital union. The first stage is an oral one, in which pleasure is derived solely from mouth contacts, such as suction. Later on comes the anal stage, in which the child derives his satisfaction from his own intestinal movements. The last and definitive phase is the genital. Freud considers it the only mature form of

—You just relax, and don't worry. You're usually such a pisser anyway. Tell me when you're finished and I'll help you clean yourself up.

— . . .

—All finished?

—I think so, but now I'm freezing.

—Let me give you my blanket. That way you'll stay warm.

—Thank you.

—But first roll over so I can clean you up. If you think you're all done.

—Better wait a little longer . . . Molina, I'm sorry for laughing that way before, at what you were saying about boleros.

—What a time you pick to talk about boleros.

—Listen, I think I'm finished now, but I'm the one to clean myself . . . if I don't start to faint again when I lift my head.

—Try slowly . . .

—No use, I'm still too weak, there's no other way . . .

—I can clean you up, don't worry about it. You just relax.

—Thank you . . .

—Okay . . . that's it, and a little over here . . . turn slowly . . . that's right. Nothing went through to the mattress, so it's not so bad. And fortunately there's plenty of water. I can just wet a clean tip of the sheet to wipe you off, that's easy enough.

—I don't know what to say.

---

sexuality, an assertion which years later would be directly attacked by Marcuse.

The same Freud amplifies his views in *Character and Anal Eroticism*, where he elaborates the following theory: certain abnormal types of personality, whose predominant traits are avarice and an obsession with orderliness, may be influenced by repressed anal desires. The pleasure which they derive from the accumulation of goods can arise from the unconscious nostalgia for the pleasure they felt when younger in retaining—a common activity among children—their feces. On the other hand, an obsession for order and cleanliness would have to be a compensation for the guilt which they have felt on account of their impulse to play with feces. As for the role which anal fixation may play in the development of homosexuality, Freud

—Don't be silly. Let's see now . . . lift up a little over here. That's right . . . very good.

—Honestly, I can't thank you enough, because I don't have the strength to make it to the showers.

—Of course not, and that's all you need is some icy water on your body.

—Uh . . . uh . . . the wet sheet's cold too.

—Spread your legs a little more . . . That's it.

—But it doesn't disgust you?

—Be quiet. Now I'll wet some more of the sheet . . . like this . . .

— . . .

—Well, you're getting to look all tidied up now . . . just a little drying with the other end . . . What a shame I've got no talcum left.

—Doesn't matter. It's so great just being dry.

—Good, and there's one more corner of the sheet to pat you off . . . Like that. Now you're good and dry.

—I feel so much better, really. Thank you, my friend.

—Wait now . . . here we go . . . let me wrap you up tight in the blankets, just like a papoose. There we go . . . lift up a little on this side.

—Okay?

—That's right . . . Wait . . . and now the other side, so you won't catch a chill. Are you comfortable now?

—Mmm-hmm, fine . . . Thank you so much.

—And don't you dare move, not until the dizziness goes away completely.

---

asserts that besides the influences already enumerated—Oedipus, Narcissus—one must take into account the fact that all of those impediments tend to interrupt the development of the child, by bringing about affective inhibitions which cause fixation in an anal phase, without the possibility of acceding to the final phase, which is to say, the genital.

To this assertion West responds that homosexuals, upon feeling themselves denied an avenue leading to normal genital relations, are forced to experiment with extra-genital erogenous zones, and in sodomy they encoun-

—We'll see, it'll probably go away soon.

—But whatever you want, I'm the one who gets it for you. You don't budge.

—And I promise not to laugh at your boleros anymore. I like the lyrics from that one you were singing before . . . they're okay.

—I especially love the part that goes, ". . . and I wonder . . . could you be remembering too, sad dreams . . . of this strange love affair . . ." Divine, isn't it?

—You know what? . . . I actually changed diapers on that poor comrade's baby boy, the guy they killed, I mean. We were all hiding out together in the same apartment, he and his wife, and their little son . . . Who knows what's to become of him now? He can't be more than three years old. What a cute little tyke . . . And the worst of it is I can't write to anyone about it, because the slightest move on my part would compromise them . . . or even worse, identify them.

—Can't you just write to your girl?

—That would be the worst choice of all. She's the head of the group now. No, not to her, not to anyone. And it's just as it says in your bolero, "because this life will never bring you back," because I'll never be able to write to that poor fellow either, or talk to him or anything.

—Actually what it says is, *"Although* life *may never* let us meet again . . ."

—"Never"! What an awful word. Until now I had no idea . . . how awful . . . that word . . . could . . . I'm sorry . . .

—It's okay, Valentin, get it off your chest, cry as much as

---

ter—after progressive adjustment—a type of mechanically direct but not exclusive form of gratification. West adds that the male who practices sodomy is not necessarily fixated in the anal phase, just as the heterosexual who kisses his mate is not necessarily fixated in an oral phase. Finally, he points out that sodomy is not an exclusively homosexual phenomenon, since heterosexual couples also practice the same behavior, while individuals with an "anal character" (which is to say, avaricious, obsessed with cleanliness and order, etc.) do not necessarily feel inclined toward homosexuality.

you want, let yourself go until you're all cried out.

—It's just that it all feels so rotten . . . And not being able to do anything, locked up here, unable to even . . . take care of his wife, his li- . . . little . . . kid . . . Oh, my friend, it's . . . so sad . . .

—But what can we do?

—Molina, help me to . . . to lift my arm out . . . from under the blanket . . .

—What for?

—Give me . . . give me your hand, tight.

—Sure, grip it as hard as you can.

—I just want to stop shaking so damn much, that's all.

—But who cares whether or not you're shaking, if it gives you some relief.

—But there's something else, and it bothers me so much. Something really terrible, something despicable . . .

—Tell me, get it off your chest.

—It's that the one I'd . . . I'd really like to write me . . . the one I'd like to be with most of all, and to hold . . . isn't my girl . . . isn't my real woman. It's the other one . . . it's the one I talk to you about that I want to see.

—But that's simply how you feel . . .

—Yeah . . . because I talk a lot but . . . but deep down inside, what I . . . what I really like is . . . is the other kind of woman. Inside I'm just the same as all the other reactionary bastards who helped to murder that poor guy . . . I'm just like them, exactly.

—That's not true.

—Oh yes it is, let's not kid ourselves.

—If you were like them you wouldn't be in here.

—". . . sad dreams of this strange love affair . . ." And you know why I became so annoyed when you started in with your bolero? Because it reminded me of Marta, not my girlfriend. That's why. And I even think that, with Marta, I don't feel attracted to her for any good reasons, but because . . . because she has *class* . . . that's right, class, just like all the class-conscious pigs would say . . . in their son-of-a-bitching world.

—Don't torture yourself . . . Close your eyes and try to rest.

—But whenever I do, I start to feel dizzy again.

—I'll heat up some water for some camomile tea. Yes, it turns out that we still have some. We just forgot about it.

—I don't believe you . . . Really?

—I swear. It was under all my magazines, so we lost track of it.

—But it's yours, and you like having tea in the morning.

—Listen, it'll help you relax. Just stay quiet for a while. You'll see what a difference a good rest makes . . .

—*a fellow with a plan on his mind, a fellow who accepts his mother's invitation to visit her in the city, a fellow who lies to his mother assuring her of his opposition to the guerrilla movement, a fellow who dines by candlelight alone with his mother, a fellow who promises his mother to accompany her on a trip to all the fashionable winter resorts like when he was a child just after the war, a mother who goes on about all the eligible young beauties of the European aristocracy, a mother who goes on about all the wealth that he will eventually inherit, a mother who proposes to already place a substantial fortune in her son's name, a mother who hides the real reason why she can't accompany him to Europe just yet, a fellow who inquires into the whereabouts of the ex-manager, a fellow who finds out that the same man is actually the brains behind the Ministry of Internal Security, a fellow who finds out that the ex-manager is actually the head of secret service in the office of counterinsurgency operations, a fellow who wants to convince his mother to go off with him to Europe, a fellow who wants to take title to his fortune and repeat his childhood European voyage in order to ski with his lovely mother, a fellow who decides to leave everything behind and fly off with his mother, a fellow whose* mother rejects his proposal, a mother who confesses to already having other plans, a mother who has plans to rebuild her own emotional life, a mother who goes to see him off at the airport and confides to him the news of her imminent marriage to the ex-manager, a fellow who pretends to be enthusiastic over the projected marriage, a fellow who gets off the plane at the first stopover and takes a return flight home, a fellow who joins up with the guerrillas in the mountains, a fellow determined to rehabilitate the good name of his father, a fellow who meets up with that same peasant girl who once led him through the sierra when he first met the guerrillas, a fellow who can see that she's pregnant, a fellow who doesn't want to have an Indian for a child, a fellow who doesn't want to mix his blood with the blood of an Indian, a fellow who feels ashamed about all his feelings, a fellow who feels revolted to caress the future mother of his own child, a fellow who doesn't know how to make up for his faults, a fellow who leads a guerrilla assault against the plantation where his mother and the ex-manager happen to be, a fellow who surrounds the mansion, a fellow who opens fire on his own home, a fellow who opens fire on his own flesh and blood, a fellow who orders the occupants of the house to surrender, a fellow who watches the ex-manager come out of the house hiding like a coward behind the mother as his hostage, a fellow who orders his men to fire, a fellow who listens to the heartrending screams of his mother as she begs for mercy, a fellow who delays the execution, a fellow who demands a full confession relating to the complete facts of his father's death, a mother who breaks loose from the arms imprisoning her and confesses to the whole truth, a mother who explains how her lover dreamed up a plan designed to make the father seem a murderer of his own faithful overseer, a mother who confesses how her husband was actually innocent, a fellow who orders his men to execute his own mother after giving the order to execute the ex-manager, a fellow who completely loses his mind and seeing his mother agonizing on the *ground picks up a submachine gun to execute the very soldiers who've just riddled her with bullets, a fellow who in turn is immediately executed, a fellow who feels guerrilla bullets burn into his stomach, a fellow who manages to glimpse the accusing eyes of the peasant girl among the faces of the firing squad, a fellow who before dying wants to beg for forgiveness but can no longer utter a word, a fellow who sees in the eyes of the peasant girl an eternal condemnation*

MINISTRY OF THE INTERIOR OF THE ARGENTINE REPUBLIC
Penitentiary of the City of Buenos Aires
Report to the Warden, prepared by Staff Assistants

Prisoner 3018, Luis Alberto Molina
   Sentenced July 20, 1974, by the Honorable Judge Justo José
   Dalpierre, Criminal Court of the City of Buenos Aires. Con-
   demned to eight years imprisonment for corruption of mi-
   nors. Lodged in Pavilion B, cell 34, as of July 28, 1974, with
   sexual offenders Benito Jaramillo, Mario Carlos Bianchi, and
   David Margulies. Transferred on April 4, 1975, to Pavilion
   D, cell 7, housing political prisoner Valentin Arregui Paz.
   Conduct good.

Detainee 16115, Valentin Arregui Paz
   Arrested October 16, 1972, along Route 5, outside Barran-
   cas, National Guard troops having surrounded group of acti-
   vists involved in promoting disturbances with strikers at two
   automotive assembly plants. Both plants situated along said
   highway. Held under Executive Power of the Federal Government and awaiting judgment. Lodged in Pavilion A, cell
   10, with political prisoner Bernardo Giacinti as of November
   4, 1974. Took part in hunger strike protesting death of
   political prisoner Juan Vicente Aparicio while undergoing
   police interrogation. Moved to solitary confinement for ten
   days as of March 25, 1975. Transferred on April 4, 1975,

to Pavilion D, cell 7, with sexual offender Luis Alberto Molina. Conduct reprehensible, rebellious, reputed instigator of above hunger strike as well as other incidents supposedly protesting lack of hygienic conditions in Pavilion and violation of personal correspondence.

GUARD: Remove your cap in front of the Warden.

PRISONER: Yes, sir.

WARDEN: No need to be trembling like that, young man, nothing bad is going to happen to you here.

GUARD: Prisoner has been thoroughly searched and has nothing dangerous on his person, sir.

WARDEN: Thank you, Sergeant. Be good enough to leave me alone with the prisoner now.

GUARD: Shall I remain stationed in the hallway, sir? With your permission, sir.

WARDEN: That will do fine, Sergeant, you may go out now . . . You look thin, Molina, what's the matter?

PRISONER: Nothing, sir. I was sick to my stomach, but I'm feeling much better now.

WARDEN: Then stop your trembling . . . There's nothing to be afraid of. We made it look like you had a visitor today. Arregui couldn't possibly suspect anything.

PRISONER: No, he doesn't suspect anything, sir.

WARDEN: Last night I had dinner at home with your sponsor, Molina, and he brought me some good news for you. Which is why I had you summoned to my office today. Oh, I know it's rather soon . . . or have you learned something already?

PRISONER: No, sir, nothing yet. I feel I need to proceed very cautiously in this kind of situation . . . But what did Mr. Parisi have to say?

WARDEN: Very good news, Molina. It seems your mother is feeling a lot better, since he spoke to her about the possibility of a pardon . . . She's practically a new person.

PRISONER: Really? . . .

WARDEN: Of course, Molina, what would you expect? . . . But stop your crying, what's this? You should be pleased . . .

PRISONER: It's from happiness, sir . . .

WARDEN: But come on now . . . Don't you have a handkerchief?

PRISONER: No, sir, but I can just use my sleeve, it's no problem.

WARDEN: Take my handkerchief at least . . .

PRISONER: No, I'm really okay. Please excuse me.

WARDEN: You know, Parisi is like a brother to me, and it was his interest in you that led us to come up with the present option, but Molina . . . we're expecting you to know how to manage things. Do you seem to be making any headway, or what?

PRISONER: I think I'm getting somewhere . . .

WARDEN: Was it helpful to have him weakened physically, or no?

PRISONER: Actually I had to eat the prepared food the first time.

WARDEN: Why? That was certainly a mistake . . .

PRISONER: No, it wasn't, because he doesn't like rice, and since one plate had more than the other . . . he insisted I have the bigger portion, and it would have been suspicious had I refused. I know you warned me that the prepared one would come in a new tin plate, but they loaded it up so much I had to eat it myself.

WARDEN: Well, good work, Molina. I commend you, and I'm sorry about the mixup.

PRISONER: That's why I look so thin. I was sick for two days.

WARDEN: And Arregui, how's his morale? Have we managed to soften him up a little? What's your opinion?

PRISONER: Yes, but it's probably a good idea to let him begin to recover now.

WARDEN: Well, that I don't know, Molina. I think the matter had best be left to our discretion. We have here appropriate techniques at our disposal.

PRISONER: But if he gets any worse there's no way he can remain in his cell, and once he's taken to the infirmary, there's no chance left for me.

WARDEN: Molina, you underestimate the proficiency of our personnel here. They know exactly how to proceed in these matters. Weigh your words, my friend.*

PRISONER: Excuse me, sir, I only want to cooperate. Nothing else . . .

WARDEN: Of course. Now another thing—don't give out the slightest hint about a pardon. Hide any sign of euphoria when you go back into your cell. How are you going to explain this visit?

PRISONER: I don't know. Perhaps you can suggest something, sir.

WARDEN: Tell him your mother came, how does that sound?

PRISONER: No, sir, impossible, not that.

WARDEN: Why not?

PRISONER: Because my mother always brings some bags of food for me.

WARDEN: We have to come up with something to justify your euphoria, Molina. That's definite. I know now, we can requisition some groceries for you, and pack them up the same way, how does that strike you?

---

*In *Three Essays on the Theory of Sexuality*, Freud points out that repression, in general terms, can be traced back to the imposition of domination of one individual over others, this first individual having been none other than the father. Beginning by such domination, the patriarchal form of society was established, based upon the inferiority of the woman and the intensive repression of sexuality. Moreover, Freud links his theory of patriarchal authority to the rise of religion and in particular the triumph of monotheism in the West. On the other hand, Freud is especially preoccupied with sexual repression, inasmuch as he considers the natural impulses of a human being much more complicated than patriarchal society admits: given the undifferentiated capacity of babies to obtain sexual pleasure from all the parts of their body, Freud qualifies them as "polymorphous perverse." As a part of the same concept, Freud also believes in the essentially bisexual nature of our original sexual impulse.

PRISONER: Fine, sir.

WARDEN: This way we can also repay you for your sacrifice, over that plate of rice. Poor Molina!

PRISONER: Well, my mother buys everything in the supermarket a few blocks from the prison, so as not to have to carry everything on the bus.

WARDEN: But it's easier for us to requisition everything from supplies. We can make the package up right here.

PRISONER: No, it would look suspicious. Please don't. Get them to go to that market, it's just down the street.

WARDEN: Wait just a minute . . . Hello, hello . . . Gutierrez, come into my office a moment, will you please.

PRISONER: My mother always brings me the stuff packed in two brown shopping bags, one for each hand. They pack it for her at the store, so she can manage everything.

WARDEN: All right . . . Yes, over here. Look, Gutierrez, you'll have to go buy a list of groceries which I'm going to give you,

---

Along the same lines, and with reference to primary repression, Otto Rank considers the long development, which runs from paternal domination to a powerful system of state run by men, to be a prolongation of the same primary repression, whose purpose is the increasingly pronounced exclusion of women. In addition, Dennis Altman, in his *Homosexual Oppression and Liberation*, addressing himself specifically to sexual repression, relates it to a need, at the very origin of humanity, to produce a large quantity of children for economic ends and for purposes of defense.

With regard to the same subject, in *Sex in History* the British anthropologist Rattray Taylor points out that, beginning with the fourth century B.C., there occurs in the classical world an increase in sexual repression and a growth of the feeling of guilt, factors which facilitated a triumph of the Hebraic attitude, sexually more repressive, over the Greek one. According to the Greeks, the sexual nature of every human being combined elements which were as much homosexual as heterosexual.

Again Altman in the above-cited work expresses the view that Western societies specialize in sexual repression, legitimized as it is by the Judeo-Christian religious tradition. Such repression expresses itself in three interrelated forms: by associating sex with (1) sin, and its consequent sense of guilt; (2) institution of the family and procreation of children as its only justification; (3) rejection of all forms of sexual behavior outside

and wrap them up in a certain way. The prisoner will give
you instructions, and it all has to be done in . . . let's say
half an hour. Take out a voucher and have the sergeant go
make the purchases with you according to the prisoner's
instructions. Molina, you dictate whatever you think your
mother would be likely to bring you . . .

PRISONER: To you, sir?

WARDEN: Yes, to me! And quickly. I have other things to attend
to.

PRISONER: . . . Guava paste, in a large package . . . Make it two
packages. Canned peaches, two roast chickens, still warm,
obviously. A large bag of sugar. Two boxes of tea, one
regular and the other camomile. Powdered milk, condensed
milk, detergent . . . a small box, no, a large box, of *Blanco,*
and four cakes of toilet soap, *Suavísimo* . . . and what else?
. . . Yes, a big jar of pickled herring, and let me think a little,
my mind's a complete blank . . .

---

of the genital and the heterosexual. Further on he adds that traditional
"libertarians"—in terms of sexual repression—fight to change the first two
forms but neglect the third. An example of the same would be Wilhelm
Reich, in his book *The Function of the Orgasm,* where he affirms that sexual
liberation is rooted in the perfect orgasm, which can only be achieved by
means of heterosexual genital copulation among individuals of the same
generation. And it is under the influence of Reich that other investigators
would develop their mistrust of homosexuality and of contraceptives, since
these would interfere with the attainment of perfect orgasms, and as a result
would be detrimental to total sexual "freedom."

Concerning sexual liberation, Herbert Marcuse in *Eros and Civilization*
points out that the same implies more than mere absence of oppression;
liberation requires a new morality and a revision of the notion of "human
nature" itself. And later he adds that every real theory of sexual liberation
must take into account the essentially polymorphous needs of human beings. According to Marcuse, in defiance of a society that employs sexuality
as a means toward a useful end, perversions uphold sexuality as an end in
itself; as a result, they lie outside the orbit of the ironclad principle of
"performance," which is to say, one of the basic repressive principles
fundamental to the organization of capitalism, and thus they question,
without proposing to do so, the very foundations of the latter.

Commenting on this manner of reasoning by Marcuse, Altman adds that at the point when homosexuality becomes exclusive and establishes its own economic norms, dispensing with its critical attitude toward the conventional forms of heterosexuals in order to attempt, instead, to copy the same, it too becomes a form of repression, as powerful a one as exclusive heterosexuality. And further on, commenting upon another radical Freudian, Norman O. Brown, as well as upon Marcuse, Altman infers that, in the last analysis, what we conceive of as "human nature" is no more than what has become the result of centuries of repression, an argument which implies, and in this respect Marcuse and Brown agree, the essential mutability of human nature.

—Look what I've got!

—No! . . . your mother came? . . .

—Yes!!!

—But how great . . . Then she's feeling better.

—Mmm-hmm, a little better . . . And look at what she brought for me. I mean, for *us*.

—Thanks, but all of that's for you, no kidding.

—You be quiet, you're convalescing, remember? Starting today a new life begins . . . The sheets are almost dry, feel . . . and all this food to eat. Look, two roast chickens, *two*, how about that? And chicken is perfect, it won't upset your stomach at all. Watch how fast you get better now.

—No, I won't let you do that.

—Please take them. I don't care for chicken anyway. I'll just be glad to do without any more stink from you and your barnyard . . . No, seriously, you have to stop eating that damn stuff they feed us here. Then you'll start feeling better in no time. At least try it for a couple of days.

—You think so? . . .

—Absolutely. And once you're better then . . . close your eyes, Valentin. See if you can guess . . . Come on, try . . .

—How do I know? I don't know . . .

—No peeking. Wait, I'll let you handle it to see whether you can guess.

—Here . . . feel.

—Two of them . . . packages . . . and heavy ones. But I give up.

—Open your eyes.

—Guava paste!

—But you have to wait for that, until you feel okay, and you can be sure you only get half of that . . . I also took a chance and left the sheets alone to dry . . . and nobody walked away with them, how about that? They're just about dry. So tonight we both have clean sheets.

—Nice going.

—Just give me a minute while I put this stuff away . . . And then I'll make some camomile tea because my nerves are killing me, and you, you have a leg of this chicken. Or no, it's only five o'clock . . . Better you just have some tea with me, and some crackers here, they're easier to digest. Delicadas, see? The ones I had as a kid whenever I was sick . . . before they came out with Criollitas.

—How about one right now, Molina?

—Okay, just one, with a dab of jam, but orange for the digestion. It's lucky, almost everything she brought is easy to digest, so you can have lots of it. Except for the guava paste . . . for the time being. Let me light the burner and presto, in a few minutes you'll be licking your fingers.

—But the leg of chicken, may I have it now?

—Come on, a little self-control . . . Let's save it for later, so when they bring us dinner you won't be tempted, because, lousy as it is, you gorge yourself every time.

—But you don't realize, my stomach feels so empty when the pains stop that it's like all of a sudden I'm starving.

—One minute, let's get this straight. I expect you to eat the chicken, no, chickens, *both* of them. On condition, though, that you don't touch the prison chow, which is making you so sick. Is it a deal?

—Okay . . . But what about you? I won't let you

just sit around and drool.

—I won't, cold food doesn't tempt me, really.

—Oh, it definitely agreed with me. And what a good idea to have camomile tea first.

—Calmed your nerves, didn't it? Same with me.

—And the chicken was delicious, Molina. To think we have enough for two more days still.

—Well, it's true. Now you sleep a little, and that will complete your cure.

—I'm not really sleepy. You go ahead and sleep. I'll be fine, don't worry.

—But don't you start dwelling again on some nonsense like before, or it'll interfere with your digestion.

—What about you? Are you sleepy?

—More or less.

—Because there is one thing that's still lacking to complete the usual program.

—Christ, and I'm the one who's supposed to be degenerate here.

—No, no kidding. We should have a film now, that's what's missing.

—Ah, I see . . .

—Do you remember any others like the panther woman? That's the one I liked best.

—Well sure, I know lots of supernatural ones.

—So let's hear, tell me, like what?

—Oh . . . *Dracula* . . . *The Wolf Man* . . .

—What else?

—And there's one about a zombie woman . . .

—That's it! That sounds terrific.

—Hmm . . . how does it start? . . .

—Is it American?

—Yeah, but I saw it eons ago.

—So? Do it anyway.

—Well, let me concentrate a minute.

—And the guava paste, when do I get to taste it?

—Tomorrow at the earliest, not before.

—Just one spoonful? For now?

—No. And better I start the film . . . Let me see, how does it go? . . . Oh, that's it. Now I remember. It begins with some girl from New York taking a steamer to an island in the Caribbean where her fiancé is waiting to marry her. She seems like a very sweet kid, and full of big dreams, telling everything about herself to this ship's captain, really a handsome guy, and he's just staring down at the black waters of the ocean, because it's night, and next thing he looks at her as if to say, "This poor kid has no idea what she's getting herself into," but he doesn't say anything until they've already reached the island, and you hear some native drums and she's like transported, and then the captain says don't let yourself be taken in by the sound of those drums, because they can often as not be the portents of death . . . *cardiac arrest, sick old woman, a heart fills up with black seawater and drowns*

—*police patrol, hideout, tear gas, door opens, submachine-gun muzzles, black blood of asphyxiation gushing up in the mouth* Go on, why did you stop?

—So this girl is met by her husband, whom she's married by proxy, after only knowing each other a few days in New York. He's a widower, also from New York. Anyway, the arrival on the island, when the boat's docking, is divine, because her fiancé is right there waiting for her with a whole parade of donkey carts, decorated with flowers, and in a couple of carts there's a bunch of musicians, playing nice soft tunes on those instruments which look like some kind of table made up out of little planks, that they whack with sticks and, well, I don't know why, but that kind of music really gets to me, because the notes sound so sweet on that instrument, like little soap bubbles that go popping one after another. And the drums

have stopped, fortunately, because they'd sounded like a bad
omen. And the two of them arrive at the house; it's pretty far
from town, off in the countryside, under the palm trees, and
it's such a gorgeous island with just some low hills, and you're
way out in the middle of these banana groves. And the fiancé
is so very pleasant, but you can tell there's a real drama going
on inside him; he smiles too much, like someone with a weak
character. And then you get this clue, that something's wrong
with him, because the first thing the fiancé does is introduce
the girl to his majordomo, who's around fifty or so, a French-
man, and this majordomo asks him right then and there to sign
a couple of papers, about shipping out a load of bananas on
the same boat that the girl arrived on, and the fiancé tells him
he'll do it later, but the majordomo, he's like insistent about
it, and the fiancé looks at him with eyes full of hatred, and
while he's busy signing the papers you notice how he can
hardly keep his hand steady to write, it's trembling so much.
Anyhow, it's still daylight, and the whole welcome party, which
rode back there in those little flowery carts, is out back in the
garden waiting to toast the new couple, and they're all holding
glasses full of fruit juice, and at this point you notice the arrival
of a couple of black peons, sort of delegates from the sugarcane
plantations, with a keg of rum to honor the master, but the
majordomo sees them too and looks furiously at them, and
grabs an ax that happens to be lying around, and he chops
away at the keg of rum until it all pours out on the ground.
   —Please, no more talk about food or drinks.
   —And don't you be so impressionable then, crybaby. Anyhow, the girl turns to the fiancé as if to ask him why all the
hysterics, but just then he's busy nodding to the majordomo
how that's exactly what he should do, and so, without wasting
any more time, the fiancé raises his glass of fruit juice and
toasts the islanders there before him, because the next morning
the two of them will be married, as soon as they go sign the
papers at some government office there on the island. But that

night the girl has to stay by herself, in the house, because he has to go to the farthest banana plantation on the whole island in order to show his gratitude to the peons and, by the way, to avoid any gossip and thus protect the girl's good name. The moon is marvelous that night, and the garden surrounding the house just stunning, with all those fabulous tropical plants which seem more fantastic than ever, and the girl has on a white satin chemise, under just this loose peignoir, it's white too but transparent, and she's tempted to take a look around the house, and she walks through the living room, and then into the dining room, and twice she comes across those folding type of frames with a picture of the fiancé on one side but with the other side blank, because the photo is gone, which must have been the first wife, the dead one. Then she wanders around the rest of the house, and goes into some bedroom which you can tell was once for a woman, because of the lace doilies on the night table and on top of the dresser, and the girl starts rummaging through all the drawers to see if some photograph might still be around but doesn't find anything, except hanging in the closet are all the clothes from the first wife, all of them incredibly fine imports. But at this point the girl hears something move, and she spots a shadow passing by the window. It scares the daylights out of her and she goes out into the garden, all lit up with moonlight, and sees a cute little frog jumping into the pond, and she thinks that was the noise she heard, and that the shadow was probably just the swaying of the palm trees in the breeze. And she walks still farther into the garden, because it feels so stuffy back in the house, and just then she hears something else, but like footsteps, and she spins around to see, but right at that moment some clouds blot out the moon, and the garden gets all black. And at the same time, off in the distance . . . drums. And you also hear more steps, this time clearly, and they're coming toward her, but very slowly. The girl is suddenly quaking with fear, and sees a shadow entering the house, through the same exact door that she'd left open. So the poor thing can't even make up her mind which is scarier at this point, to stay out there in that incredibly dark garden, or to go back into the house. Well, she decides to get closer to the house, where she peeks in through one of the windows but she doesn't see a thing, and then she hurries to another window, which turns out to look in on the dead wife's bedroom. And since it's so dark she can't make out much more than like a shadow gliding across the room, a tall silhouette, moving with outstretched hands, and fingering all the knickknacks lying around inside there, and right next to the window is the dresser with the doily and, on top of that, a really beautiful brush with the handle all worked in silver, and a mirror with the same kind of handle, and since the girl is right up against the window she can make out a very thin deathly pale hand, fingering all the bric-a-brac, and the girl feels frozen on the spot, too terrified to even budge; *the walking corpse, the treacherous somnambula, she talks in her sleep and confesses everything, the quarantined patient overhears her, he's loath to touch her, her skin is deathly white* but now she sees the shadow gliding out of the room and toward who knows what part of the house, until after a tiny bit she hears footsteps out there on the patio once more, and the girl shrinks back, trying to hide in all those vines clinging to the walls of the house when the cloud finally passes by so that the moon comes back out again and the patio's lit up once again and there in front of the girl is this very tall figure wearing a long black duster, who scares her half to death, the pale face of a dead woman, with a head of blond hair all matted up and hanging down to her waist. The girl wants to scream for help but there's no more voice left in her, and she starts backing away slowly, because her legs don't work anymore, they're just rubber. The woman is staring straight at her, but all the same it's like she doesn't see her, with this lost look, a madwoman, but her arms stretch out to touch the girl, and she keeps moving ahead very slowly, and the girl is backing away, but without realizing that right behind her there's a row of dense hedges, and when she turns around and finally realizes how she's cornered she lets out a terrible scream, but the other one keeps right on coming, with her arms outstretched, until the girl faints dead away from terror. At that point someone grabs hold of the weirdo lady. It's that the kindly old black woman has arrived. Did I forget to mention her? *a black nurse, old and kindly, a day nurse, at night she leaves the critically ill patient alone with a white nurse, a new one, exposing her to contagion*

—Yes.

—Well, this kindly old black woman amounts to more or less a housekeeper. Big and fat, her hair's already turned completely gray, and always giving the girl these sweet looks ever since she arrived on the island. And by the time the girl regains consciousness the old housekeeper's already carried her inside to bed, and she makes the girl believe that what happened was just a nightmare. And the girl doesn't know whether to believe her or not, but when she sees how nice the housekeeper treats her she calms down, and the housekeeper brings her tea to help her sleep, it's camomile tea, or something like that, I can't remember exactly. Then the following day the marriage ceremony is to take place, so they have to go see the mayor, and pay their respects to him and sign some papers, and the girl is busy getting dressed for the occasion, in a very simple tailored dress, but with a beautiful hairdo which the housekeeper fusses over, to put it up in a kind of braid, how can I explain it? well, back then the upsweep was a must on certain occasions, to look really chic.

—I don't feel well . . . I'm all dizzy again.

—You sure?

—Yes, it's not really bad yet, but I feel the same way I did when it started the other times.

—But that meal couldn't have done you any harm.

—Don't be ridiculous. What makes you think I'm blaming it on your food?

—You seem so irritated . . .

—But it's got nothing to do with your food. It's a matter of my system, there's something still wrong with it.

—Then try not to think about it. That only makes it worse.*

—I just couldn't concentrate any longer on what you were saying.

—But honestly, it must be something else, because that food was totally healthy for you. You know how sometimes, after an illness, you're still suggestible for a while?

—Why not tell a little more of the film, and just see if it goes away. Maybe it's because I'm feeling so weak. I probably ate too fast or something . . . Who the hell knows why . . .

—But that must be it, you're just very weak, and I noticed how fast you were eating, like a kid, without even chewing your food.

—Ever since I woke up this morning I've been thinking about only one thing, and it must be getting to me. I can't get it off my mind.

—What is it?

—The fact that I can't write to my girl . . . but to Marta, yes. And you know, it would probably do me some good to write her, but I can't think of what to say. Because it's wrong for me to write her. Why should I?

---

*As a variation on the concept of repression, Freud introduces the term "sublimation," understanding by that the mental operation through which problematic libidinal impulses are provided with an outlet. Such outlets for sublimation would include any activity—art, sports, manual labor—that permits use of the sexual energy considered to be excessive by the canons of our society. Freud draws a fundamental distinction between repression and sublimation by suggesting that the latter may be salutary, insofar as it is indispensable to the maintenance of a civilized community.

This position has been attacked by Norman O. Brown, author of *Life Against Death*, which on the contrary favors a return to the state of "polymorphous perversion" discovered by Freud in infants, and thus implies the total elimination of repression. One of the reasons adduced by Freud in his defense of partial repression was the necessity to subjugate the destructive impulses of man, but Brown, as well as Marcuse, refutes this argument by

—I'll go on with the film then?

—Yes, do that.

—Okay, where were we?

—It was just when they were getting the girl ready.

—Ah, that's right, she was having her hair done up in—

—Yeah, it's up, I know already, and what do I care if it is? Don't get so bogged down in details that have so little importance *crudely painted effigy, a sharp blow, the effigy is made of glass, it splinters to bits, the fist doesn't hurt, the fist of a man*

—*the treacherous somnambula and the white nurse, the contagious patient stares at them in the darkness* What do you mean don't! You just keep still because I know what I'm saying. Starting with the fact that wearing the hair up is—pay attention—important, because women only wear it up, it so happens, or they used to back then, when they wanted to really give the impression it was an important occasion, an important date. Because the upsweep, which bared the nape of the neck because they pushed all the hair up on top of the head, it gave a woman's face a certain nobility. And with that whole mass of hair pushed up like that the old housekeeper is making her a braid, and decorating her hair with sprigs of local flowers, and when she finally drives off in a little chaise—even though

---

maintaining that aggressive impulses do not exist as such, so long as the impulses of the libido—which are preexistent—find a mode of realization, that is to say, a means of satisfaction.

The criticism directed at Brown, in turn, is based upon the supposition that a humanity without bounds of restraint, that is to say, without repression, could never organize itself into any permanent activity. It is here that Marcuse interjects his concept of "surplus repression," designating by such a term that part of sexual repression created to maintain the power of the dominant class, in spite of not proving to be indispensable to the maintenance of an organized society attending to the human necessities of all its constituents. Therefore, the principal advance that Marcuse presupposes in opposition to Freud would consist of the latter's toleration for a certain type of repression in order to preserve contemporary society, whereas Marcuse deems it fundamental to change society, on the basis of an evolution that

it's modern-day times they go off in this little carriage pulled by two tiny donkeys—the whole town smiles at her, and she sees herself en route to paradise . . . Is the dizzy spell going away?

—Seems like it is. But continue the story, okay?

—So they go along, her and the housekeeper, and on the steps of that kind of Town Hall-type place they have there, in a colonial style, her fiancé is waiting for her. And then you see them later on, they're out in the dark night air, her lying in a hammock, with a good close-up of the two faces, because he bends down to kiss her, and it's all lit up by the full moon kind of filtering through the palm trees. Oh, but I forgot something important. You see, the expression on their faces is like two lovers, and so contented-looking. But what I forgot is that while the black housekeeper's still brushing her hair up for her, the girl—

—Not that hairdo again?

—But you're so irritable! If you don't make any effort yourself you'll never calm down.

—I'm sorry, go on.

—So the girl asks the housekeeper some questions. Like, for instance, where did he go to spend the night. The housekeeper tries to conceal her alarm and says he went to say hello to some

---

takes into account our original sexual impulses.

Such could be considered the basis of the accusation which representatives of the new tendencies have leveled against orthodox Freudian psychoanalysts, to the effect that the latter had sought—with an impunity that became undermined toward the end of the sixties—that their patients assume all personal conflict in order to facilitate their adaptation to the repressive society in which they found themselves, rather than to acknowledge the necessity for change in that society.

In *One-Dimensional Man*, Marcuse asserts that, originally, sexual instinct had no temporal and spatial limitations of subject and object, since sexuality is by nature "polymorphous perverse." Going even further, Marcuse gives as an example of "surplus repression" not only our total concentration on genital copulation but also such phenomena as olfactory and gustatory repression in sexual life

people out in the banana groves, including the ones that lived on the farthest plantation of all, and out there most of the peons believe in . . . voodoo. The girl knows it's some kind of black religion and she says how she'd very much like to see some of that, some ceremony, perhaps, because it must be quite lovely, with lots of local color and music, but the housekeeper gives her a frightened look, and tells her no, she better just stay away from all that stuff, because it's a religion that can get very bloody at times, and by no means should she ever go near it. Because . . . but at this point the housekeeper stops talking. And the other one asks her what's the matter, and the housekeeper tells her how there's a legend, which probably isn't even true but just the same it scares her, and it's about the zombies. Zombies? What are they? the girl asks her, and the housekeeper motions her not to say it so loud, only in a very low voice. And she explains that they're the dead people that witch doctors manage to revive before the corpses get cold, because the witch doctors themselves are the ones who kill them, with a special poison they prepare, and the living dead no longer possess any will of their own, and they obey only the orders of the witch doctors, and that the witch doctors use them to do whatever they want them to, and they make them work at anything, and the poor living dead, the zombies, they don't

---

For his part, Dennis Altman, commenting favorably in his own aforementioned book on these assertions by Marcuse, adds that liberation must not only be aimed at eliminating sexual constraint, but also at providing the practical possibility of realizing those desires. Moreover he maintains that only recently have we become aware of how much of what we considered normal and instinctive, especially with respect to family structuring and sexual relations, is actually learned, and as a result how much of what up to now has been considered natural would have to be unlearned, including competitive and aggressive attitudes outside of the sexual realm. And along the same lines, Kate Millett, the theoretician of women's liberation, says in her book *Sexual Politics* that the purpose of sexual revolution ought to be a freedom without hypocrisy, untainted by the exploitive economic bases of traditional sexual alliances, meaning matrimony.

Furthermore, Marcuse favors not only a free flow of the libido, but also

have any will at all beyond the witch doctor's. And the housekeeper tells her how many years ago some of the poor peons from a few of the plantations decided to rebel against the owners because they paid them almost nothing, but the owners managed to get together with the chief witch doctor on the island to have him kill all the peons and turn them into zombies, and so it came to pass that after they were dead they were made to work at harvesting bananas, but at night, so as not to have the other peons find out, and all the zombies work and work, without any talk, because zombies don't say a word, or think, even though they suffer so much, because in the middle of working, when the moon shines down on them you can see the tears running down their faces, but they never complain, because zombies can't talk, they haven't any will left and the only thing they get to do is obey and suffer. Well, all of a sudden the girl, because then she remembers the dream that she still thinks she had the other night, the girl asks her whether there's such a thing as a zombie woman. But the housekeeper manages to get off on a tangent somehow and tells her no, because women are never strong enough for such hard work in the fields and so that's why, no, she doesn't think there's any such thing as a zombie woman. And the girl asks her if the fiancé isn't afraid of all that business, and the

---

a transformation of the same: in other words, the passage from a sexuality circumscribed by genital supremacy to an eroticization of the whole personality. He refers therefore to an expansion more than an explosion of the libido, an expansion that would extend to other areas of human endeavor, private and social, such as work, for example. He adds that the entire weight of civil morality was brought to bear against the use of the body as mere instrument of pleasure, inasmuch as that reification was considered taboo and relegated to the contemptible privilege of prostitutes and perverts.

Differing from this position, J. C. Unwin, author of *Sex and Culture*, after studying the marital customs of eighty uncivilized societies, seems to support the very generalized assumption that sexual freedom leads to social decadence, since, according to orthodox psychoanalysis, if an individual does not perish from his neurosis, the imposed sexual constraints can help

nousekeeper answers no, but naturally he has to put up with a certain amount of superstition in order to stay on friendly terms with the peons, so he just went out there to receive the blessing from the witch doctors themselves. And then the conversation ends, and like I told you, later on you see them together on their wedding night, and happy-looking, because for the first time, you see the kid, the husband, has a look of peace on his face, and all you hear is the *bzz-bzz* of tiny bugs outside and water running in the fountains. And then later you see the two of them lying asleep in their bed, until something wakes them up and gradually they hear, louder and louder, off in the distance, the beating of the drums. She shivers, a chill runs up and down her back . . . Are you feeling any better? *night rounds for the nurses, temperature and pulse normal, white cap, white stockings, good night to the patient*

—A little . . . *but I can barely follow what you're saying. the endless night, the cold night, endless thoughts, cold thoughts, sharp slivers of broken glass*

—But I ought to stop then. *the strict nurse, the very tall cap stiff with starch, the slight smile not without cunning*

—No, honestly, when you distract me a little I feel better, please, go on. *the endless night, the icy night, the walls green with mildew, the walls stricken with gangrene, the injured fist*

—Okay. So . . . how did it go next? They hear drums way off in the distance, and the husband's expression changes, all that peace is gone, he can't sleep now, so he gets up. The girl doesn't say anything, discretion itself, she doesn't move a

to channel such energies toward socially useful ends. Unwin has concluded from his exhaustive study that the establishment of the first foundations of an organized society, its subsequent development and appropriation of neighboring terrain—in other words, the historical characteristics of every vigorous society—are evident only from the moment when sexual repression has been instated. While those societies in which freedom of sexual relations is tolerated—whether prenuptial, extraconjugal or homosexual— remain in an almost animal state of underdevelopment. But at the same

muscle, making like she's fast asleep, but she really pricks up her ears and hears this noise of a cupboard door being opened and squeaking, and then nothing more. She doesn't dare get up and actually investigate, but then it gets later and later and still no sign of him. She decides to look, and finds him lying across an easy chair, completely drunk. And she quickly eyes all the furniture and discovers a little open cabinet, hardly big enough for one bottle, the empty bottle of cognac, but the husband also seems to have another bottle, next to him, and that one is just half empty. So the girl wonders where it came from, because there's no liquor kept in the house at all, and then she notices how, just underneath the bottle in the cabinet, certain things have been tucked away, and it's a bunch of letters and photographs. And it's a job for her to drag him back into the bedroom, where she just lies down beside him, trying to cheer him up because she loves him and promises him he's not going to be alone anymore, and he looks gratefully at her and falls back asleep. She tries to get some sleep too, but now she can't, although before she was so contented, but seeing him drunk like that makes her incredibly upset. And she realizes how right the majordomo was to smash that rum keg. She puts on her negligee and goes back to the cabinet to look at the photos, because what intrigues her incredibly is the possibility of finding a picture of the first wife. But when she gets there she finds the cabinet closed, and locked too. But who could've locked it? She looks around but everything is swallowed up in complete darkness and absolute silence, except for those drums, which you can still hear. Then she goes over to shut

---

time, Unwin says that societies which are strictly monogamous and strongly repressive do not manage to last very long, and if they do in part, it is by means of the moral and material subjugation of women. Therefore, Unwin claims that, between the suicidal anguish that the minimizing of sexual necessities provokes and the opposite extreme of social disorder attributed to sexual incontinence, a reasonable medium ought to be found which might provide the solution to such a critical problem—that is to say, an elimination of the "surplus repression" about which Marcuse speaks.

the window so as not to have to listen to them, but right at that very moment they stop, as if they'd spotted her from miles and miles away. Anyhow, the next morning he looks as if he doesn't remember anything, and he wakes her with their breakfast all ready, and smiley as can be, and informs her that he's going to take her on a ride by the sea. She becomes totally infected with his excitement, and off they go into the tropics, in a great convertible with the top down, and there's a peppy musical background, calypso type, and they drive past a couple of divine beaches, and here it's a very sexy scene because she feels the urge to go for a swim, because by then they've already seen the lovely coconut groves, and rocky cliffs looking out to sea, and here and there some natural gardens with gigantic flowers, and the sun is scorching hot but she's forgotten to bring along a bathing suit, so he says, why not swim in the nude? and they stop the car, she undresses behind some rocks and then you see her off in the distance running naked to the ocean. And later on you catch them lying on the beach to-gether, under the palms, her with a sarong out of his shirt, and him with just his pants on, nothing else, and barefoot, and you have no idea where it comes from, but you know the way it happens in movies, you suddenly just hear the words of this song, saying how when it comes to love, it's a question of earning it, and at the end of some dark trail, strewn with all kinds of hardships, love awaits those who struggle to the last in order to earn that love. And you can see the girl and he are completely enchanted with each other once again and they decide to let bygones be bygones. And then it begins to get dark, and when they drive up a little ridge of road, you just manage to catch in the background, not too far from there, all glinty from the sun which is like this fiery red ball, a very old colonial house, but pretty, and very mysterious, because it's completely overrun by vegetation, which covers it up almost totally. And the girl says how some other day she'd like to go for a ride to that house, and she asks why it's been abandoned.

But at this point he seems to get very nervous and tells her like very rudely, never, never go near that house, but he doesn't offer the slightest explanation, just saying that he'll tell her why some other time. *the night nurse is inexperienced, the night nurse sleepwalks, is she asleep or awake? the night shift is long, she's all by herself and doesn't know where to turn for help* You're so quiet, you're not even making any wise-cracks . . .

—Somehow I'm not feeling very good. Just go on with the film, it's good to take my mind off things for a while.

—Wait, now I lost the thread.

—I don't understand how you manage to keep so many details in your head anyway. *the hollow head, the glass skull, filled with mass cards of saints and whores, someone throws the glass head against the putrid wall, the head smashes, all mass cards fall onto the floor*

—In spite of the great time they were having that whole day, the girl gets upset all over again now, because she saw how nervous he became the minute she asked about that house, the one that looked abandoned. Well, when they arrive back at the mansion, he takes a shower, and that's when she can't resist looking through his pockets for the keys in order to search through that cabinet of the night before. And she goes and searches through his pants, and finds a key ring, and runs to the cabinet. On the key ring there's only one tiny key; she tries it and it fits. She opens the cabinet. There's a full bottle of cognac inside, but who put it there? Because she hasn't left her husband's side for a second since the night before, so he didn't do it; she would have seen him. And underneath the bottle there's some letters, love letters, signed by him and others signed by the first wife, and underneath the letters some photographs, of him and some other woman, was that the first wife? The girl seems to recognize her, it's as if she's seen her some-where before; surely she's come upon that face before, but where? An interesting type, very very tall, long blond hair. The girl goes on looking through each and every photograph, and then she discovers one in particular that's like a portrait, just of the face, the eyes very pale, that slightly lost look . . . And the girl remembers! It's the woman who chased her in the nightmare, with the face of a madwoman, dressed all in black down to her toes . . . But at that point she notices the water isn't running in the shower, and her husband could easily catch her going through his things! So she tries frantically to put away all that stuff, setting the bottle back on top of the letters and photographs, closing the cabinet, and then going back into the bedroom, where she finds him right there! all wrapped up in this huge bath towel, but smiling away. She doesn't know what to do, so she offers to dry his back, she has no idea how to keep him busy, how to distract him *the poor nurse, so unlucky, they assign her to a patient on the critical list and she doesn't know how to keep him from dying or killing her, the danger of contagion is stronger than ever* because he's already about to start getting dressed, but she's terrified that she has the key right in her hand, and he might notice that fact any minute now. But she goes on drying his shoulders with one hand, looking over at his pants draped on the chair, and doesn't know what to do to get the key back into his pocket —until she gets an idea, and says she'd like to comb his hair. And he answers, wonderful, the comb is in the bathroom if you want to get it, and she says, that's no way for a gentleman to act, saying that, so then he goes to look for it himself and meantime she takes the chance to slip the key back into his pocket just in the nick of time, and when he comes back she starts combing his hair and massaging his bare shoulders. And the poor little newlywed, she just breathes a sigh of relief. Then a few days go by, and the girl realizes how the husband always gets up around midnight because he can't sleep, and she pretends to be sound asleep, because she's afraid of bringing up the subject face to face with him, but in the early morning she gets up to help him back into bed, because he always ends up bombed out of his mind and collapsed in the armchair. And she always checks the bottle, and it's a different one each time, and it's full, so who's putting it there in that cabinet? The girl doesn't dare ask him a thing, because when he comes back every evening from the plantations he's so happy to see her waiting there for him, embroidering something, but at midnight you always begin to hear those drums again, and he gets all obsessed about something, and can't sleep anymore unless he gets himself into a drunken stupor. So obviously, the girl gets more and more uptight about the whole thing, and at one point when her husband is outside somewhere, she tries to have a word with the majordomo, to discover some possible secret from him maybe, about why the husband seems so nervous at times, but the majordomo tells her with a big sigh how they're having lots of problems with the peons, etcetera, etcetera, and in the end he really doesn't say too much about anything. Well, the thing is, the girl, one time when the husband tells her he's going off for that whole day with the majordomo, to that plantation that's the farthest away of all, and won't be back until the following day, she decides to go off by herself on foot to that same abandoned house, because she's sure she'll find out something there. And so just after tea, around five o'clock, when the sun isn't so strong anymore, the husband and the majordomo set out on their trip, and the girl eventually goes off too. And she's looking for the road to that abandoned house, but she gets lost, and soon it's getting late, and already almost nightfall, when she manages to find that ridge in the road from where you got to see the house, and she doesn't know whether to turn back or not, but her curiosity gets the best of her, and she goes on to the house. And she sees how suddenly, inside there, a light goes on, which encourages her a little more. But once she reaches the house, which is, no exaggeration, almost buried by wild plants, she doesn't hear anything, and through the windows you can see how on the table there's a candle burning, and the girl gets up enough courage to open the door and even take a look inside, and she sees over in the corner a voodoo altar, with more candles burning, and she goes farther inside to see what's on top of the altar, and she walks right up to it, and on top of the altar she finds a doll with black hair with a pin stuck right through the middle of the chest, and the doll is dressed in an outfit made to look exactly like what she was wearing herself on her own wedding day! And at this point she almost faints with fright but spins around to run away through the same door that she came in by . . . And what's in the doorway? . . . this incredibly huge black guy, with bulging eyeballs, wearing only a ragged pair of old pants, and with the look of somebody who's totally out of his mind, staring at her and blocking any escape. And the poor thing, all she has left to do is let out a desperate scream, but the guy, who's actually what they call a zombie, one of the living dead, he keeps coming closer and closer, with his arms reaching out, just like the woman from the other night in the garden. And the girl lets out another scream, and runs into the next room and locks the door behind her. The room's almost dark, with the window almost covered with jungle growth so only a tiny bit of light comes through, a little twilight, and the room has a bed in it, which little by little the girl begins to make out, as she becomes more accustomed to the darkness. And every inch of her shudders, nearly suffocated by her own cries and her terror, as she sees there on the bed . . . something moving . . . and it's . . . that woman! Incredibly pale, all disheveled, the hair hanging down to her waist, and with the same black duster on, she slowly rises and begins to move toward the girl! in that room without escape, all locked up . . . The girl would like to drop dead she's so frightened, and now she can't even scream, but suddenly . . . from the window you hear a voice ordering the zombie woman to stop and go back to her bed . . . It's the kindly black housekeeper. And she tells the girl not to be scared, that she's going to come right in and protect her. The girl opens the door, the black woman hugs her and calms her down; and behind her, in the front doorway, is that black giant, but he's totally obedient now to the housekeeper, who tells him he must look after the girl, and not attack her. The giant black zombie obeys, and the zombie woman, too, all disheveled, because the housekeeper orders her back to her bed, and the woman completely obeys. Then the housekeeper takes the girl affectionately by her shoulders and tells her she's going to get her back safely to the main house in a little donkey cart, and along the way she tells her the whole story, because by now the girl's realized that the zombie woman with the blond hair down to her waist . . . is her husband's first wife. And the housekeeper begins to tell how it all happened. *the nurse trembles, the patient looks up at her, asking for morphine? asking to be caressed? or does he just want the contagion to be instantaneous and deadly?*

—*the skull is glass, the body is glass too, easy to break a toy made out of glass, slivers of sharp cold glass in the cold night, the humid night, gangrene spreading through the hand shredded by the punch* Do you mind if I say something?

—*at night the patient gets up and walks barefoot, he catches cold, his condition deteriorates* What? Go ahead.

—*the glass skull full of mass cards of saints and whores, old yellowed mass cards, dead faces outlined in cracked paper, inside my chest the dead mass cards, glass mass cards, sharp, shredding, spreading the gangrene into the lungs, the chest, the heart* I'm very depressed. I can hardly follow what you say. I think it'd be much better to save the rest for tomorrow, don't you? And this way we can talk a little.

—Fine, what do you want to talk about?

—I feel so awful . . . you have no idea. And so confused . . . Anyhow, I . . . I see it a little more clearly now, it's the business I was talking about that had to do with my girl, how afraid I am for her, because she's in danger . . . but that the one I long to hear from, the one I'm longing to see, isn't my girl. And longing to touch, it's not her I'm dying for, to hold in my arms, because I'm just aching for Marta, my whole body aches for her . . . to feel her close to me, because I think Marta is really the only one who could save me at all, because I feel like I'm dead, I swear I do. And I have this notion that nothing except her could ever revive me again.

—Keep talking, I'm listening.

—You're going to laugh at what I want to ask of you.

—No I won't, why should I?

—If it's not a bother, would you mind lighting the candle? . . . What I'd like is to dictate a letter to you for her, I mean for the one I always talk about, for Marta. Because I get dizzy if I use my eyes for anything.

—But, what could be wrong with you? Couldn't it be something else? Besides the stomach problem, I mean.

—No, I'm just terribly weak, that's all, and I want to unburden myself a little somehow, Molina, my friend, because I can't stand it anymore. This afternoon I tried myself to write a letter, but the page kept swimming.

—Sure then, wait till I find the matches.

—You've been really good to me.

—There we are. Shall we do a rough draft on scratch paper first, or what would you like to do?

—Yeah, on scratch paper, because I've no idea of what to say. Use my ball-point.

—Wait, I'll just sharpen this pencil.

—No, take my ball-point, I'm telling you.

—Fine, but don't start foaming at the mouth again.

—I'm sorry, I just see everything black right now.

—Okay, start dictating.

—Dear . . . Marta: It must be strange for you . . . to get this letter. I feel . . . lonely, I need you so, I want to talk with you, I want . . . to be close, I want you to . . . give me . . . some word of comfort. I'm here in my cell, who knows where you are right now? . . . and how you're feeling, or what you're thinking, or what you might be needing right this minute? . . . But I just have to write you a letter, even if I don't send it, who knows what'll happen actually? . . . But let me talk to you anyway . . . because I'm afraid . . . afraid that something is about to break inside of me . . . if I don't open up to you a little. If only we could actually talk together, you'd understand what I mean . . .

—". . . you'd understand what I mean . . ."

—I'm sorry, Molina, how did I tell her that I'm not going to send her the letter? Read it to me, would you?

—"But I just have to write you a letter, even if I don't send it."

—Would you add, "But I will send it."

—"But I will send it." Go ahead. We were at "If only we could actually talk together, you'd understand what I mean . . ."

— . . . because at this moment I could never present myself to my comrades and talk with them, I'd be ashamed to be this weak . . . Marta, I feel as if I have a right to live a little longer, and that someone should pour a little . . . honey . . . on my wounds . . .

—Yes . . . Go on.

— . . . Inside, I'm all raw, and only someone like you could really understand . . . because you were raised in a clean and comfortable house like me and taught to enjoy life, and I'm the same way. I can't adjust to being a martyr, it infuriates me, I don't want to be a martyr, and right now I wonder if the whole thing hasn't been one terrible mistake on my part . . . They tortured me, but still I didn't confess anything . . . I didn't even know the real names of my comrades, so I only confessed combat names, and the police can't get anywhere with that, but inside myself there seems to be another kind of torturer . . . and for days he hasn't let up . . . And it's because I seem to be asking for some kind of justice. Look how absurd what I'm about to say is: I'm asking for some kind of justice, for some providence to intervene . . . because I don't deserve to

just rot forever in this cell or, I get it . . . I get it . . . Now I
see it clearly, Marta . . . It's that I'm afraid because I've just
been sick . . . and I have this fear in me . . . this terrible fear
of dying . . . and of it all ending like this, with a life reduced
to just this rotten bit of time, but I don't think I deserve that.
I've always acted with generosity, I've never exploited anyone
. . . and I fought, from the moment I possessed a little understanding of things . . . fought against the exploitation of my
fellow man . . . And I've always cursed all religions, because
they simply confuse people and prevent them from fighting for
any kind of equality . . . but now I find myself thirsting for
some kind of justice . . . divine justice. I'm asking that there
be a God . . . Write it with a capital G, Molina, please . . .

—Yes, go on.

—What did I say?

—"I'm asking that there be a God . . ."

— . . . a God who sees me, and helps me, because I want
to be able, someday, to walk down streets again, and I want
that day to come soon, and I don't want to die. But at times
it runs through my mind that I'm never, never going to touch
a woman again, and I can't stand it . . . And whenever I think
about women . . . I see no one but you in my mind, and it would
be such a comfort to somehow believe that at this moment,
from here on, until I finish this letter to you, you're really
thinking about me, too . . . while you run your hand over your
body which I remember so well . . .

—Wait, don't go so fast.

— . . . your body which I remember so well, and that you're
pretending it's my hand . . . and what a deep consolation that
could be for me . . . my love, if that were happening . . . because
it would be just like my touching you, because a part of me is
still with you, right? Just the way the scent of your body is still
inside my nostrils . . . and beneath the tips of my fingers I too
have the sensation of feeling your skin . . . as if I'd somehow
memorized it, do you understand me? Even though it has

nothing to do with understanding . . . because it's a question of believing, and at times I'm convinced that I've kept something of yours with me, too . . . and that I've never lost it . . . But then sometimes, no, I feel like there's nothing here in this cell except me . . . all alone . . .

—Yes . . . "me . . . all alone . . ." Go ahead.

— . . . and that nothing leaves a trace of itself, and that the luck of having been so happy together, of having spent those nights with you, and afternoons, and mornings of pure enjoyment, is absolutely worthless to me now, and actually works against me . . . because I miss you like crazy, and the only thing I feel is the torture of loneliness, and in my nostrils there's nothing but the disgusting smell of this cell, and of myself . . . but I can't wash myself because I'm so sick, so totally debilitated, and the cold water would probably give me pneumonia, and beneath the tips of my fingers what I really feel is the chill fear of dying, and in my very marrow I feel it . . . that same chill . . . It's so terrible to lose hope, and that's what's happening with me . . . The torturer that I have inside of me tells me everything is finished, and that this agony is my last experience on earth . . . and I say this like a true Christian, as if afterward another life were waiting . . . but there's nothing waiting, is there?

—Can I interrupt? . . .

—What's wrong?

—When you finish, remind me to tell you something.

—What?

—Well, that there is something we could do, actually . . .

—What? Say it.

—Because if you wash yourself in that freezing shower it certainly will kill you, as sick as you are right now.

—But what is to be done? For the last time, tell me, goddamn it!

—Well, I could help you clean yourself. Look, we can heat some water up in the pot, we already have two towels, so one we soap up and you wash the front of yourself, I can do the back for you, and with the other towel slightly wet we sponge off the soap.

—And then my body wouldn't itch so much?

—That's right, we can do it bit by bit, so you don't catch any chill, first your neck and ears, then your underarms, then your arms, your chest, your back, and so on.

—And you'd really help me?

—Obviously.

—But when?

—Right now if you like, I'll heat up some water.

—And then I can sleep, without the itching? . . .

—Peaceful as can be, without any itching. The water will be warm enough in just a few minutes.

—But that kerosene is yours, you'll waste it.

—It doesn't matter, in the meantime we'll finish your letter.

—Give it to me.

—What for?

—Just give it to me, Molina.

—Here . . .

— . . .

—What are you going to do?

—This.

—But why are you tearing up your letter?

—Let's not discuss it any further.

—Whatever you say.

—It's just no good getting carried away like that, out of desperation . . .

—But it's good to get something off your chest sometimes, you said so yourself.

—Well, it doesn't work for me. I have to just put up with it . . .

— . . .

—Listen, you've been very kind to me, honestly, I mean that with all my heart. And someday I expect to be able to show my appreciation, I swear I will . . . that much water?

—Mmm-hmm, we'll need at least that much . . . And don't be silly, there's nothing to thank me for.

—So much water . . .

— . . .

—Molina . . .

—Mmm?

—Look at the shadows that the stove's casting on the wall.

—Mmm, I always watch them. You never saw them before?

—No, I never noticed.

—Mmm, it helps me pass the time, watching the shadows when the stove's lit.

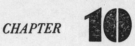

—Morning . . .

—Good morning!

—What time is it?

—Ten after ten. You know, with my mom, poor dear, I call her ten-ten, because she walks so duckfooted.

—I can't believe it's that late already.

—Mmm, when they opened up for our coffee you rolled over and stayed asleep.

—What did you say about your old lady?

—Nothing, Valentin, you're still asleep. So did you finally get a good rest?

—Yes, I feel a lot better, too.

—No dizziness?

—No . . . And I slept like a log. Even sitting up like this, I swear it's fine, no dizziness at all.

—Very good! . . . How about getting on your feet a little, to see how it feels.

—No, because you'll start laughing.

—At what?

—Something you'd notice.

—What would I notice?

—Something on any healthy man, that's all, especially when he first wakes up . . . and has a little energy in the morning.

—A hard-on, well that's healthy . . .

—So look the other way, will you? You make me feel self-conscious . . .

—Okay, I'll close my eyes.

—Thanks to that good food of yours, or I never would've gotten better.

—Well? You dizzy at all?

—No . . . not a bit. My legs are a little weak, but no dizziness.

—Very good . . .

—You can look now. I'm going to stay in bed awhile.

—I'll boil some water for a cup of tea.

—No, just reheat the coffee they left us.

—You have to be joking; I dumped that stuff when I went to the john. If you expect to get well you'll have to stick to what's good for you.

—No, listen, I can't keep using up all your tea, and everything else besides. I won't allow it, I'm fine now.

—You just be quiet.

—No, honestly . . .

—Honestly nothing. My mom has started bringing stuff again, so it's no problem.

—But it disturbs me.

—You have to learn to accept from people too, you know. And anyhow, why be so complicated?

—Okay, then.

—If you want to, you can go out to the john now while I'm making the tea. But stay in bed until I call the guard to open up first. That way you don't get chilled.

—Thanks.

—And when you come back, if you want I can go on with the zombies . . . Dying to know what happens?

—Yes, but I should try to study a little, and see if I can get back into the grind again, now that I feel better.

—Think so? That's not pushing yourself a bit too hard?

—We'll see . . .

—What a fanatic.

—How come so many sighs?

—It's no use, Molina, the page just keeps swimming in front of me.

—I told you so.

—Fine, it doesn't hurt to try.

—Dizzy now?

—No, only when I read, that's all; I just can't focus.

—You know what? It's probably a case of just being a little weak in the morning, nothing except tea for breakfast, refusing to eat any of that bread and ham I suggested.

—Think so?

—I know so. After lunch, you take a little nap and you'll see that then you can study.

—I feel so lazy, you wouldn't believe it. I have this urge to just lie around in bed some more.

—But you shouldn't, because they say it's important to try and strengthen yourself by walking around a little bit or at least sitting up, because lying in bed eventually makes you weak.

—What about the film? Give me a break . . .

—Know what I better do? Put the potatoes on to boil, because they take a year.

—What are you making?

—We have some ham, and I'll open up a tin of olive oil, so we can have a couple of boiled potatoes, with just a drop of oil and salt, together with the ham: nothing could be healthier.

—The film was up to where the black housekeeper's about to tell the protagonist the whole story about the zombie wife, about the living dead woman.

—You're really into it, aren't you? Admit it.

—It's entertaining.

—Oh sure. Baloney. It's more than entertaining, it's superb. Tell the truth.

—Come on, what happens?

—Okay, okay, but wait . . . This thing's not lighting, . . . there, I got it. So, now, where were we? Right, the housekeeper is on the way home with the girl and starts telling her the whole story. It turns out the husband had been happy enough with his first wife, but at the same time tormented by the fact that he was guarding a terrible secret, because when he was a kid he had witnessed a really ghoulish crime. It turns out his own father was an unscrupulous type of guy, but a real monstrosity, and he came to the island to get himself rich and started off by treating his peons like dirt. But the peons on the plantations began to organize a rebellion, so his father got together with the local witch doctor, who always held his ceremonies and voodoo stuff out on the farthest plantation of them all, and one night the witch doctor called a meeting of all the leaders from the rebel peons, supposedly in order to put his blessing upon them. But in fact it was actually an ambush; they went and massacred all of them right on the spot, with arrows dipped in a special poison made by the witch doctor himself. And from there they dragged the bodies off to hide them way out in the jungle, because a few hours later they opened their eyes and became living dead. And the witch doctor ordered them to stand up, and little by little the bodies started getting up, all of them, with their eyes wide open—you've seen how whenever Negro eyes are like that, really big—but these ones had their eyes rolled up, all completely white, and the witch doctor ordered them to pick up machetes and get themselves in line and walk out to the banana groves. And once he got them there he gave them orders to start working at cutting down bunches of bananas all night long, and the kid's father felt fiendish ecstatic about the whole thing and put up some little huts, like cabanas, made with a lot of old dried cane stalks so during the day they could hide the living dead inside the huts, all of them stuffed together on the floor like a pile of garbage, but every night they ordered them out to work at cutting down bananas, and that's how the kid's father managed to accumulate his vast fortune. And the son witnessed all of that but was still a young kid at the time. But eventually he grew up and married a tall blond co-ed he met away at college in the United States, and brought her back to the island, same as a few years later he did with the other girl, the one he married later on, the brunette . . . the leading lady. Anyhow, the first wife, she made him happy, in the beginning, and when the old man died the kid decided he had to call it quits with the witch doctor, so he sends for him to come to the main residence, but meantime he himself heads off to the farthest-away plantation, where they kept the zombies at, he goes and surrounds the zombie huts, and nails stakes across all the doorways, and pours turpentine all over the place and sets fire to the bunches of zombies caught inside, and burns them to a crisp which was the only way to make the poor black living dead stop suffering. But while all that's going on, the witch doctor, who's arrived at the main residence to wait for him, with the first wife there, the witch doctor gets a message about what's happening—the jungle tom-toms bring it to him, because they work like a telegraph system. So then the witch doctor decides to threaten the wife, saying he's going to waylay her husband on the road somewhere and kill him. So the tall blonde, poor thing, she gets absolutely desperate, and promises him anything—money, her jewels—just so he'll go away and let her husband alone. Then the witch doctor tells her, yes, there is a way he might be willing to spare her husband's life, and his eyes roam all over her from top to bottom, as if undressing her. And he shows her a poisoned dagger, putting it down on the table, and tells her if she ever gives him away, I mean the witch doctor, he'll use that knife on her husband. And at this point the husband arrives back at the house and through the open window he spots the two of them there with her already half undressed, and then the wife tells him she's leaving him and running away with the witch doctor, and the

husband goes crazy blind with infuriation, and spots the dagger
there and sinks it into his wife in an outburst of pure insanity.
Then the witch doctor tells him no one could possibly have
seen what just happened, and being as he was the only witness
to the wife's murder, if the kid lets him just go on with his
voodoo and stuff, he'll lie to the police and claim that the two
of them showed up just as somebody was finishing off his wife,
some fanatic from somewhere out of the jungle, anybody, just
trying to rob the place. So that's the story that the kindly old
housekeeper tells the girl, who's now completely terrified, but
anyway at least she's been saved from getting herself killed
back there in that old abandoned house by a couple of zombies,
I mean that giant black guy and then the creepy blond. *the
nurses on the dayshift, joking and smiling with nice patients
who obey directions and eat and sleep but when they recover
they leave for good*

—*a dog's cortex, a mule's, a horse's cortex, a monkey's, a
primate's cortex, a chick's from suburbia hanging out at the
movies when she's supposed to be in church* And that's how
the first wife got turned into a zombie.

—Right. And now comes the part that really thrilled me,
because the girl and the kindly housekeeper made it back to
the main house, safe and sound for the time being, but—

—And the witch doctor? What does he look like? You never
said.

—Ah, well I forgot to tell you, but actually you never get
to see him, because when the old housekeeper is busy telling
the girl how all that stuff happened, you see like a spiral of
smoke, which means you're moving backwards in time and you
actually get to see everything she's talking about pass before
you but with the housekeeper's voice in the background, a
deep voice but sweet, and very trembly.

—And the housekeeper, how did she get to know all that?

—Well, the girl asks her that very same question: but
how do you know about it, Mammy? And the housekeeper

with her head lowered, she confesses: her husband was the witch doctor. But through all that part you never once got to look at the witch doctor's face.

—*the learned executioner's cortex, factory girl heads roll, zombie heads, impassive gaze of the learned executioner down upon the poor innocent cortex of a chick from suburbia, of a fag from suburbia* What was it you were about to tell me, about a part that knocked you out or something?

—Yes, because once the girl and the housekeeper get back to the main residence, you switch back to seeing the other house again, the one that's abandoned, and the black zombie guy standing like a sentinel in the doorway, and a shadow slowly making its way through the jungle foliage, and creeping right up to the zombie guy, there at the door. And the zombie guy steps aside and lets the shadow go in right past him. And the shadow, whoever's entering the house, keeps going, into the bedroom and over to where the poor blonde is still lying in bed. And the poor thing is just lying there unable to move, with her eyes so gigantically open, without looking at anything though, and a white hand, which isn't the husband's because it's not shaking at all, the hand begins to undress her. And the poor dead woman, she's right there without the slightest possibility of defending herself or doing anything. *the youngest and prettiest nurse, all alone in a huge pavilion with the young patient, if he hurls himself upon her the poor novitiate could never escape him*

—Go on. *the poor rolling head of the fag from suburbia, nothing more to be done now, now it won't attach anymore to the body, when it's dead you must simply shut the eyes in the head, and caress the little narrow forehead, kiss the forehead, the little narrow forehead encasing the brains of that poor chick from suburbia, and who gave the order to have her guillotined? the learned executioner obeys an order which comes from no one knows where*

—And when the girl gets back to the main residence she

finds out the husband's already there, too, and he's incredibly upset. When he first sees her he throws his arms around her, he's so relieved she's safe, but then his rage comes right back and he forbids her ever to go out without his permission. And they sit down to supper. Naturally there's no alcohol around on the table, not even a drop of wine. And the husband, you see how incredibly nervous he is, and how he's trying to pretend not to be, and she asks him how the harvests are going, and he answers, going very well, but at that point he suddenly explodes, flings down his napkin and leaves the table in a huff, going off to his study where that cabinet is, locking the door behind him, and starts guzzling away again like a complete maniac. And her, before she goes to bed, she calls in to him, because she can see the light on under the door, but him, he just mumbles, leave me alone. The girl runs into her bedroom and changes her clothes, puts on a nightie or, no, it's a bathrobe, so she can go take a shower because the heat is so unbearable, and she steps into the shower, but without noticing how she's left all the doors open, and next thing you know, you start to hear these heavy footsteps, of some man somewhere in the house. She comes running back into the bedroom, soaking wet, to shut her door, but then stays glued to the door and hears someone out there unlocking another door and entering the room where her husband is still probably sulking. She bolts the bedroom door shut and locks all the windows. Well, finally she gets to sleep somehow, but then the next morning when she wakes up he's nowhere to be found, and she throws herself out of bed all frantic and asks one of the servants where her husband went, and the servant says he left not speaking a word to anyone, but heading off in the direction of that farthest-away plantation. And the girl remembers that that's exactly the place where the witch doctor has some kind of hideout. She summons the majordomo and asks him for his help; he's the only person that she feels she can trust. He says how his

own last hope had been her arrival there on the island, because maybe his master would finally be happy for a change;
but now even that's gone. Then the girl asks him whether
any doctor there on the island ever paid her husband a visit,
and the majordomo answers yes, but the master always
refuses to follow any instructions, so now there was only one
more alternative. And he looks at the girl right in the eye.
And she realizes, the majordomo is hinting about actually
going to see the witch doctor who's on the island, and she
answers, never. But the majordomo explains how the only
thing really needed in a case like this is simply for someone
to plant the suggestion deep in her husband's mind and for-
tify his willpower, that's all, and anyway he only came up
with the idea because it seemed to be the last resort, and of
course, it was up to her to decide. And the majordomo claims
that her husband insulted him again that very morning as he
was leaving the house, and says he's not about to put up with
that type of thing any longer, because as a matter of fact her
husband is nothing less than a total monster, and she ought
to leave him flat and look for someone who was more of a
man and might actually deserve her, and now the girl begins
to think the majordomo is looking a little too strange for
comfort, because his eyes are drilling right into her eyes. The
girl, totally confused, runs out to look for her husband,
frightened now that something has really happened to him
and that he really needs her. But the old housekeeper absolutely refuses to accompany her, saying it's just too dangerous, above all for the girl herself, because she's a white
woman. So the girl winds up with no alternative but to ask
the majordomo if he'll go with her, in spite of the weirdo way
their last conversation was going. So the majordomo agrees
to come along; he harnesses the cart with the fastest pair of
horses, loads a shotgun and off they ride. The kindly old
housekeeper, busy out in the garden cutting the morning's
bunch of fresh flowers, she sees them drive off like that and

shudders from head to foot, and then screams, but like a crazy person, so the girl would hear and not go, but the girl doesn't hear a thing at that point because the ocean waves are pounding against the shore like deafening rolls of thunder. The girl begs him not to drive so fast, the horses seem like they're running wild, but the majordomo pays no attention. The only thing he bothers to shout is that she'll find out soon enough what a miserable wretch her husband is. They don't exchange another word, the girl scared to death at each bend in the road, because the carriage sometimes careens around the curves on one wheel, and the horses seem to obey the majordomo in the eeriest way. Eventually they reach someplace in the thick of the jungle, and the majordomo tells her he has to go over into that hut over there a minute, to ask something from somebody, and he gets down from the cart. And some time goes by, and he doesn't come back and doesn't come back. And the girl begins to get scared of staying by herself, when what's even worse, the drums start beating, and they sound incredibly close by. The girl gets down from the buggy and goes over to the hut, afraid somehow that the majordomo has been attacked. And she calls out, but no one answers. She reaches the hut and discovers it's deserted, it's a place where nobody seems to have been for years, because the plants have all totally overrun the place. Then the girl begins to hear singing, voodoo chants, but since at this point she's more afraid to be by herself, she begins to walk toward where the voices are coming from. But I'll tell you the rest next time.

—Cut it out.

—What do you mean? I'm just hungry, you know? And somebody's got to make lunch, so long as you don't want to poison yourself again with that stuff they serve us . . . Anyway, the potatoes are almost done.

—But if there's not much left to go, let's finish it now.

—No, there's still a lot more left.

—————————

—Morning . . .

—How are you? Sleep well?

—Mmm, unbelievably well.

—You did too much reading though. And since that candle is mine, I'll decide when to put it out next time.

—It's just that I can't believe I'm actually able to read again.

—Yes, okay, it's fine to read in the afternoon and all that; you could read and that was great . . . in the afternoon. But after the lights went out, first thing, you go and overdo it for two more hours with that tiny candle.

—Okay, but I'm a big boy now, right? So let me tend to my own affairs.

—But at night we could have just gone on with the zombies, right? Which I know you liked, don't tell me you didn't.

—What time is it?

—It's eight-fifteen.

—And the guard didn't come by yet?

—He came with the coffee but you didn't wake up. Sleeping like a log, you were.

—How fantastic! . . . what a way to sleep . . . But where are the mugs? . . . Say, are you putting me on or something? They're right where you left them last night.

—Okay, I lied to you, so what? I just thought the guard should stop bringing us coffee in the mornings. And I told him so.

—Look, you can decide for yourself whatever you want, but me, I want my coffee, even if it's pisswater.

—You don't have any sense, do you? Whenever you take the prison stuff you get sick, but this way you don't have to worry, because as long as I have provisions you have provisions, too. And besides I'm expecting a visit from my lawyer today, and my mom'll probably show up with him like usual, so that means another package for us.

—Honestly, my friend, I don't like anybody running my life for me.

—What my lawyer has to say today could be important. To tell you the truth, I don't put much stock in appeals and all that, but if he's got the kind of pull he says he has, then there may be something to it.

—Let's hope so.

—Say, if I get out . . . who knows what you'll wind up with for a cellmate.

—Have you had your breakfast already, Molina?

—No, because I didn't want to disturb you, while you were sleeping.

—I'll put some water on for both of us then.

—No! You just stay put, you're barely recovering. I'll fix it. And the water's already on.

—But this is the last day I allow any of this. What are you making?

—A surprise. What were you reading last night?

—Nothing. Political stuff.

—Boy are you communicative . . .

—What time is the lawyer coming?

—He said at eleven . . . And now . . . we open up the little secret package . . . which I've been hiding from you . . . something really delicious . . . to have with our cup of tea . . . marble cake!

—Thanks, I don't want any.

—You don't want any . . . oh, I've heard that before . . . Look, the water's already starting to boil, so out you go and hurry back, now that the water's almost ready!

—Don't be telling me what I have to do . . .

—But, hey, can't I just coddle you a little bit? . . .

—Cut it out! . . . Christ almighty!!!

—You gone crazy? . . . What the hell's wrong with you?

—Shut up!!!

—But the marble cake . . .

— . . .

—Look what you did . . .

— . . .

—If we don't have a stove, we're done for. And the plate . . .

— . . .

—And the tea . . .

—I'm sorry.

— . . .

—I lost my head, I'm sorry, honestly.

— . . .

—The stove isn't broken. But the kerosene got knocked over.

— . . .

—Molina, please forgive my damn temper.

— . . .

—Can I pour more kerosene into the bottle?

—Yes.

—And please forgive me, honestly.

—Nothing to forgive.

—Yes there is. All that time I was sick, if it weren't for you, who knows how I'd have ended up?

—You don't have to thank me for anything.

—Yes I do. And for a lot, too.

—Forget it, nothing's the matter.

—Yes there is, obviously, and I'm terribly ashamed.

— . . .

—I'm a real bastard.

— . . .

—Molina, look, I'll call the guard and while I'm out I'll fill the pitcher up with water because we're almost empty. Look at me, will you? Lift your head up.

— . . .

—See, I'm going for some water now. You forgive me?

— . . .

—Please, Molina.

— . . .*

---

*In a survey quoted by the sociologist J. L. Simmons, in his book *Deviants*, it was established that homosexuals are subject to a considerably stronger rejection on the part of people than are alcoholics, compulsive gamblers, ex-convicts and former mental patients.

J. C. Flugel, in his *Man, Morals and Society*, claims with respect to those who during infancy have strongly identified themselves with paternal or maternal figures of a particularly stern disposition, that as they grow up they will embrace conservative causes and will be fascinated by authoritarian regimes. The more authoritarian the leader, the more confidence he will awaken in them, and they will also feel very patriotic and loyal when fighting in support of traditions and class distinctions, as well as in favor of rigidly disciplinary educational systems and religious institutions, while at the same time wholly condemning sexual abnormalities of any type. On the other hand, those who in infancy somehow reject—on an unconscious, emotional or rational level—such rules of parental conduct will favor radical causes, repudiate distinctions of class and treat understandingly those who exhibit any unconventional inclinations: homosexuals, for example.

For his part, Freud, in "Letter to an American Mother," says that homosexuality, while certainly not an advantage, ought not to be considered a reason for shame, since it is neither a vice nor degrading, but simply a variation in sexual functions produced by a certain arrest in sexual development. In effect, Freud judges that the overcoming of the "polymorphous perverse" stage of childhood—in which bisexual impulses are present—due to socio-cultural pressures, is actually a sign of maturity.

Several contemporary schools of psychoanalysis would disagree with that judgment; they would instead see in the repression of the "polymorphous perverse" one of the principal reasons behind the malformation of personality, especially in terms of the hypertrophy of aggressiveness. As for homosexuality itself, Marcuse points out that the social function of the homosexual is analogous to that of the critical philosopher, since his very presence is a constant reminder of the repressed elements of society.

With reference to the repression of "polymorphous perversity" in the West, Dennis Altman states in his work, cited above, that the principal components of such repression are on the one hand the elimination of the erotic from all human activity that is not definitely sexual, and on the other hand the negation of the inherent bisexuality of all human beings: society assumes, without pausing to reflect at all, that heterosexuality equals sexual normality. Altman observes that the repression of bisexuality is effected by the forced implantation of seemingly prestigious historico-cultural concepts of "masculinity" and "feminity" which manage to suffocate our unconscious impulses and mask themselves in the consciousness as the only appropriate forms of conduct, at the same time that they succeed in upholding, down through the ages, the supremacy of the male—in other words, clearly delineated sexual roles which are learned during childhood. Moreover, Altman adds, the sense of being male or female is established, above all, by means of the other: men feel that their masculinity depends upon a capacity to conquer women, and women feel that fulfillment can only come about through being coupled with a man. On the other hand, Altman and the whole Marcusian school condemn the "strong man" stereotype which is presented to males as the most desirable model for emulation, since the said stereotype tacitly implies an affirmation of masculinity through violence, which explains the constant presence of the aggressiveness syndrome in the world. Finally, Altman underscores the lack of any form of identity for the bisexual in contemporary society, and the pressures that he suffers from both sides, given that bisexuality threatens equally the exclusively homosexual forms of bourgeois life as well as heterosexual forms, and this characteristic would explain the reason why avowed bisexuality is so uncommon. And as for the convenient but—until a few years ago—merely potential parallelism between the struggle for class liberation and the one for sexual liberation, Altman emphasizes that in spite of Lenin's concern for sexual liberty in the USSR, his rejection of anti-homosexual legislation for example, such legislation was reintroduced in 1934 by Stalin, and as a result, the prejudice against homosexuality—as a type of "bourgeois degeneration"—held fast in a number of Communist parties of the world.

It is in different terms that Theodore Roszak comments upon the sexual liberation movement in his work entitled *The Making of a Counter Culture.* There, he expresses the concept that the kind of woman who is most in need of liberation, and desperately so, is the "woman" which every man keeps locked inside the dungeons of his own psyche. Roszak points out that this and no other is the form of repression that needs to be eliminated next, and the same with respect to the man bottled up inside of every woman. Furthermore, Roszak has no doubt that all of the above would represent the most cataclysmic reinterpretation of sexual life in the history of humanity, inasmuch as it would involve a restructuring of all that concerns sexual roles and concepts of sexual normality that are currently in force.

CHAPTER 11

WARDEN: Fine, Sergeant, you can leave now.

SERGEANT: Yes, sir.

WARDEN: Well, Molina, how is it going?

PRISONER: Fine, sir. Thank you . . .

WARDEN: What news have you got for me?

PRISONER: Not much to tell, I'm afraid.

WARDEN: Hmmm . . .

PRISONER: But I promise you one thing—each day he opens up more and more with me, that I can tell you . . .

WARDEN: Hmmm . . .

PRISONER: Yes sir, that much is for sure . . .

WARDEN: The unfortunate thing, Molina, is that they're pressuring me from all sides. And I'm going to let you in on something confidential, so you can understand my position. The pressure is coming right from the top . . . from the Presidency. They want to hear something up there, and soon. What's more, they're insisting upon Arregui's being interrogated again, and thoroughly. You understand my meaning? . . .

PRISONER: Yes, sir . . . But give me a few more days, don't interrogate him yet; say he's too weak, which is true. Because it'll be worse if he drops dead on them, tell them that.

WARDEN: Yes, I tell them, but they're not very convinced.

PRISONER: Give me just another week, and I'm sure I'll have some information for you.

WARDEN: All the information possible, Molina, all of it.

PRISONER: I have one idea though, sir.

WARDEN: What's that?

PRISONER: I don't know whether you'll . . .

WARDEN: Speak up . . .

PRISONER: Well, it's true, Arregui is very tough, but he also has his weaker side . . .

WARDEN: Yes? . . .

PRISONER: So . . . for example, if he should find out, for instance . . . Say a guard comes along and announces that they'll be shifting me into a different cell, because I'm now under a special category, on account of the pardon, or . . . Not so fast yet, on account of the fact that my lawyer has just presented an appeal, then if he thinks they're putting us into different cells, he'll probably soften up a lot. Because I think he's gotten a bit attached to me, so this way he's bound to loosen up and talk . . .

WARDEN: You think so?

PRISONER: I think it's worth trying.

WARDEN: I still suspect it was a mistake to tell him about the possibility of a pardon. It's probably made him put two and two together.

PRISONER: No, I don't think so.

WARDEN: Why not?

PRISONER: Oh, just a feeling I have . . .

WARDEN: No, tell me why. You must have some reasons for thinking that.

PRISONER: Well . . . that way I cover myself too a little.

WARDEN: How do you mean?

PRISONER: In the sense that if I finally get out of prison he wouldn't suspect something and then, next thing I know, get some of his comrades to come looking for me, and take reprisals.

WARDEN: You know perfectly well he has no contact whatsoever with his comrades.

PRISONER: That's what we think.

WARDEN: He can't even write them without our seeing the letter first, so what are you frightened about, Molina? You're getting carried away with yourself.

PRISONER: But I'm still sure it's better if he thinks I'm about to be released . . . Because . . .

WARDEN: Because what?

PRISONER: Nothing . . .

WARDEN: I'm asking you a question, Molina. Speak up!

PRISONER: What can I say . . .

WARDEN: Speak up, Molina, I want it straight! If we're not straight with one another, we won't get anywhere.

PRISONER: Okay, but it's nothing, sir, I swear. Just a hunch, that's all, that maybe if he thinks I'm leaving, he might feel like getting a few things off his chest. That's the way it goes with prisoners, sir. When a buddy leaves . . . it makes you feel more helpless than ever.

WARDEN: Have it your own way, Molina, we'll see you here in a week.

PRISONER: Thank you, sir.

WARDEN: But from then on we'll have to start looking at things in a different light, I'm afraid . . .

PRISONER: Yes, of course.

WARDEN: Very good, Molina . . .

PRISONER: Sir, I'm sorry to . . . well, try your patience . . . but . . .

WARDEN: What's the matter?

PRISONER: Well, I ought to return to my cell with some kind of package, so I've made up a small list here—that is, if it's all right with you. I wrote it while we were waiting outside. Sorry about my handwriting.

WARDEN: And you think this sort of thing helps?

PRISONER: I promise you nothing helps more, especially at this point, absolutely . . . I promise you.

WARDEN: Let me see it.

List of things to go in the package for Molina, please, with everything packed in two brown shopping bags, like my mother carries it:

2 roast chickens
4 baked apples
one pint egg salad
¾ pound fresh ham
¾ pound cooked ham
4 fresh rolls, seedless
one package of tea & a tin of ground coffee
one loaf of rye bread, sliced
2 large packages guava paste
one jar orange marmalade
quart of milk & a Holland cheese
small box salt
4 large pieces assorted glazed fruits
2 marble cakes
one stick butter
jar of mayonnaise and a box of paper napkins

—This is the fresh ham, and this is the cooked. I think I'll make a sandwich just to have the bread while it's fresh. But you have what you want.

—Thanks.

—Me, all I'll do is open up one of these rolls, put a little butter on it, with some ham. And some egg salad. Then afterwards a nice baked apple. And some tea.

—Sounds good.

—And you, break off a piece of chicken if you want and have it while it's still warm, just go right ahead.

—Thanks, Molina.

—Better that way, right? Each one fixes whatever he wants; that way I don't aggravate you.

—Whatever you prefer.

—I put water on the stove in case you want something. Have what you like, tea or coffee.

—Thanks.

— . . .

—Delicious-looking food, Molina.

—And we also have some glazed fruit. Only thing I want you to leave me is that piece of glazed pumpkin because it's my favorite. We also got glazed pineapple, and a large glazed fig, and this reddish piece, I wonder what it is?

—Probably watermelon, or maybe not, I really don't know . . .

—Well, we'll get to find out when we bite into it.

—Molina . . . I'm still ashamed . . .

—Of what?

—About this morning . . . about my temper.

—Nonsense . . .

—Whoever doesn't know how to receive . . . he's the mean one. It's because he doesn't want to give anything either.

—Think so? . . .

—Yes, I've been thinking, and that's what it is. If I got all uptight because you were being . . . generous with me . . . it's because I didn't want to see myself as obligated to treat you the same way.

—You think? . . .

—Yes, I do.

—Well, look . . . I've been thinking, too, and I remembered about some of the stuff you said, Valentin, and I understood from that why you acted the way you did. I mean it.

—What was it that I told you?

—That all of you, when you're involved in a struggle the way you are, you're not supposed to . . . well, become attached . . . to anyone. Oh, maybe attached is saying too much, but why not, yes, to become attached . . . like a friend.

—That's a very generous interpretation on your part.

—See, sometimes I really do understand the things you tell me . . .

—Yes, but in this case, the two of us are locked up here, so there is no struggle, no fight to win, you follow me?

—Mmm, go ahead.

—Then are we so pressured . . . by the outside world, that we can't act civilized? Is it possible . . . that the enemy, out there, has so much power?

—I don't follow you . . .

—Well, that everything that's wrong with the world . . . and everything that I want to change . . . is it possible all that won't allow me to . . . behave . . . even for a single minute, like a decent human being?

—What do you want to have? The water's boiling.

—Put tea on for both of us, okay?

—Fine.

—I don't know if you understand me . . . but here we are, all alone, and when it comes to our relationship, how should I put it? We could make any damn thing out of it we want; our relationship isn't pressured by anyone.

—Yes, I'm listening.

—In a sense we're perfectly free to behave however we choose with respect to one another, am I making myself clear? It's as if we were on some desert island. An island on which we may have to remain alone together for years. Because, well, outside of this cell we may have our oppressors, yes, but not inside. Here no one oppresses the other. The only thing that seems to disturb me . . . because I'm exhausted, or conditioned or perverted . . . is that someone wants to be nice to me, without asking anything back for it.

—Well, about that I don't know . . .

—What do you mean you don't know?

—I can't explain it.

—Come on, Molina, don't try to pull that on me. Concentrate, and you'll know what it is you're thinking, soon enough.

—Well, don't get the idea anything's strange, but if I'm nice to you . . . it's because I want to win your friendship, and, why not say it? . . . your affection. Same as I want to be good to my mom because she's a nice person, who never did anybody any harm, because I love her, because she's nice, and I want her to love me . . . And you too are a very nice person, very selfless, and you've risked your life for a very noble ideal . . . And don't be looking the other way, am I embarrassing you?

—Yes, a little . . . But I'm looking at you, see? . . .

—And because you're that way . . . I respect you, and I'm fond of you, and I want you to feel the same about me, too . . . Because, just look, my mom's affection for me is, well, it's the only good thing that's happened to me in my whole life, because she takes me for what I am, and loves me just that way, plain and simply. And that's like a gift from heaven, and the only thing that keeps me going, the only thing.

—Can I take some bread?

—Of course . . .

—But haven't you . . . haven't you any close friends . . . who also mean a lot to you?

—Yes, but look, my friends have always been . . . well, faggots, like I am, and among ourselves, well, how can I put it? We don't put too much faith in one another, because of the way we are . . . so easy to scare, so wishy-washy. And what we're always waiting for . . . is like a friendship or something, with a more serious person . . . with a man, of course. And that can't happen, because a man . . . what he wants is a woman.

—And all homosexuals are that way?

—No, there's the other kind who fall in love with one another. But as for my friends and myself, we're a hundred percent female. We don't go in for those little games—that's strictly for homos. We're normal women; we sleep with men.

—Sugar?

—Please.

—Delicious this fresh bread, isn't it? . . . Best thing there is.

—Mmm, it is delicious . . . But I have to tell you something . . .

—You bet you do, the end of the zombie movie.

—Mmm, that too. But there's something else, too . . .

—What's the matter?

—Well, my lawyer told me things are moving along.

—What a jughead I am, I didn't even ask. What else did he tell you?

—Well, that it seems like everything's going to work out for me, but that when they put you up for a pardon, I mean when you're being considered for a pardon, not when you already have one . . . anyway, you get switched to some other section of the penitentiary. So, before the week is out they're going to move me into a new cell.

—Really? . . .

—It seems so.

—And the lawyer, how did he know?

—They told him in the parole office, when he brought the papers in to be processed.

—That's great news . . . Wow, you must feel so happy . . .

—I don't want to think about it yet. Or build up any hopes . . . You should try the egg salad.

—Should I?

—Honestly, it's delicious.

—I don't know if I should; my stomach clenched after what you said.

—Look, act like I never said a word, because nothing is certain at all. As far as I'm concerned they haven't told me a thing.

—No, it's all looking up for you; we should be celebrating.

—No, I don't buy any of it . . .

—But I'm very happy for you, Molina, even though you'll be leaving and . . . Anyway, that's the way it goes . . .

—Have a baked apple . . . easier to digest.

—No, maybe we'll leave it for later, or I'll just leave mine. You go ahead and eat, as long as you're in the mood.

—No, I'm not very hungry either. Know something? . . . probably if I finish the zombies, we'll be hungrier then, so let's eat later.

—Fine . . .

—It's fun, the film, isn't it?

—Mmm, it's really been entertaining.

—In the beginning I didn't remember a lot of it, but now it's all coming back to me.

—Mmm . . . but wait awhile. Actually I . . . I don't know what's come over me, Molina, suddenly I'm . . . I'm all messed up.

—How come? Something hurting you? Your stomach?

—No, it's my head that's messed up.

—From what?

—I don't know, maybe because you're leaving, I don't know exactly.

—Ah . . .

—Maybe I'll just lie down and rest a little bit.

—Okay.

—Talk to you later.

—Right, we can talk later.*

—Molina . . . what time is it?

—It's after seven. I already heard them making the dinner rounds.

---

*The qualification "polymorphous perverse" which Freud applies to the infantile libido—referring to the indiscriminate pleasure derived by the child from his own body or the body of others—has also been accepted by more recent scholars, like Norman O. Brown and Herbert Marcuse. The difference between them and Freud, as already indicated, lies in the fact that Freud considered it proper that the libido is sublimated and channeled into an exclusively heterosexual direction, definitely a genital one, while

—I can't get a thing done . . . And I should be taking advantage of this last hour or so, before lights-out.

—Mmm . . .

—But my head's not screwed on right or something.

—So rest then.

—You still haven't told me the end of the film.

—You didn't want me to.

—I hated to waste it, when I couldn't get totally into it.

—You didn't feel like shooting the breeze either.

—If I don't know what I'm saying, I don't like to talk. I don't want to come out with just any old bullshit, you know . . .

—So rest.

—And what about finishing the film?

—Now?

—Why not?

—Okay, if you like.

—I studied awhile but I don't even know what it was I studied.

—I can't remember where we left off, what were we up to?

—With what, Molina?

—The film.

—That the girl's all by herself in the jungle, and she hears the drums.

—Ah, right . . . The jungle is blazing with the noonday sun,

---

more recent thinkers approve and even favor a return to polymorphous perversity and to an eroticization that goes beyond the merely genital.

In any case, affirms Fenichel, Western civilization imposes on the girl or boy the models of their own mother or father, respectively, as the only possible sexual identities. The probability for a homosexual orientation, according to Fenichel, is all the greater the more the child identifies with the progenitor of the opposite sex, instead of what would generally occur. The girl who does not find the model offered by her mother to be satisfactory, and the boy who does not find the model offered by the father to be satisfactory, would as a consequence be prone to homosexuality.

the girl decides to risk going in the direction of where they seem to be playing those spooky drums. And she keeps plunging ahead, and loses one shoe, and then stumbles and rips her blouse, and then her face gets smudged with dirt, and she pushes her way past all these thorny plants tearing her skirt to shreds. And as she gets closer to where all the initiates in voodoo are singing, the jungle gets darker and darker, and the only light comes from all the candles they've got burning. And there's an altar loaded with candles, nothing but candles from top to bottom, and a rag doll at the foot of the altar, with a pin stuck through its heart. The doll looks exactly like her husband. And all the native men and women are kneeling there, praying, and every now and then letting out these weird cries because of the great sorrow each one of them feels inside themself. But the girl looks around trying to spot the witch doctor; she's incredibly scared of actually seeing him but at the same time her curiosity's killing her from wanting to know what he looks like. And the drums are beating more furiously, and the natives are breaking into louder and louder howling, and the girl's a complete mess—her hair's all straggly, not to mention the condition of her clothes, and she keeps standing there right outside the circle of everybody who's so busy praying. Suddenly the drums stop, the natives quit their wailing, a chill wind rises out of the tropical jungle and the witch doctor appears, with a kind of white tunic on down to his feet, but

---

It is appropriate here to note a recent work of the Danish doctor Anneli Taube, *Sexuality and Revolution*, where it is suggested that the rejection which a highly sensitive boy experiences toward an oppessive father—as symbol of the violently authoritarian, masculine attitude—is a conscious one. The boy, at the moment when he decides not to adhere to the world proposed by such a father—use of weapons, violently competitive sports, disdain for sensitivity as a feminine attribute, etc.—is actually exercising a free and even revolutionary choice inasmuch as he is rejecting the role of the stronger, the exploitative one. Of course, such a boy could not suspect, on the other hand, that Western civilization, apart from the world of the father, will not present him with any alternative model for conduct, in those

open at the chest, the chest of a young man matted with curly hair, but the face is of an old man—the majordomo. With a completely vicious expression, hypocritical as can be, he gives his blessing to all the natives, and with the other hand gives a signal to the drummers. Then a different rhythm begins, this one openly diabolical, and he looks toward the girl, but this time without bothering to conceal his lust, and he does some kind of abracadabra with his hand, and fixes his eyes on the girl, hypnotizing her. She looks away so as not to fall into his power, but she can't resist his magnetism and little by little starts letting her head turn back, until finally she's looking right at the witch doctor face to face. And she falls into a trance and while the drums are wildly beating out a rhythm that seems more sexy than anything else, she begins walking slowly toward where the witch doctor is, and the natives all start falling into a strange trance, they're down on their knees and throwing their heads way back, until they almost touch the ground. And when the girl is within arm's length of the witch doctor, like a hurricane wind gusts through the palms, blowing out all the candles, and the darkness is total, right at noon. The witch doctor grabs the girl by the waist and then his hands begin to slide up toward her breasts, and then he caresses her cheekbones, and lifts her up in his arms to carry her into his hut.

---

first dangerously decisive years—above all from three to five—other than his mother. And the world of the mother—tenderness, tolerance, and even the arts—will turn out to be much more attractive to him, especially because of the absence of aggressivity: but the world of the mother, and here is where his intuition would fail him, is also the world of submission, since the mother is coupled with an authoritarian male, who only conceives of conjugal union as a subordination of the woman to the man. In the case of the girl, on the other hand, who decides not to adhere to the world of the mother, her attitude is due to the fact that she rejects the role of being submissive, because she intuits it as humiliating and unnatural, without realizing that once that role has been excluded, Western civilization presents her with no other role than that of oppressor. But the act of rebellion by such a girl or boy would be a sign of undeniable strength and dignity. On the other hand, Doctor Taube asks why such occurrences are not

And then . . . Oh . . . wait, how did it go? Oh . . . what was it then? Oh, right, the kindly housekeeper, seeing the girl go off in the carriage, goes herself to find the girl's husband and drags him off with her, pretending that the witch doctor had asked him to come immediately. Because, what was it now? she, the housekeeper, was actually the wife of the witch doctor, you know? of the majordomo. And when the girl sees her husband arrive, it breaks the spell, because the housekeeper yells to her, over and over. And that was just as the girl was about to go into the hut.

—Go on. *the poor one gives money to the rich one, the rich one asks the poor one for a handout and laughs at him, scoffs at the poor one and insults him for having nothing more to give, one phony coin*

—The girl and her husband go back to the main house in the jeep. Neither one of them says anything. Obviously, the husband has already figured out that the girl knows everything. And finally they reach their house. The girl, in order to show him she wants to do everything in her power to work things out, she goes in to get them to prepare dinner, just as if nothing had happened, and by the time she goes to the kitchen and comes back, he's already hitting the bottle again. She begs him not to be so weak, not to completely abandon her in the effort

---

more common, given that the Western couple, in general, exemplifies such exploitation. Here she suggests two factors which act as checks: the first would be present whenever in a home the wife—because of lack of education, intelligence, etc.—is actually inferior to the husband, which would make the authority of the latter seem more justifiable; the second factor would depend upon a slow development of the intelligence and sensitivity of the boy or girl, which would not permit them to grasp the situation. Implicit in this observation is the probability that if, on the other hand, the father is extremely primitive and the mother quite refined but nonetheless submissive, the extremely sensitive and precociously intelligent boy almost inevitably will reject the paternal model. And likewise, the girl will reject the maternal model as arbitrary.

As for the question of why in the same home there can be found homosexual and heterosexual children, Doctor Taube suggests that in every social

KISS of the SPIDER WOMAN

to save their marriage, because the fact that the two of them
love each other will have the capacity to overcome whatever
obstacles are set in their path. But he gives her a wild shove
and knocks her to the floor. Meanwhile, the witch doctor arrives at the old abandoned house, where the zombie woman is,
and finds her being cared for by the housekeeper, who used
to be his wife, but she's old now, and he completely despises
her. And the witch doctor tells her to get out, but the
housekeeper says she's not going to let him use the poor
zombie for his wickedness any longer. And she pulls out the
dagger to stab him. But he manages to grab her by the wrist
and seize the knife, and kill her with it, stabbing her right in
the heart. The zombie woman doesn't make a move, but you
can see in her eyes what a deep pain there is, even though she
doesn't have any will of her own to do something about it. Then
the witch doctor orders the zombie woman to follow him, and
he proceeds to tell her these outrageous lies, about how her
husband was a complete fiend and how it was him who ordered
her to be turned into a zombie, not the witch doctor, and how
he's now trying to pull the same business with the second wife,
mistreating her so terribly, and that's why she, the zombie
woman, has got to just go and kill the husband with a knife,

---

cell there is a tendency toward the division of roles, and for this reason one
of the children will take charge of the parental conflict and keep the other
siblings in a rather neutralized field.

Nonetheless, Doctor Taube, after evaluating the primary impulse toward
homosexuality and pointing out the character of its revolutionary noncon-
formity, observes that the absence of other models for conduct—and in this
respect she agrees with Altman and his thesis concerning the uncommon-
ness of bisexual behavior, due to the lack of available bisexual models for
conduct—causes the future male homosexual, for example, after rejecting
the defects of the repressive father, to feel anguished about the necessity
for identification with some form of conduct and to "learn" to be submissive
like his mother. The process is identical for the girl: she repudiates exploitation, and because of that she hates to be like her submissive mother, but
social pressures make her slowly "learn" another role, that of the repressive father.

to put an end to all his wickedness. And you can see in the eyes of the zombie that she doesn't believe a bit of what the witch doctor's telling her, but there's nothing she can do, because she's not the master of her own will, and she can't do anything but obey the order. And when they get to the big mansion, they enter through the garden very quietly. It's getting toward dusk now and almost night out. And through the window the zombie sees the husband is drunk and yelling his head off at the girl, grabbing her by the shoulders and shaking her and pushing and shoving her. The witch doctor puts the knife in the zombie's hand. The husband looks for more liquor, but the bottle's empty, he shakes it anyway trying to get one last drop out of it. The zombie can only obey. The majordomo tells her to go in and kill the husband. The zombie walks closer and closer. You see in her eyes, though, how much she still loves the guy, and doesn't want to kill him, but the order is implacable. The husband doesn't see her coming. The majordomo calls in to the girl, he says madame, sounding very respectful, but the girl locks herself up in her room with the key, until suddenly she hears the fatal outcry of her husband, stabbed by the zombie. Then the girl comes rushing back out and finds him agonizing, sprawled out on the sofa where he'd just been lying in a

---

From five years of age until adolescence there occurs in these "different" kinds of children an oscillation in their original bisexuality. But the "masculinized" girl, for example, because of her identification with the father, although feeling sexually attracted to a male, will not accept the role of passive toy that a conventional male would tend to impose, and will feel uncomfortable and therefore cultivate, as the only means of overcoming her anxiety, a different role that will merely permit play with women. On the other hand, the "femininized" boy, because of his identification with the mother, although feeling sexually attracted to a girl, will not accept the role of intrepid assailant that would tend to be imposed by a conventional female, will feel uncomfortable and therefore cultivate a different role that will only permit play with men.

Anneli Taube thus interprets the imitative attitude practiced, until very recently, by a high percentage of homosexuals, an attitude imitative, above all, of the defects of heterosexuality. What has been characteristic of male

half-drunken stupor, but now with the most tragic look on his face you could ever imagine. And then the majordomo walks in, and calls the servants to act as witnesses to the crime, so he can wash his hands of the whole affair. But the husband in his final death throes confesses to the zombie woman how much he's really loved her always and how it was all due to the fiendishness of the witch doctor, who has always wanted to be ruler of the island and lord of all its properties, and the husband tells the zombie woman to go back to her chamber and lock herself inside it and set fire to the old house, so that way she'll cease to be the pawn of someone else's perversity. And the sky is all black now but once in a while everything flickers into view because of the approaching torrential storm, and the husband with his dying breath tells the servants, who by then have already gathered around, how so many of their own kin have been sacrificed by the infamous witch doctor, turning them into living dead. Then they all look furiously at the witch doctor, and he starts to back out of the room slowly and makes it as far as the garden, and tries to escape, out in the raging storm, with the hurricane winds lashing the palms, and the lightning exploding repeatedly, like daylight, and when the witch doctor pulls out his revolver, the servants are forced to halt, so he's just about to get away, out through the garden, but at this point a deafening bolt of lightning slams the witch doctor down to the ground and strikes him dead. Soon after, the rains die down. No one has noticed, though, how the zombie woman is taking the road out to the old abandoned house. You hear the whistle of a steamship about to sail, and

---

homosexuals is a submissive spirit, a conservative attitude, a love of peace at any cost, even the cost of perpetuating their own marginality; whereas what has been characteristic of female homosexuals is their anarchical spirit, violently argumentative, while at the same time basically disorganized. Yet both attitudes have proven not to be deliberate, but compulsive, imposed by a slow brainwashing in which heterosexual bourgeois models for conduct participate—during infancy and adolescence—and later on, at

the girl flings a few things into a suitcase and races off to the boat; she leaves all the rest behind for the servants, because the only thing she wants to do is forget. She reaches the boat just as they're lifting the gangplank. The captain spots her from on deck; luckily, it's the same handsome captain who delivered her to the island in the first place. The boat casts off; they leave the harbor lights behind. The girl is down in her cabin; someone knocks at the door. She opens up and it's the captain himself; he asks her if she enjoyed her stay on the island. She answers no, and then he mentions the drums they heard on that first day she arrived, those drums that always forebode terrible sufferings, not to mention death itself. She tells him it's possible those drums will never be heard again. The captain suddenly tells her to be quiet a moment, he seems to hear something strange. The two go up on deck to listen and it's an incredibly beautiful melody, and they see hundreds of islanders gathered along the docks to sing to the girl, and tell her goodbye with a chant of love and gratefulness. The girl is trembling with emotion. The captain puts his arm around her so she'll feel protected. And way up the island, off behind the town, out there in the jungle, is a towering bonfire. The girl clings to the captain to try and stop trembling, the chills running up and down her spine, because she knows that out there in that fire is the poor zombie woman burning to ashes. The captain tells her not to be afraid, all that's left behind now, and the music of love from the whole town is bidding her goodbye forever, and wishing her a future filled with happiness . . . And that's all, folks . . . How'd you like it? *back in the*

---

the point of adopting homosexuality itself, "bourgeois" models for homosexual conduct.

This prejudice, or perhaps truthful observation, concerning homosexuals placed them on the periphery of movements for class liberation and political action in general. The socialist countries' mistrust of homosexuals is notorious. Much of the—fortunately, suggests Doctor Taube—began to change throughout the decade of the sixties, with the emergence of the woman's

pavilion the critically ill patient is now out of danger, the nurse will keep watch throughout the night over his tranquil sleep

—Very much. *the rich one sleeps peacefully after bestowing his wealth upon the poor one*

— . . . Oh . . . well . . .

—Why the big sigh?

—It's a hard life . . .

—What's the matter, Molina?

—I don't know, I'm scared of everything, scared of kidding myself about getting out of here, scared they'll never let me. And what scares me most is that they might separate us and stick me in another cell and keep me there forever, with who knows what sort of creep . . .

—Best not to think about it, especially since nothing depends upon us.

—But you see, I don't agree with that. I think that maybe if we think about it we might come up with something, Valentin.

—With what?

—Well . . . at least some way not to be separated.

—Look . . . Don't you go spoiling things for yourself at this point, think about just one thing: what you want is to get out of here in order to take care of your mother. Nothing else. Don't think about anything else. Because her health is what's most important to you, right?

—Yes . . .

—Concentrate on that, and only that.

—But I don't want to concentrate on it . . . I won't . . .

—Hey . . . what's up?

—Nothing . . .

---

liberation movement, when the resulting judgments tended to discredit— in the eyes of such sexual marginals—those unattainable but tenaciously imitated roles of "strong male" and "weak female."

The subsequent formation of homosexual liberation fronts is one proof of that.

—Come on, don't get like that . . . Take your head out of the pillow . . .

—Leave me alone . . .

—But what's up? Are you hiding something from me?

—No, not hiding anything . . . But it's just . . .

—Just what? When you're out of here, you'll be free, you'll be with people. If you want you can even join up with some kind of political group.

—That's ridiculous and you know it; they'd never trust some faggot.

—But I can tell you who to go see . . .

—Not on your life, never, you hear? Never, never tell me anything about your comrades.

—Why? Who would ever figure you'd go to see any of them?

—No, I could be interrogated or something, and as long as I don't know anything I can't tell anything.

—Anyway, there's a lot of different types of groups for political action. And if you find one that appeals to you, join it, even if it's a group that just does a lot of talking.

—I don't know anything about that stuff . . .

—And don't you have any close friends? . . . good friends?

—Oh, I have silly girlfriends like myself, but just in passing, good for a laugh once in a while, and that's all. But as soon as we start getting a little dramatic . . . then we can't stand the sight of each other. Because I already told you what it's like; you see yourself in the other ones like so many mirrors and then you start running for your life.

—Things could change for you once you're outside.

—No, they'll never change . . .

—Come on, don't cry . . . don't be that way . . . Look how many times you make me listen to you cry . . . Well, I suppose you had to put up with my blubbering that time, too . . . But enough is enough. God . . . you . . . you make me nervous with your crying.

—I just can't help it . . . I always have such rotten . . . luck . . .

—Hey, they shut off the lights . . .

—Of course they did, what do you think? It's already eight-thirty. And just as well anyway, so you can't see my face.

—That picture really made the time fly, Molina.

—And I won't ever get to sleep tonight.

—Now listen to me, because there must be something I can help you with. It's just a matter of discussing it a little. First of all, you have to think about getting into some group, and not be alone all the time. That's bound to help you.

—Get into what group? I tell you I don't understand any of those things, and I don't believe in them very much either.

—Then you have no right to complain.

—Let's just . . . stop talking . . .

—Come on . . . don't be that way . . . Molina.

—No . . . don't touch me . . .

—Can't a buddy even pat your back?

—It makes me feel worse . . .

—Why? . . . Come on now, say something. It's time for us to be honest with each other. Really, Molina, I want to help you, tell me what's wrong.

—I just want to die. That's all I want.

—Don't be saying things like that. Think how sad it'd make your mother, and your friends, and me.

—You? It wouldn't matter to you . . .

—What do you mean it wouldn't! Come on, what a thing to say . . .

—I'm tired, Valentin. Tired of hurting. You don't know, I hurt so much inside.

—Where does it hurt you?

—In my chest, and my throat . . . Why does the sadness always jam up right there, in that one spot?

—It's true . . .

—And now . . . you made me stop crying, so I can't even

cry anymore. And that makes it worse, the knot in my throat, it's so tight there, so tight . . .

—. . .

—. . .

—Is it hurting you right now? that knot I mean?

—Yes.

—. . .

—. . .

—Right here?

—Yes.

—Can I massage it for you?

—Yes.

—Here?

—Yes.

—Does that feel better?

—Yes . . . it feels better.

—Me too, I feel better.

—Honestly?

—Mmm . . . It's restful . . .

—How come restful, Valentin?

—Because . . . I don't know.

—But why?

—Maybe because I'm not thinking about me . . .

—You do me a lot of good, Valentin.

—Maybe because I feel like you really need me, so I can do something for you.

—You're always looking for explanations, Valentin . . . You're crazy . . .

—I don't like to just go along with things . . . I want to know why they happen . . .

—Valentin . . . Can I touch you too?

—Yes.

—I want to touch the mole there . . . right above your eyebrow.

—. . .

—And this way, can I touch you this way?

— . . .

—And this way?

— . . .

—It doesn't disgust you to have me caress you?

—No . . .

—You're kind to me . . .

— . . .

—Really, you are . . .

—No, you're the one who's kind.

—Valentin . . . If you like, you can do whatever you want with me . . . because I want you to.

— . . .

—If I don't disgust you.

—Don't talk like that. It's better if it's quiet.

—I'm squeezed up against the wall a little.

— . . .

—I can't see at all, not at all . . . it's so dark.

— . . .

—Slowly now . . .

— . . .

—No, that way it hurts a lot.

— . . .

—Wait . . . no, it's better like this, let me lift my legs.

— . . .

—A little slower . . . please . . .

— . . .

—That's better . . .

— . . .

—Thank you . . . thank you . . .

—And you . . .

—No, you . . . This way I hold you in front of me, even if I can't see you there, it's so dark. Wait, it still hurts . . .

— . . .

—Now, yes . . . now it's beginning to feel better, Valentin.

It doesn't hurt.

—Does it feel better?

—Yes.

— . . .

—And you, Valentin? . . . Tell me . . .

— . . . I don't know, don't ask questions . . . Because I don't know anything.

—Oh, it's good . . .

—Don't talk, Molina . . . for a little while.

—It's that I . . . I feel such strange things . . .

— . . .

—Just then, without thinking, I put my hand up to my face, trying to find the mole.

—What mole? . . . I have it, not you.

—Mmm, I know. But I put my hand to my forehead, to feel the mole that . . . I haven't got.

— . . .

—It looks so handsome on you, it's a shame . . . why can't I see you?

— . . .

—Are you enjoying it, Valentin?

—Just quiet . . . just quiet a little while.

— . . .

— . . .

—And know what else I felt, Valentin? But only for a second, no more.

—What? Talk to me, but just . . . don't move . . .

—For just a second, it seemed like I wasn't here . . . not here or anywhere out there either . . .

— . . .

—It seemed as if I wasn't here at all . . . like it was you all alone.

— . . .

—Or like I wasn't me anymore. As if now, somehow . . . I . . . were you.

—Morning . . .

—Good morning . . . Valentin.

—Sleep well?

—Mmm . . .

— . . .

—How about you, Valentin?

—What?

—Did you sleep well, too?

—Yes I did, thanks . . .

— . . .

—I heard the coffee going around just now, you really don't want any?

—No . . . I don't trust it.

— . . .

—What'll you have with breakfast? Tea or coffee?

—What are you going to have, Molina?

—Me, oh, some tea. But if you want coffee it's no more trouble . . . it's no trouble at all. Whatever you'd like.

—Thanks a lot. Coffee, please.

—You want to be let out first, Valentin?

—Thanks, yes. I would like to go out first.

—Fine . . .

— . . .

— . . .

—You know why I chose coffee, Molina?

—No . . .

—To wake up so I can study. Not too much, a couple of hours or so, but of concentrated studying. So I get back into the swing of it.

—Sure.

— . . . And then a nice break before lunchtime.

— . . .

—Molina . . . How did you wake up, okay?

—Fine . . .

—Not feeling gloomy anymore, are you? . . .

—No, but I'm like really out of it . . . I can't think . . . about anything.

—That's good . . . once in a while.

—But I'm fine . . . I'm okay.

— . . .

— . . . I'm even afraid to speak, Valentin.

—Well don't, then . . . There's no need to speak, or to think.

— . . .

—If you're feeling good, just don't think about things, Molina. Whatever you think about is just going to bring you down.

—And you?

—Me? I'm not going to think about things either, I'm just going to study. That's my remedy.

—Remedy for what? Regrets about last night?

—No, I don't have any regrets about anything. The more I think of it the more I'm convinced that sex is innocence itself.

—Can I ask you a favor . . . very seriously?

— . . .

—Let's not . . . let's not talk about anything, let's not discuss anything today. Just for today I'm asking.

—If you want that.

— . . . You're not going to ask me why?

—Why?

—Because I . . . feel good . . . really good . . . and I don't want anything to spoil this sensation.

—If you want that . . .

—Valentin . . . I think I haven't felt so happy since when I was a kid. Since when my mom used to buy me a toy, or something like that.

—You know what? Think up a good film . . . and when I'm all finished studying you can start telling it to me while the meal is cooking.

—Okay . . .

— . . .

—What kind of film would you like to hear?

—One that you really like a lot yourself, don't think up one for me this time.

—But what if you don't like it?

—No, if you like it yourself, Molina, I'm going to like it, too, even if I don't like it.

— . . .

—Don't be so silent. I just mean that if you like something, that makes me happy, because I feel like I owe you something, no, what am I saying? because you were nice to me, and I'm grateful. And knowing that something made you feel good . . . it's a relief to me.

—Honestly?

—Honestly, Molina. And you know what I'd like to hear? It seems ridiculous . . .

—Tell me . . .

—I want to know if you remember a toy you really liked, the one you even liked most of all . . . of all the toys your mother bought you.

—A dolly . . .

—Ugh, I don't believe it . . .

— . . . Why are you laughing so much?

—Oh, if they don't let me out fast I'll do it in my pants . . .

—But why are you laughing so much?

—Because . . . Oh, I'm dying . . . oh, some psychologist I turn out to be . . .

—What's wrong?

—Nothing . . . I just wanted to see if there was any relation between myself and . . . and that toy . . .

—You asked for it . . .

—You're sure it wasn't like a toy soldier or something else?

—No, a dolly with very blond hair, all braided up, and she could blink her eyes, and wore a Bavarian costume.

—Oh, tell them to open up . . . This is too much; I can't believe it . . .

—I think this is the first time you've laughed since I had the great misfortune to end up in your cell.

—That's not true.

—I swear, I've never seen you laugh before.

—But come on, I have so laughed, lots of times . . . even at you.

—Yes, but it's always been when the lights were already out. I swear I never *saw* you laugh before.

—It takes place in Mexico, some city on the coast, very tropical. The fishermen are already heading out in their boats; it's just before daybreak. They hear the echoes of some music drifting out to them. The only thing they see from out on the water is this spectacular villa, all lit up, with several stunning balconies overlooking a sumptuous walk, full of jasmine, then a row of palms, and below that the beach itself. Most of those who were invited to the masked ball have already left. The orchestra's playing a very rhythmic melody, with maracas and bongos, but nice and slow, a kind of habanera. Only a few couples are left dancing, and one in particular, with their masks still on. The famous Mardi Gras of Veracruz is finally drawing to a close, and unfortunately the sun is beginning to rise and announce the coming of Ash Wednesday. The couple wearing the masks, they look fabulous, her in a kind of gypsy costume, very tall-looking, wasp-waisted, dark, with her hair parted in the middle and hanging loose down to her waist, and he's very strong and swarthy, with dark sideburns and the hair swept to one side in like a wave, and a heavy mustache. She's got a petite little nose, very straight, with a delicate profile that at the same time reveals lots of character. She's wearing a band of coins across her forehead, and one of those full blouses with the elasticized necks, so they can stretch and be worn off the shoulder, or off both shoulders, one of those gypsy-type blouses, know what I mean?

—More or less, it doesn't matter though, go on.

—And then a very fitted waist. And the skirt . . .

—What about the neckline. Don't skip around.

—Well, back then it was that period when a very low neckline was in fashion, and you got to see some cleavage, but they didn't prop the bosom up like buoys. Because they didn't really show you that much but you still got the idea; they just left it more to your imagination.

—Well how much is there then? a lot or a little?

—Lots, and the skirt she has on is all billowy; it's made of kerchiefs, loads of kerchiefs, all chiffon, in lots of different colors, and when she's dancing, now and then you catch a glimpse of her legs, but just a glimpse. And him, he's in a domino costume, which is like a black cape, that's all, and with a suit and tie on underneath. He tells her that's the last dance the orchestra's going to play, and so now it's time to unmask themselves. But she says, no, the night must end without his knowing who she is, or her knowing who he is. Because they won't ever see one another again; it's been a perfect encounter, but it's just one night of carnival and that's that. He insists and takes off his mask, he's divine-looking, and he tells her all over again that he's spent his whole life waiting for her, and he's not about to let her just slip through his fingers now. And he stares at the fabulous-looking gem set in the ring she's wearing,

and asks whether it signifies anything like a serious engagement. And she says, yes, it does, and asks him to wait out in
his car, while she goes to the powder room to freshen up her
makeup. And that's the fatal moment, because he goes outside
to wait and he waits and she never shows. So, next thing, the
action switches to the capital city of Mexico, and it turns out
that the guy works as a reporter for a big afternoon daily. Oh,
wait! I forgot to tell you that while they were dancing she says
how lovely the melody is that the orchestra's playing, and what
a pity there are no lyrics to that tune, and then the guy tells
her he's a kind of poet. And so one afternoon he's there at the
city desk of the paper he works for, where everything's a
madhouse, with people running in and out, and he notices this
article being put together about some peppery scandal, with
lots of photos, concerning some actress-singer who went into
retirement a while back, and who now lives in total seclusion
with some incredibly powerful tycoon, a magnate feared by
many important people, a semi-mafia type, but whose name is
nowhere mentioned. And looking at the photos, the guy starts
thinking to himself: this incredibly beautiful woman, who
started her career in theatrical revues, and then became a very
successful dramatic actress, but only for a short time, because
she retired—anyway, this woman turns out to look totally
familiar to him, and when in one photo he discovers on the
hand in which she's holding up her champagne glass . . . an
incredibly rare gem, there's no doubt left in his mind. And by
playing dumb, he manages to find out just how much of a
scandal is brewing, and they tell him it's bound to create a
sensation when the story breaks, and they just have to get hold
of a few more photographs, of when she undressed on stage,
and that stuff they'll have in just a couple of days more. He
also sees her address there, because they've been busy spying
on her as well, and so he manages to take it down and go pay
her a visit at her home. He stares in astonishment, for she's
wearing only a black tulle negligee. It's an ultramodern apart-

ment, with recessed lighting fixtures that create a kind of diffuse light so you can't tell where it's coming from, and everything's all in white taffeta—the drapes taffeta, the lounges taffeta, and the hassocks, too, round, with no legs. She's sitting back on the divan and listening to him. He relates the whole story of what's going on and promises her to get rid of all the photographs and squash the story that's been put together, so the article's never going to see the light of day. She thanks him profusely. He asks her if she's happy inside this gilded cage. She says she doesn't like to hear him talk like that. Then she tells him the truth, how, exhausted by the terrible ordeal of the theater, where she'd managed to climb to the very pinnacle, she let herself be taken in by a man she thought was decent. That man, incredibly wealthy, took her around the world on a long voyage, but once they got back home he became more and more jealous, to the point of reducing her to a virtual prisoner in her own house. She soon got bored with just doing nothing all the time and asked him to allow her to return to acting, but he refused. Then the reporter tells her he's ready to do anything for her, and he's not afraid of the other guy. But, well, she keeps looking straight at him, from over there on the divan, and takes out a cigarette. He goes and lights it for her, and then kisses her. She throws her arms around him, for a minute letting herself be carried away by an impulse, and says, I need you . . . But then he asks her to go away with him. And she's too afraid to do it. The guy tells her, don't be a coward, because together they can go to the ends of the earth. She asks for a little time, a few days. He insists it's now or never. She tells him to go away then. He says, no, he's not leaving without her, and he takes her by the arms and shakes her, to make her let go of her fears. Well, then she does react, but it's against the guy, telling him, all you men are the same, and she's not a belonging, something for them to manipulate whatever way they like, all at their own choosing, and she's going to make up her own mind. Then he tells her he never wants to see her again, and marches over to the door. Furious, she says to wait a minute, and goes into her bedroom and comes back with a pile of banknotes, and says it's to pay for the favor he's done for her, by destroying the article. He throws the money down at her feet and walks out. But down on the street he regrets the fact that he acted so impetuously. He doesn't know what to do, and goes off to have a couple of rounds at a bar, where through the heavy smoke all you can make out is some blind fellow sitting at the piano, playing that same very slow, very sad, tropical song, the one they danced to at the Mardi Gras ball. The guy drinks, and drinks, and starts composing lyrics for the song, while he's thinking about her, and starts singing, because he's actually a singer, the leading man, the reporter: "Even though you're . . . a prisoner, in your solitude . . . your heart whispers still . . . I love you." And how does the rest go? Let me see, there's something else and then comes, "Your eyes cast a shadow, your smile brings such pain, your lips . . . I remember . . . they once used to lie . . . and I ask my darkest self, if those lips I adore, with their fervent kiss . . . with their fervent kiss . . ." then what else? something like ". . . could ever lie to me again." And then it goes, "Black flowers . . . of fate, cruelly keep us apart, but the day will come, when you'll be . . . mine forever . . . mine alone . . ." You remember that bolero?

—No, I don't think so. I don't know . . . Go on.

—Next day, at the paper, the guy sees how everyone's busy trying to find the article on her, and they can't. Obviously, because he's got it locked up in his desk. And since they can't find any of the stuff, the editor-in-chief decides to forget the whole story, because it'd be practically impossible to gather so much material all over again. So the guy's relieved, and after hesitating a little . . . he dials her number. And he tells her she can relax, there's no chance the article is ever going to be printed. She thanks him, he asks her to forgive him for all he said yesterday, and to see him again, and suggests where and when. And she accepts. He asks the boss if he can leave work early; the editor-in-chief gives him the rest of the day off, saying he's been looking overworked for a couple of days now. All this time she's busy getting ready to go out, in a black two-piece suit, those really smart ones they wore back then, very fitted, and without any blouse on underneath, and a diamond brooch on the lapel, and a white tulle hat, like a white cloud behind her head. And her hair in a bun. And she's already got her gloves on, white to match the hat, when she suddenly thinks twice about the risk involved in this rendezvous, because the magnate walked in just at that minute, while she was busy trying to figure out whether or not to go. And the magnate, who's middle-aged, with gray hair, about fifty or so, a little heavy, but presentable enough as a guy, he asks her where she's running off to. She says shopping, he offers to come along, she says it'll be such a bore for him, she has to pick out fabrics. The magnate looks like he suspects something, but doesn't openly reproach her. Then she responds by telling him he has no right to put on a bad face, because she always does whatever he asks, she's dropped the idea of returning to the theater, hasn't she? and of radio singing, but it's really the limit when he dares to look at her like that just because she's going out shopping. Then the magnate tells her to go ahead, to buy anything she wants, but if he ever catches her lying . . . it won't be her he takes his revenge out on, he knows well enough he can't live without her, but he'll wreak his vengeance on any man who dares to go near her. The magnate leaves, and moments later she does, too, but she doesn't know what to tell the chauffeur, because the magnate's threat is still ringing in her ears: "I'll wreak my vengeance on any man that dares to go near you." Meantime the guy is waiting for her at some posh bar, and he's looking and looking at the time, and begins to realize she's not coming. He orders another whiskey, a double. Another hour goes by, two hours, and by then he's totally drunk, but tries to pretend not to be,

getting up and walking stiffly out of the bar. He goes back to
the office, sits at his desk and asks the errand boy to go get
him two containers of coffee. And he sets himself to work,
trying to forget everything. Next day he shows up earlier than
usual, and the editor-in-chief is happy to see him, and pats him
on the back for coming in so early to help out, because it's a
tough day ahead of them. He buries himself in his work and
even finishes up early, and hands in the assignment to the
chief, who congratulates him on how it's written, and tells him
he can have the remainder of the day off. So then the guy
leaves, and goes off to have a few glasses with some reporter
friend who asks him along; he refuses at first, but the other guy
insists—but no, wait, it's the boss himself that invites him to
have a drink, right there in his private office, because since the
guy's managed to solve the whole day's problem, which happened to be an article on some gigantic embezzlement high up
in the government, the boss wants to celebrate a little. Then
after a drink or two, the guy goes down into the street, feeling
gloomy, the scotch gave him the blues, and before he realizes
what he's done he's standing in front of her house. He can't
resist and goes in and rings the buzzer of her apartment. The
maid asks, who is it? He says he wants to talk to the lady of
the house, it's just five o'clock then, so she's having tea with
the magnate, who has brought her an extravagant surprise, an
emerald necklace, to ask her forgiveness for the scene he made
yesterday. She orders the maid to tell the reporter she's not at
home, but he's already barged into the room. Then she tries
to handle the situation by telling the magnate what happened
with the business of that article, and thanks the guy, and tells
the magnate how he wouldn't accept any money, so she really
doesn't know what more to say in order to settle the affair, but
him, the guy, furious at seeing her holding on to the magnate's
arm like that, he says the whole thing makes him sick and all
he wants is for them to forget him once and for all. Neither she
nor the magnate have a word to say; the guy walks out, but

leaving a piece of paper on the table, with the lyrics of the song written for her. The magnate stares at the girl; her eyes are flooded with tears, because she's in love with the reporter and can't deny it any longer, especially to herself, which is worst of all. The magnate looks hard at her eyes and asks her to say exactly what she feels for that creep of a newspaperman. She can't answer, there's a knot in her throat, but then she sees how red in the face he's getting; well, she has to swallow somehow and say, that creep of a newspaperman means absolutely nothing to me, but I just met him over the problem of that news article. And the magnate asks her for the name of the newspaper, and when he finds out it's the one that's been relentlessly investigating his ties with the mafia, he asks her for the name of the guy, too, so as to in some way try to bribe him. But the girl, terrified that what the magnate actually wants to do is revenge himself on the guy . . . refuses to tell him his name. Then the magnate gives her a heavy slap across the face, knocking her to the floor, then leaves. She just lies there sprawled on the carpet that's made of real ermine, her pitch black hair against the snowy white ermine, and the tears twinkling like stars . . . And she looks up . . . and sees over on one of those taffeta hassocks . . . a sheet of paper. She gets up and reaches for it, and reads . . . "Even though you're a prisoner, in your solitude your heart whispers still . . . I love you. Black flowers of fate . . . cruelly keep us apart, but the day will come when you'll be . . . mine forever, mine alone . . ." and presses the paper all crumpled to her heart, which is probably just as crumpled inside as that piece of paper, just as much . . . or even more.

—Go on.

—The guy, for his part, is destroyed, he doesn't return to work and wanders around from bar to bar. At the newspaper they look for him but can't find him; they call him on the phone and he answers, but as soon as he hears the boss's voice he hangs up on him. Days go by, until suddenly he finds on the newsstands, in the same daily paper he was working for, an announcement promising for the next edition an exclusive inside story about the private life of a famous star now retired from show business. He trembles with rage. He goes to the press office, where everything is all closed because it's very late. The nightwatchman lets him in without suspecting a thing; he goes up to his old office and discovers they've jimmied the locks on his drawers to put another reporter at his old spot, and so of course they found all the material there in the desk. Then he goes to the printers, which is a long way from there, and so by the time he arrives at the place, it's already morning and he sees that the afternoon edition has already started rolling off the presses. So out of despair he grabs a sort of hammer and smashes up the machinery destroying the whole printing of the afternoon edition, because the inks get dumped all over, and everything, everything is totally ruined. Damage running into thousands and thousands of pesos, into the millions, it's an act of outright sabotage. He disappears from the city, but they kick him out of the union so he can never again work as a newspaperman in his life. Drifting from drunken binge to drunken binge he one day arrives at a beach, in search of his memories: Veracruz. In some crummy dive, facing the sea, right at the foot of the harbor, a colorful local orchestra, they're playing on that instrument that's like a table full of sticks . . .

—A xylophone.

—Valentin, you know everything . . . How do you do it?

—Go ahead. I want to know what happens.

—Okay, right on that same instrument, they're playing a very sad song. And the guy, with his penknife he's scrawling into the table, which is full of carved hearts, names, dirty words, too, and he's inscribing some lyrics to the song while he's singing it. And it goes: "When they speak to you of love, and its fascination . . . and they offer you the sun, the moon and the stars . . . If you still think of me . . . don't say my name!

because your lips might recall . . . what love is about . . . And if they ask about your past, just go ahead and lie, say you come from a very strange world . . ." and then he begins to imagine her, and actually to see her at the bottom of that glass of brandy, and she starts swirling around there, until she swells up to a normal size and starts walking around the miserable dive, and looking at him, she sings the rest of the stanza . . . something suggesting that she doesn't know what love is, and that she doesn't know what pain is, and that she has never, never cried . . . And then he sings back to her, looking at her, right in the middle of all those stumblebums that are too drunk to see or hear anything, and he tells her that wherever he goes, he talks about her love, like some golden dream, and then she comes in with something like that he should forget his bitterness and never tell people that her farewell was what really broke his heart, and then he caresses the transparent memory of her, sitting beside him there at the table, as he answers her, ". . . and if they ask about my past, I'll make up another lie, and say I come from a very strange world . . ." and the two of them then, looking at each other with tears in their eyes, they end on like a duet but in a low, low voice that's barely a whisper, ". . . because I've triumphed in love, and I've conquered all heartaches, and I've never . . . never cried . . ." and when he dries his eyes, because he's ashamed to be a man and crying like that, and he can see clear now, she's obviously nowhere beside him. Desperate, he grabs the glass to hold it up to the light, and doesn't see the reflection of anything but himself all disheveled there in the bottom of the glass, and then with his whole strength he hurls it against the wall, smashing it to bits . . .

—Why are you stopping?

— . . .

—Don't start doing that . . .

— . . .

—Goddamn it! I said there's not going to be any unhappy

feelings here today, so there's not going to be any!

—Don't shake me like that . . .

—Because today we don't let the outside in.

—You frightened me.

—And don't get sad on me, and don't be frightened either . . . The only thing I want is to keep my promise to you, and make you forget about anything that's ugly. I swore it this morning; you're not going to have to brood about things. And I'm going to keep my word, damn it, because it doesn't cost me anything. It's so easy to make you stop that brooding . . . and while it's in my power, for at least this one day . . . damn it, I'm not going to let you brood about things . . .

—I wonder how it is outside tonight.

—Who knows? Not cold, but very humid, I guess. So it must be kind of cloudy, Molina, with most likely a low ceiling, enough to block the street light and send it back down.

—Mmm . . . probably.

—And the streets damp, especially the cobblestones, even if it's not raining, and a little fog in the distance.

—Valentin . . . with me the humidity makes me nervous, because it makes me itchy all over, but not tonight.

—I feel good, too.

—The meal sit well with you?

—Yes, the meal was . . .

—Boy, not much left . . .

—It's my fault, Molina.

—We're both to blame; we ate more than usual.

—How long has it been since you got that last package?

—Four days. Well, for tomorrow there's at least a little cheese, a little bread, some mayonnaise . . .

—And there's orange marmalade. And half a marble cake. And some guava paste.

—And nothing else, Valentin?

—Yes, a piece of glazed fruit. The glazed pumpkin you put aside for yourself.

—I can't bring myself to eat it, it looks so pretty. But tomorrow we'll split it in half.

—No, it's for you.

—No, tomorrow we have to eat the prison food, and for dessert we'll share the glazed pumpkin.

—We'll discuss that tomorrow.

—Mmm, I don't want to think about anything now, Valentin. Just let me dawdle.

—You sleepy?

—No, I'm fine, I feel peaceful . . . No, I'm more than peaceful . . . But don't get angry if I tell you the silly truth of it. I'm really happy.

—That's the way it should be.

—And the good thing about feeling really happy, you know, Valentin? . . . It's that you think it's forever, that one's never ever going to feel unhappy again.

—I feel really good, too. Even this rotten piece of cardboard they call a mattress feels nice and warm, and I know I'm going to sleep fine.

—I feel nice and warm in my chest, Valentin, that's the good thing. And my head feels so empty—no, that sounds stupid: my head's like filled with warm mist. All of me feels like that inside. I don't know, maybe it's that I still . . . can feel . . . how you touch me.

— . . .

—Does it bother you if I say things like that?

—No.

—It's that when you're here, like I already told you, I'm not me in a way, and that's a relief. And afterwards, until I sleep, even though you're back on your little cot, I'm still not me. It's a strange thing . . . How can I explain it?

—Go on, tell me about it.

—Don't hurry me, let me concentrate . . . And it's like when I'm alone here in my bed I'm no longer you either, I'm someone else, who's neither a man nor a woman, but someone who feels . . .

— . . . out of danger.

—Yes, that's exactly it, how did you know?

—Because it's what I feel.

—Why is it we feel like that?

—I don't know . . .

—Valentin . . .

—What?

—I want to tell you something . . . but don't laugh.

—Tell me.

—Each time you've come to my bed . . . afterwards, I've wanted . . . not to wake up again, once I was asleep. Sure it upsets me about my mom, that she'd be all alone . . . but if it was just me, I wish I wouldn't wake up ever again. But it's not just some notion that's gotten into my head or something; I'm telling you the only thing I want is to die.

—First you have to finish the film for me.

—Ugh, well there's a lot left; I won't finish it tonight, anyway.

—If you'd told me a little more the last couple of days, we'd almost be finished tonight. Why didn't you want to go on with it?

—I don't know.

—Don't forget, it could be the last film you'll get to tell me.

—It just might be, God only knows.

—Tell me a little before it's time to go to sleep.

—Just until you get tired.

—Okay. Where were we?

—The part when he's singing in that miserable dive, singing to her, after she appears at the bottom of his tequila glass.

—Right, and they sing together. In the meantime, the girl . . . she's actually left the magnate, she felt so ashamed of going on and living that way, and decided to go back to work. She's going to appear in a nightclub, as a singer, and tonight she's supposed to make her debut; she feels very nervous, because it's the first night she's going to appear in front of the public once again, and that afternoon it's dress rehearsal. She shows

up in a long gown, like all the ones she wears, strapless, very
fitted in the bust, the wasp waist and the incredibly full skirt,
all in black sequins. But the shine of the sequins is like only
a glow. The hair very simple, parted down the middle and
flowing over the shoulders. An accompanist on the piano, the
props nothing more than a curtain in white taffeta tied by a
sash of the same fabric, because wherever she goes she always
wants to have that lustrous finish of taffeta, and to one side a
Greek column faked in white marble, the piano white, too, a
baby grand, and the pianist in a black tuxedo. Everyone there
in the nightclub is working feverishly to arrange the tables,
polish the floors, hammering all sorts of things, but when she
appears and you hear a few introductory notes on the piano,
of course, everybody in the place quiets down. And she sings
—or no, not yet, it begins with those few chords on the piano,
and, almost imperceptibly, the rhythm of the maracas in the
background, and she sees her own hands trembling, and her
eyes fill with tenderness, she reaches out for a cigarette from
the prompter down in front, takes her position next to the
Greek column, and begins with a deep but melodious voice to
start the introduction, almost spoken, thinking about her reporter: ". . . Everyone says absence makes you forget, but I
swear . . . it's not that way at all . . . From that last moment
we spent together, my life has known . . . only regrets," and
at this point the whole invisible orchestra starts to accompany
her as loud as can be and she, she belts it out with "You, you
stole away the kiss, that I kept in my heart, for you? . . . Was
it you? . . . You, you took with your eyes, that whimsical world
that you saw in my eyes . . . for you . . . yes, for you . . ." and
then there's a short interlude, of just the orchestra, and she
strolls rhythmically across to the middle of the floor, then spins
around and lets it out again, with her whole voice, "How could
you leave then, when love was on fire! . . . when you discovered
my heart held out . . . so much, so much ecstasy . . . You,
although you're far away, you'll cry just like a child, looking

for the same love, that I gave you that day . . ."

—I'm listening, go ahead.

—And as she finishes the song she's like completely wrapped up inside herself, and everyone breaks into applause, everyone who's been working there and setting up the room for the evening. And she walks happily off to her dressing room because she imagines to herself how he will find out she's working again, and therefore . . . she's not with the magnate anymore. But she's got a terrible shock in store for her. The magnate has bought out the whole nightclub, and he's ordered them to close it down, immediately, before her debut. And there's also a writ of attachment against her jewelry, because the magnate has bribed the jewelers to pretend that none of the jewels has been paid for, and so on. She realizes immediately that the magnate has decided to prevent her from being able to work, to make her life really impossible, obviously, so she'll go right back to him. But she doesn't let it get her down and decides with her agent to fill in with any work at all, until a good contract comes along. The newspaper guy, for his part, down in Veracruz, realizes now that he's running out of funds and has to look for work. He can't be a reporter anymore because he's been put on the blacklist by the union; and as for other kinds of work, without a recommendation, and with that spongy face of his from so many drunken binges, and the sloppy appearance, they're not going to take him either. Finally he gets a job as a laborer in a sawmill, and he works there a few days, but he doesn't have any strength left; his physique has been totally undermined by drinking, he no longer has any appetite, the food never goes down. One day on their lunch hour break, a fellow worker insists that he take something to eat, and he tries a mouthful, but he can't even swallow it; the only thing he feels is thirst, always that thirst. And that afternoon he collapses. They have to take him to a hospital. Delirious with fever he calls out her name. His fellow worker goes through all his papers, trying to find her address, and calls her in Mexico City, and of course she's no longer in that luxurious apartment, but the housekeeper, who was very kindly, delivers the message to the girl, now living at a cheap boardinghouse. The girl immediately prepares to rush to Veracruz—but now comes the toughest part of all, and it's that she doesn't have the money for the fare, and the owner of the boardinghouse is this repulsive guy, old and fat, and she asks him to lend her the money, and he says no. So then she begins to warm up to him, and the filthy slob immediately tells her, yes, he'll lend the money but in exchange for . . . dot, dot, dot. And you see him entering her room, something the girl had never let the slob ever do. And meanwhile the guy's there in the hospital, and the doctor comes in, along with a nun, and he looks at the chart they always have to note how the patient's doing, and takes his pulse, and looks at the whites of his eyes, and tells him he's responding fairly well to treatment, but he needs a lot of caring for, no more alcohol, lots of good food, and rest. And he tells himself sure, lots of luck . . . seeing how he's completely broke, when he spots this incredible figure suddenly appearing from out of the hallway, way over at the other end of the pavilion. She's coming slowly, glancing at each patient, slowly coming toward the guy, and all the patients are staring up at her like she was some kind of apparition. She's clothed very simply, but divine-looking, all in white, a very simple but flowing dress, with her hair tied back and not a single piece of jewelry. Obviously, because she doesn't have any, but for the guy it all has a very special significance, it means she has broken away from the life of luxury she was caught up in with the magnate. When she sees him, she can't believe her eyes, because he's been changed so much by the drinking, and her eyes are flooded with tears, and it's just at the point when the intern is telling him that he's been discharged, and he's telling the intern that he doesn't have anywhere to go, but she says, yes, he does, because there's a sweet house with a garden, very tiny, very modest but shaded with coconut trees and caressed by the salt sea air. And they go off together, where she has rented that house, almost out in the country, just outside the suburbs of Veracruz. He's kind of faint with weakness, so she prepares his bed but he says he'd rather rest on a hammock, out in the garden, hung between two of the palm trees surrounding the little house. And he stretches out there, and they hold hands, they can't stop looking into each other's eyes, and he says he will soon recover because of the joy of having her there with him, and he'll manage to find a good job, and won't be a burden to her, but she answers not to worry, she has some money saved up, and she will only let him return to work after he is totally cured, and they stare in silent adoration at each other and echoes drift up to them from the distant songs of the fishermen, melodious strings, very delicate, you don't know if it's on the guitar or the harp. And the guy, in almost a whisper, begins to think up some lyrics to the song, talking more than singing, and the rhythm is very slow, like the one they're strumming on those instruments playing way off in the distance, ". . . I live in you . . . you live in me . . . All sorrow is ended . . . why suffer more . . . Be still, my happiness . . . let the world never guess . . . how it cries out within me . . . this yearning to live . . . to love . . . I'm happy now, you're happy, too . . . You love me now, I love you more . . . Let the past drift away, let life begin today . . . when I feel such happiness, because . . . just now I saw you . . . cry for me . . ."

—Don't stop.

—The days go by, and he's feeling much better, but he's disturbed because she won't let him go to the luxurious hotel where she has been singing every night, or even accompany her as far as the door. Little by little jealousy begins to worm its way into his mind. He asks her why there's never any ads in the papers for a star attraction like herself, and she says it's in order to prevent the magnate from pursuing her again, and also the magnate might try to send someone to kill him if he were seen at the hotel, and he begins to suspect that she's seeing the magnate again. And one day he goes over to the ultra-luxurious hotel with its downstairs supper club, featuring international attractions. And she's not mentioned anywhere on the billboard, and no one knows her and no one's ever seen her either—they recall the name, yes, but like a star from some time ago. Then, desperate, he starts prowling the harbor districts, trying to find a cheap tavern. And he can't believe what he sees: on a corner, under a streetlamp, it's her: a hooker ... that's how she made the money to support him! So he hides, not to let her spot him, and goes back to the house a broken man. When she gets there toward morning, he pretends to be —for the first time—asleep when she arrives. Next day he gets up early to look for work, giving her some excuse or other. And he gets back toward evening and of course without having found anything, but she was really getting worried. He just pretends to her everything is fine, and when it's time for her to go back out on the street, or as she puts it, to go sing, he begs her not to go, the night feels rife with dangers, and please stay with him tonight, he feels so afraid of never seeing her again somehow. She asks him to control himself, it's absolutely necessary for her to go out, because the rent has to be paid. And the doctor, without his knowing it, has suggested the possibility of a new, very costly treatment, and tomorrow they have to visit his office together. And she leaves ... He realizes then what a dead weight he is on her shoulders, to the point that she needs to humiliate herself in order to save him. The guy watches the fishing fleet return to their anchorage at sundown; he walks along the shore, there's a gorgeous full moon, and the moon quivers apart as it shimmers reflected in the soft surging tide of the tropical night. There's no wind at all, everything is quiet, except his heart. The fishermen sound like they're humming together, droning this sad, sad melody, and the guy sings to it; the words seem to be dictated by his own desperation ... I don't remember the song much, but it's something about him asking the moon to take her a message, because he thinks the moon's going off to spend the night on the town just like she does. And the message is to take care of herself, because those nights on the town cause nothing but pain and in the end only make people cry. I can't remember the words. Anyway, the next morning when she returns he's no longer there; he left a note saying he loves her like crazy, but can't go on being a burden to her, and she shouldn't try to find him, because if God wants to bring them back together again . . . they'll meet even if they don't try to . . . And she sees a lot of cigarette butts lying around, and a book of matches forgotten there, the kind you pick up in the bars along the harbor district, and at that point she realizes he has somehow seen her . . .

—And that's it?

—No, there's more still, but we'll leave the final part for another day.

—You're sleepy.

—No.

—Then what is it?

—This film really gets me down, I don't know why I ever started it.

— . . .

—Valentin, I have a bad premonition.

—Of what?

—That they're going to just dump me in another cell, and nothing else, that they're not going to let me out of here, and I'm not going to see you again.

— . . .

—I was feeling so contented . . . but telling you this film threw me right back down in the dumps.

—It's no good trying to anticipate the future, Molina, you don't know what might happen . . .

—I'm afraid it's something bad, whatever it is.

—Like what?

—Look, getting out is important to me, but for the sake of my mother's health mostly. But then I worry, no one's going to be around . . . to take care of you.

—And you don't think about yourself?

—No.

— . . .

— . . .

—Molina, there's something I'd like to ask you.

—What?

—It's complicated. Well . . . it's like this: you, physically you're a man as much as I am . . .

—Mmm . . .

—Sure, you're not in any way inferior. Then why doesn't it occur to you to ever be . . . to ever act like a man? I don't say with women, if they don't attract you. But with another man.

—No, that's not for me . . .

—Why?

—Because it's not.

—That's what I don't really understand very well . . . All homosexuals, they're not that way.

—Right, there's all kinds. But me, no, I don't . . . I don't enjoy it any other way.

—Look, I don't understand anything about this, but I want to explain something to you, even if I just bumble my way through it . . . I don't know.

—I'm listening.

—I mean that if you enjoy being a woman . . . you shouldn't feel any the less because of it.

— . . .

—I don't know if you follow me . . . how do you see it?

— . . .

—I just mean that you don't have to make up for it with anything, with favors, or excuses. You don't have to . . . submit.

—But if a man is . . . my husband, he has to give the orders, so he will feel right. That's the natural thing, because that makes him the . . . the man of the house.

—No, the man of the house and the woman of the house have to be equal with one another. If not, their relation becomes a form of exploitation.

—But then there's no kick to it.

—Why?

—Well, this is very intimate, but since you're asking about it . . . The kick is in the fact that when a man embraces you . . . you may feel a little bit frightened.

—No, that's all wrong. Whoever put that idea in your head? It's absolutely wrong.

—But that's the way I feel.

—You don't feel that way, you've been fed an old wives' tale by whoever filled your head with that nonsense. To be a woman you don't have to be . . . I don't know . . . a martyr. Look . . . if it weren't for the fact that it must hurt a hell of a lot, I'd tell you to do it to me, to demonstrate that this business of being a man, it doesn't give any special rights to anyone.

—Let's not talk about it anymore, because this conversation isn't getting anywhere.

—To me it is, I want to talk more about it.

—But I don't.

—Why not?

—Because I don't, and that's that. Please, I'm asking you . . .

CHAPTER 14

WARDEN: Hello, Miss? I'd like to talk to your boss, please . . . Thank you.   How are you! How are things there? No, nothing new here.   Yes, that's why I called you, actually.
I see him again in a few minutes.   I don't know if you remember, Molina was allowed another week. In addition, Arregui was given the impression that any day Molina was going to be shifted to another cell, because he was recommended for parole.   Exactly, Molina's own idea, yes. Christ . . .   Of course, time is crucial then.   Yes, if they want to know before launching a counteroffensive, I understand, of course.   Right, I see him in just a few minutes, but that's why I wanted to talk to you first. Tell me, in case he has nothing . . . absolutely nothing to pass on, in case there's no progress whatsoever, what then with Molina? You think so? . . .   How many days from now?   First thing tomorrow?   Why tomorrow?   Yes, of course, there is no time to lose then.   Yes, I understand, not today, that way Arregui has time to plan something.   Perfect, if he gives him a message, Molina can lead us right to their door. The problem will be not to let him know he's being followed.
But listen . . . There is something strange about our Molina, there's something tells me, I don't know how to explain it, but I can't help thinking . . . that Molina isn't coming clean with me . . . that he's hiding something.   You think Molina has gone over to them?   Right, out of fear

of reprisals from Arregui's people, that could be the thing.

Yes, and Arregui might have been working on him, using who knows what sort of methods.   That's also a possibility too. It's hard to fathom the reactions of a type like Molina, a pervert, after all.   There's also another possibility: that Molina hopes to leave here without compromising himself with anyone, either with us or with Arregui. That Molina's out for Molina, plain and simple.   Yes, it's definitely worth the trouble of trying.   And there is one other possibility too.   Yes, excuse me for interrupting . . .

It's just this: if Molina doesn't lead us to anything . . . that is to say, if he doesn't furnish us with any information today, or at the latest tomorrow before he's out on the street . . . well, we're still left with one other possibility . . .   And it's the following: have it published in the papers, or let the word out, whatever . . . that Molina, or perhaps just some agent, has furnished the police with information regarding the activities of Arregui's group, and that the agent actually operated surreptitiously, as a prisoner in this penitentiary. Then when Arregui's people hear of it, they'll come looking for him to square up accounts, and at that point we close in. So it opens up a lot of possibilities, once Molina is out on the street.   Ah, well, I'm very glad.   Don't mention it. Of course, I'll give you a call the moment Molina leaves my office.   Perfect, we'll leave it at that.   Fine, fine . . . I'll call you immediately . . .   My pleasure. So long.

WARDEN: Come on in, Molina.

PRISONER: Good afternoon, sir.

WARDEN: That's fine, Sergeant, you can go now.

SERGEANT: Yes sir, as you wish, sir.

WARDEN: How goes it, Molina?

PRISONER: Okay, sir.

WARDEN: So what have you to tell me?

PRISONER: Well, here we are, sir.

WARDEN: Any progress?

PRISONER: I'm afraid not, sir . . . I thought . . . I wanted so much to . . .

WARDEN: Nothing at all? . . .

PRISONER: Nothing.

WARDEN: Look, Molina, I've had everything arranged to obtain your release, provided you brought us some information. I'll speak frankly: the papers granting your parole have already been prepared. The only thing missing is my signature.

PRISONER: Oh, I see . . .

WARDEN: It's a pity.

PRISONER: I did everything I could, sir.

WARDEN: But wasn't there at least a hint of something? perhaps the slightest clue? . . . Because any element would be enough . . . for us to take action. And that minimal element would already be enough to justify my signing your papers.

PRISONER: You can imagine, sir, what more could I want than to get out of here? . . . But the worst thing would be for me to invent something to you. Honestly, you can't get near him —Arregui is like a tomb, sir, and suspicious of everything . . . I don't know, he's impossible, he's not . . . he's not human.

WARDEN: Look at me, Molina. Let's talk like human beings, since that's what we are, you and I, human . . . Think about your mother, about the happiness you can bring her. And rest assured nothing is going to happen to you once you're out on the street, because we will be right there to protect you.

PRISONER: It'll be enough just to be out, never mind the rest.

WARDEN: Honestly, Molina, you needn't fear reprisals of any kind, we will provide you with twenty-four-hour protection, you'll be perfectly safe.

PRISONER: I know that, sir. And I appreciate it very much, your thinking about that, that I might need protection . . . But what can I do? The worst thing would be to make something up that wasn't true.

WARDEN: Well . . . I'm very sorry, Molina . . . In that case there's nothing I can do for you.

PRISONER: So it all comes to nothing then? . . . My parole, I mean. There's no hope for anything?

WARDEN: No, Molina. If you don't furnish us with any information, then I'm powerless to help you.

PRISONER: No recommendation for good conduct? Nothing?

WARDEN: Nothing, Molina.

PRISONER: And my cell? Are they going to let me stay in the same cell at least?

WARDEN: Why? Wouldn't you rather be with someone . . . more communicative than Arregui? It must be rather upsetting to stay with a fellow who never talks.

PRISONER: It's just . . . I still have the hope of someday his telling me something.

WARDEN: No, I think you've already done enough to help us, Molina. We're moving you to another cell.

PRISONER: Please, sir, for the love of God . . .

WARDEN: But what's all this? . . . One would think you were attached to Arregui.

PRISONER: Sir . . . As long as I'm there, I'll at least have the hope of his telling me something . . . And if he ever talks there's a hope of somehow getting myself out of here.

WARDEN: I don't know, Molina. I'll have to give it some consideration. But I don't think it's feasible.

PRISONER: Sir, please, for the love of God . . .

WARDEN: Control yourself, Molina. We have nothing more to discuss. You may leave now.

PRISONER: Thank you, sir. For doing whatever you could for me, thanks anyway.

WARDEN: You can go.

PRISONER: Thank you, sir . . .

WARDEN: So long, Molina.

SERGEANT: You rang, sir?

WARDEN: Yes. You may take the prisoner back.

SERGEANT: At your orders, sir.

WARDEN: But first, I want to say one more thing to him. Molina
. . . tomorrow have your things ready to leave your cell.

PRISONER: I beg you . . . Don't, don't take away my only chance
to . . .

WARDEN: Just a minute, I haven't finished speaking. Tomorrow
have everything ready because you will be paroled.

PRISONER: Sir . . .

WARDEN: That's right, tomorrow, first thing in the morning.

PRISONER: Thank you, sir . . .

WARDEN: And good luck, Molina.

PRISONER: Thank you, sir. Thank you . . .

WARDEN: It's nothing, just see that you take care now . . .

PRISONER: But you really mean it?

WARDEN: Of course I mean it.

PRISONER: It's so hard to believe . . .

WARDEN: Well, believe it . . . and behave yourself, once you're
on the street. Because you had better stay away from any
more nonsense with little kids, Molina.

PRISONER: Tomorrow?

WARDEN: Yes, first thing tomorrow.

PRISONER: Thank you . . .

WARDEN: All right, now get going, because I'm very busy.

PRISONER: Thank you, sir.

WARDEN: Don't mention it.

PRISONER: Oh! . . . one thing, though . . .

WARDEN: What is it?

PRISONER: Even though I'm getting out tomorrow . . . if anyone
came to see me today, from my house, or the lawyer . . .

WARDEN: Speak up . . . or do you prefer I have the sergeant
leave the room for a minute?

PRISONER: No, I just mean . . . if they came to see me, they
couldn't be so sure I was getting out tomorrow . . .

WARDEN: What do you mean? . . . I don't understand you. Make yourself clear, I'm much too busy to spend any more time . . .

PRISONER: Well, if they came to visit me they'd bring another package . . . So, to cover it with Arregui . . .

WARDEN: No, that's not important anymore. Tell him they didn't bring anything, because the lawyer knew you were going to be paroled. Tomorrow you'll already be eating in your own house, Molina.

PRISONER: It wasn't for me, sir. It was for Arregui . . . to cover things.

WARDEN: No need to overdo it, Molina. It'll be fine like it is.

PRISONER: Excuse me, sir.

WARDEN: Good luck to you.

PRISONER: Thank you so much. For everything . . .

—Poor Valentin, you're staring at my hands.

—I didn't realize. I did it automatically.

—Your poor eyes betrayed you, precious love . . .

—Such language . . . So? Quick! tell me something!

—You'll have to forgive me, but they didn't bring me any package.

—That's not your fault . . .

—Oh, Valentin . . .

—What's wrong?

—Oh, you won't believe it . . .

—Come on . . . Why all the mystery?

—You'll never guess . . .

—Come on . . . what happened? Tell me!

—Tomorrow I leave.

—Another cell, huh? . . . What a pisser.

—No, they're letting me out, I'm free.

—No! . . .

—They're releasing me on parole.

—But that's wonderful . . .

—I don't know . . .

—But it isn't possible . . . It's the nicest thing that could happen for you!

—But what about you? . . . Now you're all alone.

—No, it's not possible, such a piece of luck, Molina! This is fantastic, really fantastic, do you hear? . . . Tell me, it's actually the truth, or are you putting me on?

—No, honestly.

—This is fantastic news.

—You're nice to be feeling happy on my account.

—Yes, I am happy for you, but it's also for another reason . . . This is fabulous!

—Why, what's so fabulous . . .

—Molina, you're going to do something fabulous for me, and I assure you you won't run the slightest risk in doing it.

—What is it?

—Look . . . in the last few days an extraordinary plan of action has occurred to me, and it was killing me not to be able to pass it on to my comrades. I was racking my brains trying to find some solution . . . and you come along and hand it to me right on a silver platter.

—No, Valentin. I'm no good for that, you'd have to be crazy.

—Listen to me for a minute. It'll be easy. You just memorize the whole thing, and that's all there is to it. You'll be all set.

—No, you're out of your mind. They can follow me, or anything, just to see if I'm in cahoots with you.

—That'll be taken care of. You can let a few days go by, a couple of weeks. And I'll explain to you how to tell if you're being followed or not.

—No, Valentin, I'll be out on parole. The least thing and they could lock me up again.

—I swear you won't be running the slightest risk.

—Valentin, I'm telling you. I don't want to hear a word of it. Not where they are, not who they are, nothing!

—Wouldn't you like me to get out of here someday, too?

—Out of here?

—Yes, out of here, free . . .

—Oh, wouldn't I like that . . .

—Then you have to help me.

—There's nothing in the world I want more than that. But listen, it's for your own good I'm telling you . . . Don't give me any information, don't tell me anything about your comrades. Because I'm no good at that sort of thing, and if they catch me I'll wind up telling them everything.

—I'm the one, not you, who is responsible for my comrades. If I ask you to do something, it's because I know there is no risk involved. All you have to do is let a few days go by, and make a call from a public phone somewhere, not from your house. And arrange to meet at some fake location.

—Some fake location?

—Yes, in case the lines are being tapped on my comrades. That's why you have to arrange the location by code, for instance you tell them at the Rio Coffee Shop, and they know where that really means, because we always do that over the telephone, you understand? If we mention one place it's that we're really saying somewhere else. For instance, the Monumental Theater is actually the house of one of our people, and the Plaza Hotel is a corner in the Boedo district.

—But it scares me, Valentin.

—After I explain it you won't feel afraid at all. You'll see how simple it is to pass along a message.

—But if the lines are tapped I'll be caught myself, won't I?

—Not if you're talking from a public phone, and you disguise your voice properly, which is the easiest thing in the world; I'll teach you how. There are thousands of ways to do it, with a caramel in your mouth, with a toothpick under the tongue . . . Listen, that's nothing.

—No, Valentin . . .

—We'll discuss it again later.

—No!

—Whatever you say . . .

— . . .

—What's the matter?

— . . .

—Don't turn away . . . Look at me, please.

— . . .

—Don't bury your head in the pillow, please, I'm asking you.

—Valentin . . .

—What is it?

—It hurts me to leave you all alone.

—None of that. Be happy that you'll be able to see your mother again, to take care of her. That's what you wanted, isn't it?

— . . .

—Come on, look at me.

—Don't touch me . . .

—All right, fine, Molina.

— . . . Will you miss me at all?

—Yes, I'll miss you.

—Valentin, I made a promise, I don't know who I promised, God, maybe, although I'm not a believer.

—Mmm . . .

—And it was that what I wanted more than anything in life was to get out of here in order to take care of my mom. And that I'd sacrifice anything for that, that everything to do with me came second, that what I wanted above all was to be able to care for mom. And my wish has been granted.

—Be happy then. You, you're very generous to think first about someone else, and not yourself. You ought to be proud of that.

—But is it fair, that, Valentin?

—What?

—That I always end up with nothing . . . That I don't have anything truly my own in life.

—Well, but you have your mother, that's your responsibility, and you have to assume it.

—I suppose you're right.

—So then?

—Listen, though. My mom has already had a life, and lived it, and had her husband, and her son, too . . . She's old already, her life is almost finished now . . .

—Yes, but she's still alive.

—Yes, and I'm alive, too . . . But when does my life start? When do I strike it lucky, and have something for my own?

—Molina, one has to adjust. You got lucky, you're getting out of here. Be happy with that. Outside you've got the chance to start all over again.

—I want to stay with you. Right now the only thing I want is to stay with you.

— . . .

—Do I embarrass you when I talk like that?

—No . . . Well, yes . . .

—Yes what?

—What you said, it embarrasses me.

—Valentin . . . if I pass along the message you think it can help you get out of here faster?

—Well, it would be a way of helping our cause.

—But it's not something that could get you out of here right away. You're telling me that it's just going to make the revolution happen faster, right?

—Yes, Molina.

—Not that it's going to get you out for some other reason.

—No, Molina.

— . . .

—Don't rack your brains over it, forget it. Later we'll talk.

—There's not much time left for talking.

—We have the whole night.

—

—And you have to tell me the rest of the film, don't forget. The last few days you haven't wanted to tell any more of it.

—It's that the film makes me really sad.

—Everything's making you sad.

—You're right . . . Everything except one thing.

—None of that crap.

—Yes, it's unfortunate, but that's how it is. Everything makes me sad, if they change my cell it makes me sad, if they let me out of jail it makes me sad. Everything except one thing.

—On the outside you'll do fine, you can forget all you went through in prison, you'll see.

—I don't want to forget.

—Okay . . . enough of this nonsense! Lay off, please!!!

—I'm sorry.

— . . .

—Please, Valentin, say you forgive me.

— . . .

—I'll tell you the film, I'll finish the whole thing if you want. And afterwards I promise I won't pester you with my problems.

— . . .

—Valentin . . .

—What do you want?

—I'm not going to pass on the message.

—So, fine.

—It's because I'm afraid that before they let me go they'll interrogate me, about you.

—Whatever you think.

—Valentin . . .

—What?

—Are you mad at me?

—No.

—Want me to finish the film?

—No, you're not in the mood.

—Yes I am, if you want I'll finish.

—It's not worth it, I can already guess how it ends.

—It ends happily, right?

—I don't know, Molina.

—See, you don't know. I'll finish it for you.

—Whatever you want.

—Where were we?

—I don't remember.

—Let's see . . . I think we left off when he discovers that she's become a prostitute, in order to have money to feed him, and then she realizes that he's found out about it. Because when she comes home in the morning he's no longer there.

—Right, that's where we were.

—So. During all this time the magnate has been searching high and low for her, because he found out how she's been living in complete poverty, and the guy feels awful about what he's done to her. And that morning a showy-looking car pulls up in front of the little house by the sea. And it's the magnate's chauffeur; he sent him out to look for her. She refuses to talk to him, and awhile later the magnate himself arrives. He tells her to forgive him, because everything he did was out of love, out of desperation from losing her. She tells him what's happened, crying inconsolably. Then the magnate repents everything, and says that if she's been capable of such sacrifices, it means she loves that man and she'll love him forever. And he says, "This belongs to you," and hands her a case, with all her jewels inside, then kisses her on the forehead and goes away. Then she starts searching madly everywhere for her love, because with the sale of her jewelry she now has plenty of money for him to take the cure with the finest doctors in the very best sanatoriums. But she can't find him anywhere, until she begins to comb the jails, and all the hospitals. And in a roomful of critically ill patients finally, she spots him. His system is completely shattered, first because of the alcohol, and then because of hunger and exposure. The cold nights spent sleeping on the beach, without anyplace to go. When he sees her he smiles, and asks her to come closer so he can hold her.

She kneels down beside the bed and they fling their arms around each other. He tells her how last night he was afraid of dying, because his illness got much worse, but this morning, when he seemed out of danger, he thought, as soon as he felt strong enough he was going to look for her, because nothing was important enough to come between them, and somehow they would manage to start a new life together. Then the girl turns to the sister of mercy standing there at the foot of the bed, as if looking for some confirmation of what he says, that he'll soon be better. But the nun, almost imperceptibly, shakes her head no. And he goes on talking, saying that he's been offered some new jobs, on important newspapers, and even the possibility of becoming a correspondent overseas, so now they can go far away, and forget about any more suffering. Slowly the girl begins to realize he is actually delirious from the fever, and terribly ill. He tells her that he's even composed some new lyrics, but that she'll have to be the one, for the time being, to sing them, and he whispers one by one the words, and she repeats them, and music plays in the background, as if coming from the sea, because, in his delirium, he imagines he's with her out on some fishermen's wharf in the sunlight of a late afternoon. And he tells her the words, and she repeats, ". . . The times I feel sad . . . it's you I remember . . . The times I feel glad . . . it's you I remember. If I look at other eyes, if I kiss another's lips, if I smell some perfume . . . it's you I remember . . ." and from the wharf they look out on to the horizon, and a schooner is approaching, ". . . I carry you within me, deep inside of me . . . I carry you in my heart, you are a part of me . . ." and the schooner docks alongside there at the little pier for the fishermen, and the captain signals for them to come aboard because they're going to weigh anchor immediately, to take advantage of the favorable wind, which is going to carry them far off, on a calm sea, and the words continue, ". . . I never thought . . . I could become . . . so obsessed with you . . . I never thought . . . you could steal

. . . my heart from me . . . That's why, my life . . . it's you I remember . . . whether near or far away, it's you I remember . . . Whether by night or by day, like a melody . . . that lingers within me . . . it's you I remember . . ." and he imagines that they're both there together, on board the schooner, holding one another and staring into the infinite distance, nothing but sea and sky, because the sun's just gone down below the horizon. And the girl tells him how beautiful she thinks the song is, but he doesn't answer, he still has his eyes open, and probably the last thing he saw in this life was the two of them on board ship, arm in arm forever, en route to happiness.

—How sad . . .

—But it's still not finished. She just holds him, and cries in desperation. And leaves all that money from her jewelry there with the sisters in the hospital, to care for the poor, and she walks, and walks, like a sleepwalker, a somnambula, and reaches the little house where they lived together for just a few days of happiness, and she begins to walk along the shore, and it's already getting dark, and you hear the fishermen singing songs, but they're his songs, because the fishermen all heard them and learned them, and you see several young couples watching the sunset and they listen to the happy words he once sang to her when they first arrived there, words that the fishermen sing now while the couples in love are listening, ". . . I live in you . . . you live in me . . . All sorrow's ended . . . why suffer more . . . Be still, my happiness . . . let the world never guess . . . how it cries out within me . . . this yearning to live . . ." and an old fisherman asks after him, and she tells him he's gone away, but it doesn't matter, because he'll always be with them, even if it's nothing more than in the memory of his songs, and she goes on walking and walking all alone, with her face toward the sun disappearing over the horizon, and you hear: ". . . I'm happy now . . . you're happy, too . . . You love me now . . . I love you more . . . Let the past drift away . . . let life begin today . . . when I feel such happiness, because

. . . just now I saw you . . . cry for me . . ." And, since it's almost dark now, you see only her silhouette, way off in the distance, which keeps walking but with no direction, like a wandering soul. And then suddenly you see a giant giant close-up of just her face, with her eyes flooded with tears, but with a smile on her lips . . . And well . . . that's all . . . folks . . .

— . . .

—Such an enigmatic ending, isn't it, Valentin?

—No, it's right, it's the best part of the film.

—Why is that?

—It means that even if she's left with nothing, she's content to have had at least one real relationship in her life, even if it's over and done with.

—But don't you suffer even more, after having been so happy but then winding up with nothing?

—Molina, there's one thing to keep in mind. In a man's life, which may be short and may be long, everything is temporary. Nothing is forever.

—Yes, but let it last a little while, at least that much.

—It's a question of learning to accept things as they come, and to appreciate the good that happens to you, even if it doesn't last. Because nothing is forever.

—Yes, it's easy to say. But feeling it is something else.

—But you have to reason it out then, and convince yourself.

—Yes, but there are reasons of the heart that reason doesn't encompass. And that's straight from a French philosopher, a very great one. I got you that time . . . And I think I even remember his name: Pascal. So put that in your pipe!

—I'm going to miss you, Molina.

—At least the films.

—Yes, at least the films . . .

— . . .

—Every time I see a piece of glazed fruit, I'm going to remember you.

—. . .

—And every time I see a chicken on a spit, turning in a deli oven.

— . . .

—Because someday I'll strike it lucky, too, and they'll let me out of here.

—I'm going to give you my address.

—Good.

—Valentin . . . If something happened here once, I was always careful about beginning it, because I didn't want to ask you for anything, if it didn't arise from yourself. Spontaneously, I mean.

—Yes.

—Well, but as a farewell, I do want to ask you for something . . .

—What?

—Something you never did, even though we did a lot worse things.

—What?

—A kiss . . .

—You're right . . .

—But tomorrow, before I go. Don't get scared, I'm not asking for it now.

—Fine.

— . . .

— . . .

—I'm curious . . . would you feel much revulsion about giving me a kiss?

—Mmm . . . It must be a fear that you'll turn into a panther, like with the first movie you told me.

—I'm not the panther woman.

—It's true, you're not the panther woman.

—It's very sad being a panther woman; no one can kiss you. Or anything.

—You, you're the spider woman, that traps men in her web.

—How lovely! Oh, I like that.

— . . .

—Valentin, you and my mom are the two people that I've loved most in the world.

— . . .

—And you, are you really going to remember me?

—I learned a lot from you, Molina . . .

—You're crazy, I'm just a dope.

—And I want you to go away happy, and have good memories of me, like I have of you.

—And what is it you're supposed to have learned from me?

—It's kind of hard to explain. But you've made me think about so many things, of that you can be sure . . .

—Your hands are always warm, Valentin.

—And yours, always cold.

—I promise you one thing, Valentin . . . that whenever I remember you, it will always be with happiness, like you taught me.

—And promise me something else . . . that you're going to make them respect you, that you're not going to allow anyone to treat you badly, or exploit you. Because no one has the right to exploit anyone. Forgive me if I'm repeating this to you, because the last time I said it, you didn't like it.

— . . .

—Molina, promise me you won't let anybody push you around.

—I promise you.

— . . .

—You're putting your books away, so early?

— . . .

—Aren't you going to wait for when lights go out?

— . . .

—You're not cold taking your clothes off?

— . . .

—How good you look . . .

—. . .

—Ah . . .

—Molina . . .

—What?

—Nothing . . . I'm not hurting you?

—No . . . Ow, yes, that way, yes.

—It hurts you?

—Better like last time, let me lift my legs. This way, over your shoulders.

—. . .

—Like this . . .

—Quiet . . . quiet a little while.

—Yes . . .

—. . .

—Valentin . . .

—What?

—Nothing . . . nothing . . .

—. . .

—Valentin . . .

—. . .

—Valentin . . .

—What's the matter?

—Oh, nothing just some nonsense . . . that's all.

—What?

—No, better nothing.

—. . .

—. . .

—Molina, what is it? Did you want to ask for what you asked for before?

—What?

—The kiss.

—No, it was something else.

—You don't want me to give it to you now?

—Yes, if it doesn't disgust you.

—Don't make me angry with you.

— .

—

—Thanks so much

—Thank you.

—Valentin . . .

— . . .

—Valentin, are you asleep?

—What?

—Valentin . . .

—Tell me, what is it?

—You have to give me all the information . . . for your friends . . .

—If you want.

—You have to tell me everything I have to do.

—Okay.

—So I can learn it all by heart . . .

—Sure . . . Was that what you wanted to tell me awhile ago?

—Yes . . .

— . . .

—But one thing, and this is very, very important . . . Valentin, are you sure they won't interrogate me before I leave?

—I'm sure.

—Then I'll do whatever you tell me.

—You don't know how happy that makes me.

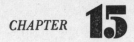

*Report on Luis Alberto Molino, prisoner 3.018, paroled on the
9th, placed under surveillance by CISL in conjunction with wiretap unit of TISL*

9. *Wednesday.* Subject released 8:30 A.M. and arrived home
   approximately 9:05 A.M., alone by taxi. Spent entire day at
   home, Calle Juramento 5020, appeared at the window a
   number of times, peering out in various directions, but con-
   centrating several minutes in a northwesterly one. Apartment situated on third floor with no tall buildings opposite.
   Telephoned 10:16 A.M., asking for Lalo, and when latter
   responded conversed several minutes together, in feminine
   gender, using various different names interchangeably
   throughout the conversation, for example: Teresa, China,
   Perla, Caracola, Pepita, Carla, Tina, etc. With the above Lalo
   insisting vehemently that subject relate any "conquests"
   while imprisoned. Subject answered to the effect that what
   was said about sexual behavior in prisons was hardly the
   truth and that there had in fact been no "diversions." Exchanged promises to get together over the weekend to see a
   movie. Each time one addressed the other with a new name,
   it was followed by laughter.
6:22 P.M., subject telephoned a woman he called Aunt Lola.
   Talked to her at length, evidently a sister of the mother's,
   with the conversation focused especially on health problems

of subject's mother and aunt's impossibility of looking after her because of her own illnesses at the time.

10. *Thursday.* Subject left home, 9:35 A.M., stopped at a dry-cleaners located on corner of Pampa and Triunvirato, which is to say, two blocks from home. Delivered a large bundle of clothing. Next proceeded to a grocer's, half a block away, located around the corner on Gamarra. On the way back stopped to buy cigarettes at newsstand, over on Calle Avalos just below Pampa. From there, subject returned directly home.

11:04 A.M., subject received phone call from relatives, Uncle Arturo and Aunt Maria Esther, welcoming him back. Immediately afterwards, a party with a much younger voice also called, her name Estela, presumably a cousin because she passed receiver to her mother whom subject addressed sometimes as Chicha and sometimes Aunt Chicha. Subject was congratulated on his release, because of good conduct, before serving out full sentence. Callers invited him to lunch the following Sunday, certain unintelligible phrases were then exchanged which apparently were meant to suggest idiosyncratic speech habits of subject as a child, when requesting food. Subject, for instance, when questioned in said fashion about his preference for food on Sunday, requested "camel only" (?). All of which would seem to be nothing more than babytalk, but nevertheless we call attention to same. At 5 P.M., in spite of cold weather, subject opened the window, and remained there a considerable period of time and—as on previous day—looking northwest. At 6:46 P.M. a call from the same Lalo of day before, inviting subject to come for a ride in the car with his girlfriend, subject accepting with one proviso: to get back no later than 9 P.M., in order to have supper with mother and aunt. The latter, name: Cuca, also inhabiting the same apartment, generally leaves premises mornings to stop in at a local bakery and deli, and evenings sometimes, for shopping at the local supermarket situated six blocks away on the corner of Avenida Triunvirato and Roosevelt. Subject came out a few minutes after call, and waited in the doorway until two males arrived in a Fiat, not a man in the company of a woman as announced. One of the two, around forty, quickly got out of the car and flung arms around subject, kissing the latter on both cheeks and seeming to be visibly moved, whereas second male did not leave the car, instead, remained at the wheel with the motor left running, and gave the impression of being unfamiliar with subject, given the way in which he extended his hand to same. Second male about fifty. Drove them together straight to Avenida Cabildo, along Pampa, up Cabildo as far as Pacifico and next along Santa Fe, then Retiro, Leandro Alem, Plaza de Mayo, Avenida de Mayo, Congreso, Callao, Corrientes, Reconquista, and various streets in the San Telmo district, stopping the car for brief moments in front of several new cabaret-nightclubs which lately seem to be proliferating in the area. Also in front of various antique shops. With subject continually turning around to look out rear window, obviously suspicious, evidently aware of being followed. From San Telmo district car proceeded without additional stops directly back to subject's own home.

With respect to suggestion of yesterday from unit deployed by TISL concerning the possibilities of a hidden code based upon the various feminine names employed by the subject in addressing the above-mentioned Lalo, it should be stressed that the tone of the conversations was continually bantering and the conversations themselves extremely disordered. Nonetheless, the matter will be watched further.

11.Friday. 11:45 A.M., a call from someone with a raspy voice, whom subject addressed as "godfather," and from the tension in the voice the phone call might have been construed to be suspicious, the voice sounding slightly fake, but topic of conversation turned out to be subject's future conduct.

The "godfather," who in reality appeared to be that, recommended good behavior on the street and above all at work and reminded subject of the fact that his recent incarceration stemmed from carrying on sexually with a minor in the very shop where he worked as windowdresser. Conversation ended on a very cool note, with both parties apparently offended. Godfather saying: "You never spoke to me in that tone before, is that what you learned in prison?" Minutes later a call from the above-mentioned Lalo, during which the two again proceeded to address one another by a number of feminine names, this time actresses, or so it seemed: Marilyn, Gina, Greta, Marlene, Merle, Heady (?). It should be reiterated that it did not seem to pertain to any code, but rather a running joke between the two. The tone of the conversation was animated, with the friend advising subject that a few acquaintances were about to open a boutique with a fair amount of windowspace but couldn't come to any agreement with another windowdresser because of budget difficulties. Lalo then supplied subject with address and phone number, suggesting he call them on the following Monday, Berutti 1805 and 42-5874 respectively. At 3 P.M., subject went out and walked as far as Cabildo, a little over twenty blocks, and went inside the Cine General Belgrano, not many people in the audience, subject sat alone, spoke to no one, before leaving stopped in men's room, but to avoid suspicion was not followed at that point, given the close quarters. Left immediately afterwards. Walked home, along a street running parallel to the previous above, stopping on several corners, gazing at houses and shops. Entered own premises a little before 7 P.M. Later on, subject telephoned party which answered "Restaurant" something or other, impossible to pick up because of the background noises and voices, apparently originating at the counter of a bar or place to eat. Subject asked to speak to Gabriel. The latter picked up the receiver immediately, sounded quite shocked and surprised, but went on to talk in very friendly tone. His voice quite manly, and his accent attributable to lower-class neighborhoods of Buenos Aires. Finally agreed to call each other the hour that the said Gabriel, whom we suspect to be a waiter there, usually arrived at work, if it turned out subject couldn't get to the restaurant around the same time. We call attention to certain ambiguities in passages of conversation, making it definitely mandatory to establish identity of Gabriel. Immediately afterwards subject appeared in window without bothering to open same, obviously due to the cold temperature outside, did however open curtain, remained there for several minutes staring attentively out, but as per usual not at the streets below but somewhere higher up. As on previous occasions, so this time staring in a northwesterly direction, which is to say toward intersection of Calle Juramento and Bauness, or—to give more precise location—the existing site of the present penitentiary.

12. *Saturday.* Subject left with mother and aunt, caught a cab, arrived at Gran Savoy Cinema on Avenida Cabildo, 3:25 P.M. Sat together and spoke to no one. Left 5:40 P.M., but this time caught a bus at the corner of Monroe and Cabildo. Got off together, one block from home, walking with occasional outbursts of laughter. Stopped in at bakery to buy eclairs. At 7 P.M., subject telephoned the restaurant, and this time it could clearly be heard "Restaurant Mallorquin," where presumed Gabriel picked up to talk and subject explained that he was unable to come to the restaurant because he needed to stay with his mother. Gabriel suggested the following Monday, when he would be on dayshift, because tomorrow, being Sunday, restaurant would be closed, as per usual. Also seemed somewhat put off by the change in plans. As was already stated in a previous report, attempts are being made, through units of the CISL operating in that district, to establish identity of Gabriel. Tomorrow a report on the above is to be delivered to our office, as per arrangement.

13.Sunday. In possession now of said report. Manager of the Mallorquin, a Spanish restaurant in business for almost fifty years, located at Calle Salta 56, affirms that Gabriel Armando Solé has in fact been in his employ for over five years, as a waiter, and that he hasn't the slightest doubts as to the honesty of the said person. That Solé seems not to exhibit any extremist political tendencies and does not attend union meetings nor is he known to have friends who are active in politics at all.

Only one phone call at subject's home, time: 10:43 A.M. Same individual who called once before, Aunt Chicha, once again persisting with more babytalk, but this time we could make out that they were expected to come to her house at 1 P.M., and shouldn't arrive late because she was cooking something for them which was first referred to by some peculiar phrases, but which subsequently we were able to interpret as "cannelloni." At 12:30 P.M., subject left house, with mother and aunt, hailing a taxi on corner of Avenida Triunvirato and Pampa. All three were driven to number 1998, on Calle Dean Funes, a one-story dwelling, in the Patricios district, where they were greeted by a very stout, gray-haired woman, who showed obvious signs of affection for all three as they mounted the front steps. Left there approximately 6:25 P.M., driven home by a young girl of uncertain age who took them in a Fiat 600. It should be noted prior to this that the taxi driver had looked back several times during the rather long drive, trying to determine if he was being followed, and subject also exhibited the same behavior, but not the two ladies. On the way back, however, the driver of the Fiat seemed not to notice anything.

14.Monday. At 10:05 A.M., subject called number, belonging to said boutique, wiretapped since Friday the 11th, and duly corresponding to above-named location on Calle Berutti, not searched to avoid suspicion in expectation of events. Answering party stated that they did in fact have need of the subject's services and asked him to stop by on the following Monday, the 21st, in order to discuss possible salary, at the same time complaining that the contractor had far exceeded his original estimate for renovations which would be completed within the week but that as a result they wouldn't be able to offer a windowdresser as high a salary as they had intended. Following this, subject telephoned waiter Solé at same restaurant. Told him there was no chance for him to get into town today because he had to stay with his mother. Solé sounded uninterested, no new date was arranged, subject promised to call later in the week. Solé has already been dismissed as a possible suspect but we still recommend continuing the wiretap of Mallorquin telephone. 3 P.M., subject appeared in window again and stood there for a long time with his attention directed as per usual in the northwest direction. 4:18 P.M., left house and went to newsstand, bought two magazines, and because of the large typeface we were able to establish one of them as the fashion monthly *Claudia.* No political magazines are vended at this location.

20. *Sunday.* Phone call from Lalo at 11:48 A.M., who suggested another ride in the car with Mecha Ortiz, as on the previous Sunday. We suppose the latter to be the nickname of the driver of the Fiat on last auto ride together. Additional names exchanged, but which we do not believe to constitute any sort of code. Names were Delia, Mirta, Silvia, Nini, Liber, Paulina, etc., almost certainly referring to actresses, like said Mecha, from older Argentine movies. Subject, however, turned down invitation due to previous plans which involved mother. 3:15 P.M., went out with mother, catching a bus on corner of Pampa and Avenida Triunvirato, getting off at Avenida de Mayo and Lima, walking a distance of two more blocks to the Avenida Theater, where two seats were purchased to the Spanish operetta, then crossing the street

to peer into shop windows while waiting for showtime, i.e., 6:15 P.M. During one intermission, subject went to men's room but spoke to no one. After sitting together in the orchestra, where for the whole show they spoke to no one, the two left together at 8:40 P.M. At the tearoom on Avenida de Mayo corner of Santiago del Estero had hot chocolate with churros, spoke to no one. Took same bus back, from corner of Avenida de Mayo and Bernardo de Irigoyen.

21. *Monday.* Subject went out at 8:37 A.M., took bus to Avenida Cabildo, from there another to Sante Fe and Callao, walking the last five blocks to intended destination: Calle Berutti 1805. Spoke with two males, examined space to be given over to window decoration, had coffee together. Left, alone, and repeated identical bus rides in opposite direction, returning home. At 11:30 A.M. called his friend Lalo at Banco de Galicia, where the latter works 11 A.M. to 7 P.M., talked together but seriously this time, obviously due to the fact that the friend was there at work. Subject simply related that he had arranged to begin work on the following day, in spite of not having settled the question of salary. The only other phone call that day came from Aunt Lola, who talked at length with subject's mother, both rejoicing over the prospect of employment.

22. *Tuesday.* Subject left home at 8:05 A.M., and arrived at boutique almost at 9 A.M., running the last two blocks. At 12:30 P.M. went out to lunch, coffee shop on Calle Juncal between Ayacucho and Rio Bamba. Made a call there, from a public phone. It should be pointed out that subject dialed the number three times and hung up immediately, then spoke for a period of some three minutes. All that very peculiar considering fact that a phone also exists at his place of employment, whereas subject had to stand on line and wait to use phone at the coffee shop. Phones at the subject's home, the Restaurant Mallorquin and the Banco de Galicia were immediately checked, verifying the fact that it was not

with any of the above locales that subject had made contact. Subject left work at 7 P.M. and arrived home a few minutes after 8 P.M.

23. *Wednesday*. Subject left house at 7:45 A.M. and arrived work 8:51 A.M. Around 10 A.M. telephoned his friend Lalo at the latter's home, thanking him for the job recommendation, and passed the receiver to one of his employers there in boutique who then spoke to Lalo as well, calling him Soraya of Persia, and eventually clarifying the meaning of said nickname, by remarking, "Soraya, that must be your name because you can never have children." In turn, the other one, Lalo, called the first Queen Fabiola of Belgium, for same reason. We should again point out that the matter of constantly switching names for each other suggests no premeditation, but rather a simple game which conceals no code of any kind. At 12:30 P.M., subject left work, hailed a cab and was driven to the main branch of Banco Mercantil, where subject proceeded to savings window, took out a sum of cash and from there took a second cab to Calle Suipacha 157, entering the office of a notary public, where it was deemed inadvisable to pursue him, for obvious reasons. Left 18 minutes later and caught still another cab to shop on Calle Berutti. There unwrapped sandwich brought from home that morning, and ate standing up while measuring fabrics with one of the two shop owners. Left 7:20 P.M. and arrived home by about 8:15 P.M. using customary means of transportation. At 9:04 P.M. left premises again, took bus to corner of Federico Lacroze and Alvarez Thomas, then second bus as far as Avenida Cordoba and Medrano. From there walking as far as Soler and Medrano. Paused near the corner, on Medrano, waited almost one hour. It should be pointed out that said corner, separated only by a few yards distance from a second crossing, that of Costa Rica, offers an excellent overall view to whoever would arrive at the above location from any one of four different vantage points,

and as a consequence must be thought to be a site selected by party or parties expert at dodging police surveillance. Subject waited and spoke to no one, several cars did pass but none stopped. Subject returned directly home, with no awareness on his part, or so it seemed, of our continuous surveillance. It is the opinion of staff headquarters that subject had arranged a meeting with party or parties who did, however, notice surveillance.

24. *Thursday.* According to separate report, subject withdrew total savings from bank, leaving only minimum deposit required in order not to close account. Money withdrawn had been deposited at intervals prior to term of imprisonment. At notary public's office, "José Luis Neri Castro," subject left sealed envelope in the name of the mother, containing only the above savings, this according to sworn declaration of named executive of said enterprise. Subject's activities minimal, left for work at regular morning hour, ate lunch at work, with coffee, which subject drank continuously on and off throughout day, there on premises. Arrived home directly, at 8:10 P.M. We also note, as per decision at command level, cancellation of project to leak to press imaginary confession, by Arregui to Molina, along with the latter's supposed undercover work as intelligence agent. Cancellation based upon the probability of pending or possible imminent contact between subject and partisans of Arregui.

25. *Friday.* Subject arrived at place of employment in the morning, left 12:30 P.M., and went to have lunch, alone, a few blocks away, at a pizzeria, number 2476 on Las Heras. Subject first spoke by public phone at same location, after dialing three times and hanging up immediately, as on previous occasion. Talked for a few minutes. Then ate by himself, or rather had a bite or two, leaving the plate almost untouched. Returned to work. Left there at 6:40 P.M., at Callao caught a bus to Congreso, where then went by subway as far as José Maria Moreno station. Walked to Riglos and For-

mosa. Waited there approximately thirty minutes, which is to say the amount of time alloted by Central Bureau until subject was to be picked up, if he had not been met by party or parties beforehand, and then taken away for interrogation. Therefore, two agents of the CISL, already in close contact with our patrol unit, proceeded to make the arrest. Subject demanded to see credentials. At that moment, however, several shots were fired from a passing automobile, wounding CISL agent Joaquin Perrone, along with subject, both of whom immediately fell to the ground. The arrival of our patrol unit, minutes later, was too late for pursuit of extremist vehicle. Of the wounded, Molina expired before arriving patrol unit could administer first aid. The above agent, Perrone, suffered thigh wounds plus serious contusions caused by his fall. The impression of other members of the patrol unit is that the extremists preferred to eliminate Molina to avoid the possibility of a confession. In fact, the recent activities of the subject, the matter of the bank account, etc., suggest that he himself feared something might actually occur. Furthermore, if he was in fact aware of our continued surveillance, his plan—in the event of being surprised in an incriminating position—may in fact have been one of the following: either he expected to escape with the extremists, or he was ready to be eliminated by same.

The present compilation of reports has been typed up in quadruplicate, for distribution only to authorized personnel, with the original to remain in this office permanently on file

CHAPTER 16

—Which part of your body hurts you the most?

—Agh . . . aghhh . . . aghhh . . .

—Don't try to talk, Arregui . . . if it hurts you that much.

—Ov- . . . over . . . here . . .

—Third-degree burns, what animals.

—Aiee . . . Agh, no . . . please . . .

—And how many days since you had any food?

—Th- . . . thr- . . . ee . . .

—Bastards . . .

— . . .

—Listen . . . you won't tell anyone, promise me.

— . . .

—Nod your head whether you want it or not. God, what they did to you it's barbaric, you'll be in a lot of pain for quite a few days . . . Listen to me. Nobody's around here in first aid right now, so I can take a chance and give you some morphine, that way you'll be able to rest. If you want it, nod your head. But you're never to tell anyone, because they'll throw me right out of here.

— . . .

—Okay, you'll get some relief in just a minute.

— . . .

—There, just a little pinch, and now you'll start feeling less pain.

— . . .

—Count to forty.

—*One, two, three, four, five, six, seven, eight, nine, ten, eleven, twelve, thirteen, fourteen, fifteen . . .*

—The way they've worked you over is unbelievable. Those burns in the groin . . . It will take weeks to heal up. But don't tell about this or I'm finished. By tomorrow it'll begin to hurt less.

— . . . *twenty-nine, thirty, thirty-one, thirty-two, thirty-th- . . . thirty-three, th- . . . what number am I on? don't hear any steps anymore, is it somehow possible they're not following me anymore? if it weren't for your knowing the way out of here, doctor, and leading me, I couldn't go on, I'd be afraid of falling into some hole, and is it possible that I've covered such a long stretch if I'm so exhausted? from not eating? it must be, and since I keep falling off to sleep, how is it possible that I go on walking without stumbling? "Don't be afraid, Valentin, the intern is a kind person and he's going to take care of you," Marta . . . where are you? when did you get here? I can't open my eyes because I'm asleep, but please come closer to me, Marta . . . don't stop speaking to me, can't you touch me? "Don't be afraid, I'm listening, but only on one condition, Valentin," what's that? "That you don't hide anything of what you're thinking, because the moment you do that, even though I want to listen to you I won't be able to anymore," no one can overhear us? "No one," Marta, I've been in terrible pain . . . "I want to know how you are now," and no one could be listening? someone waiting for me to denounce my comrades? "No," Marta, darling, I hear you speaking inside of me, "Because I'm inside of you," is that really true? and will it be that way always? "No, that can be only as long as I don't keep any secrets from you, just as you're not going to keep any from me," then I'll tell you everything, because this very kind intern is leading me to some way out of here through this long, long tunnel, "Is it very dark?" yes, and he told me that at the end* there'll be a light, very far away, but I don't know if it's true because I'm asleep and hard as I try, I can't seem to open my eyes, "What are you thinking about this very minute?" my eyelids are so heavy that it's impossible to open them, I'm so very sleepy, "I hear water running, and you?" water when it runs over stones is always clean and if I could reach over to where the water is with my hand, I could wet the tips of my fingers and then moisten my eyelashes to unseal them, but I'm afraid, Marta, "You're afraid of waking up and finding yourself in your cell," then it's not certain that someone is going to help me to escape? I can't remember, but this warmth that I'm beginning to feel in my hands and on my face is like the sun's, "It's possible that it's beginning to be light," I don't know if the water is clean, do I dare take a sip? "Moving ahead in the direction of the water, surely it'll be possible to get to wherever it empties," it's true, but it looks like what I see is really a desert, there are no trees, or houses, nothing more than the dunes that follow each other as far as the eye can see, "Instead of a desert, couldn't it be the sea?" yes, it is the sea, and there's a stretch of very hot sand, I have to run so that I don't burn the soles of my feet, "What else can you see?" from one end of the coast to the other there's no sign of that painted ship made of cardboard, "And what is it that you hear there?" nothing, you don't hear any maracas, the pounding of the waves and nothing else, sometimes the waves are so big they crash on the shore and reach up as far as where the palm trees begin, Marta . . . it looks like a flower fell in the sand, "A wild orchid?" if the waves reach it they'll carry it out too far, and is it possible for the wind to carry it off just as I was about to pick it up? and carry it way far out to sea, and it doesn't matter if it disappears because I can swim and I'll dive in, but right in the place where I'm sure that the flower sank . . . what you see now is a woman, a native girl, I could reach her if she didn't try to escape me by swimming so fast, I don't reach her though, Marta, and it's impossible to shout under the water and tell her

not to be afraid, "Underwater you hear whatever one is think-
ing," she looks at me unafraid, a man's shirt is tied across her
chest, but I'm so tired already, I have no more oxygen left in
my lungs after such a long swim underwater, but Marta, the
native takes my hand and lifts me up to the surface, she puts
a finger to her lips as a sign that I shouldn't speak, the wet knot
is tied so tightly that she can't undo it without my help, and
while I untie the knot she looks the other way . . . I didn't
remember that I was naked and I'm brushing against her, the
island girl flushed with embarrassment now puts her arms
around me, my hand is warm and I touch her and it dries her
right away, I touch her face, her long hair down to the waist,
her hips, her navel, her breasts, her shoulders, her back, her
tummy, her legs, her feet, and again her tummy, "Can I ask
you to pretend that she's me?" yes, "But don't tell her any-
thing, don't be critical of her, let her think she is me, even if
she fails in some way," with a finger to her lips the native
signals me not to say a word, but to you, Marta, I'll tell
everything, since I feel the same as I felt with you, because
you're with me, and soon this jet will spurt out of me, white
and warm from my insides and I'm going to flood her, oh,
Marta, such joy, yes I will tell you everything so that you won't
go away then, so that you'll be with me every minute, especially
now, in this instant, don't think of leaving me, this precise
instant! the most beautiful of all, now, yes, don't move, it's
better quiet, now, now, and later on, in a while, I'll also tell
you that the native is closing her eyes because she's sleepy, she
wants to rest, and if I close my eyes, who knows when I'll be
able to open them again? my eyelids are so heavy, when it gets
dark I'm not going to be able to tell because my eyes are closed,
"And you're not cold? it's night and you're sleeping out in the
open, the sea air is cool, didn't you feel cold during the night?
tell me," no, I didn't feel cold, my back touched this sheet
that's so smooth and warm on which I slept every night since
I came to the island, and I don't know how to explain it, my

love, but the sheet seems like . . . like in reality it's very smooth and warm skin, of a woman, and you don't see anything more in this place than that skin which reaches as far as the eye can see, you don't see anything else but the skin of a woman lying down, I'm like a grain of sand in the palm of her hand, she's lying in the sea and she lifts her hand and from up here I can see that the island is a woman, "The native?" I can't make out the face, it's too far, "And the sea?" just the same as always, I keep swimming underwater and you can't see the bottom it's so very deep but underwater my mother hears every word I'm thinking and we're talking, do you want me to tell you what she's asking? "Yes," well . . . she's asking me if it's true all that stuff in the papers, that my cellmate died, in a shootout, and she's asking if it was my fault, and if I'm not ashamed of having brought him such awful luck, "What did you answer her?" that yes, it was my fault, and that yes, I am very sad, but that there's no point in being so sad because the only one who knows for sure is him, if he was sad or happy to die that way, sacrificing himself for a just cause, because he's the only one who will ever have known, and let's hope, Marta, how much I wish it with all my heart, let's hope that he may have died happily, "For a just cause? hmmm . . . I think he let himself be killed because that way he could die like some heroine in a movie, and none of that business about a just cause," that's something only he can know, and it's possible that even he never knew, but in my cell I can't sleep anymore because he got me used to listening to him tell films every night, like lullabies, and if I ever get out of here sometime I'm not going to be able to call him and invite him over to dinner, he who had invited me so many times, "And what would you like to have most to eat this minute?" I'm swimming with my head above the water now so that way I won't lose sight of the island coast, and I'm very tired by the time I reach the sand, it doesn't burn anymore because the sun isn't so strong any-more and before it starts to get dark I have to look for some fruit, you don't know how beautiful it is here with this mixture of palm trees, and lianas, at night it's all silvery, because the film is in black and white, "And the music in the background?" very soft maracas, and drums, "Isn't that a sign of danger?" no, it's the music that announces, when they switch on a strong spotlight, the appearance of such a strange woman, with a long dress on, that's shining, "Silver lamé, that fits her like a glove?" yes, "And her face?" she's wearing a mask, it's also silver, but . . . poor creature . . . she can't move, there in the deepest part of the jungle she's trapped in a spider's web, or no, the spiderweb is growing out of her own body, the threads are coming out of her waist and her hips, they're part of her body, so many threads that look hairy like ropes and disgust me, even though if I were to touch them they might feel as smooth as who knows what, but it makes me queasy to touch them, "Doesn't she speak?" no, she's crying, or no, she isn't, she's smiling but a tear rolls out from beneath the mask, "A tear that shines like a diamond?" yes, and I ask her why she's crying and in a close-up that covers the whole screen at the end of the film she answers me that that's just what can never be known, because the ending is enigmatic, and I answer her that it's good this way, that it's the very best part of the film because it signifies . . . and at that point she didn't let me go on, she said that I wanted to find an explanation for everything, but that in reality I was just talking from hunger although I didn't have the courage to admit it, and she was looking at me, but every minute she seemed sadder and sadder, and more and more tears fell, "Mmm, more diamonds," and I didn't know what to do to get rid of her unhappiness, "I know what you did, and I'm not jealous, because you're never going to see her again in your whole life," it's just that she was so sad, don't you see? "But you enjoyed it, and I shouldn't forgive you for that," but I'm never going to see her again in my whole life, "And is it true that you're very hungry?" yes, it's true, and the spider woman pointed out to me the way through the forest with her finger, and so I don't know where to even begin to eat so many things I've found now, "Are they very tasty?" yes, a leg of roast chicken, crackers with big chunks of fresh cheese and little rolled up slices of cooked ham, and a delicious piece of glazed fruit, it's pumpkin, and later with a spoon I get to eat all the guava paste I want to, without worrying about finishing it all because there's so much, and I'm getting so sleepy, Marta, you can't imagine how much I just feel like sleeping after eating all that food I found thanks to the spider woman, and after I have one more spoonful of this guava paste and after I sleep . . . "You want to wake up already?" no, much, much later, because after eating all these rich foods such a heavy sleep has come over me, and I'll just go on talking with you in my sleep, will it be possible? "Yes, this is a dream and we're talking together, so even if you fall asleep you don't have to be afraid, and I think now that nothing is ever going to separate us again, because we've realized the most difficult thing of all," what's the most difficult thing of all to realize? "That I live deep inside your thoughts and so I'll always remain with you, you'll never be alone," of course that's it, that's what I can never let myself forget, if the two of us think the same then we're together, even if I can't see you, "Yes, that's it," so when I wake up on the island you're going to go away with me, "Don't you want to stay forever in such a beautiful place?" no, it's been so good up to now, but enough resting, once I've eaten everything up and after some sleep I'm going to be strong again, because my comrades are waiting for me to resume the age-old fight, "That's the only thing that I don't ever want to know, the name of your comrades," Marta, oh how much I love you! that was the only thing I couldn't tell you, I was so afraid you were going to ask me that and then I was going to lose you forever, "No, Valentin, beloved, that will never take place, because this dream is short but this dream is happy."

THE END

A NOTE about the AUTHOR

Manuel Puig was born in 1932 in a small town in the Argentine pampas. He studied philosophy at the University of Buenos Aires, and in 1956 he won a scholarship from the Italian Institute of Buenos Aires and chose to take a course in film direction at Cinecittà in Rome. There he worked as an assistant director until 1962, when he began to write his first novel. Puig's novels, *Betrayed by Rita Hayworth, Heartbreak Tango, The Buenos Aires Affair,* and *Kiss of the Spider Woman* (the last two are banned in Argentina), have been translated into fourteen languages. Manuel Puig now lives in New York City.

A NOTE on the TYPE

This book was set in Bodini Book, so-called after Giambattista Bodoni (1740–1813), son of a printer of Piedmont. After gaining experience and fame as superintendent of the Press of the Propaganda in Rome, Bodoni became in 1768 the head of the ducal printing house at Parma, which he soon made the foremost of its kind in Europe. His *Manuale Tipografico,* completed by his widow in 1818, contains 279 pages of specimens of types, including alphabets of about thirty languages. His editions of Greek, Latin, Italian, and French classics are celebrated for their typography. He was an innovator in type design, making his new faces rounder, wider, and lighter, with greater openness and delicacy, and with sharper contrast between the thick and thin lines.

Composed, printed and bound by The Haddon Craftsmen, Inc.,
Scranton, Pennsylvania.
Typography and binding design by Camilla Filancia